PLAYING
the Spy

Maggie Brown

BELLA
BOOKS
2018

Bella Books, Inc.
P.O. Box 10543
Tallahassee, FL 32302

Printed in the United States of America on acid-free paper.

First Bella Books Edition 2018

Editor: Cath Walker
Cover Designer: Judith Fellows

ISBN: 978-1-59493-575-6

Other Bella Books by Maggie Brown

I Can't Dance Alone
In the Company of Crocodiles
Mackenzie's Beat
Piping Her Tune
The Flesh Trade

Acknowledgments

Thank you once again Bella Books for the production of this book. Many thanks also to Cath Walker for her editing skills to make this a polished work.

I had fun writing this novel. The islands in the Great Barrier Reef are truly a slice of paradise. There are seventy-four islands in the Whitsunday group, only eight inhabited.

About the Author

Maggie Brown is a writer who thinks wit and humor go a long way. Is she intelligent, model-like, mega-super-important? Hell no!

She is an Australian alien life form, who drinks too much coffee, sits too long at the computer, and sometimes is a hot mess when struck down by writer's block.

She hopes you enjoy her story.

Dedication

To my family

All the world's a stage, and all men and women merely players: they have their exits and their entrances; and one man in his time plays many parts, his acts by seven ages.
-William Shakespeare, *As You Like It*

CHAPTER ONE

The *Morning Globe* pressroom buzzed with frantic activity. It was nothing new. Before an edition went to print, the chaotic last-minute scramble was a matter of course.

Sophie Marsh loved it all: the adrenaline rush, the smell of percolating burnt coffee, the tinge of panic in the air. It was her battlefield. Today, though, she wasn't amongst it. She sat in her editor's office, engaged in a different war. A verbal one.

"You've been assigned the job so dig up some dirt," Owen Cameron said flatly.

"But…"

"I don't want any further argument, Marsh."

She ignored the urge to sweep from the room in a grand gesture of defiance, but instead, hunched into her chair. Her dreams scurried further into the background at his words. Was this what the iconic Brisbane publication had become, a tabloid? But in today's world of social media, it was harder to find a story that wasn't old hat by the time the edition hit the streets. The *Globe*, like many papers, was struggling.

Silently, she watched him pop the antacid tablet into his mouth and chew it distastefully. A film of white frothed across his bottom lip. After a convulsive swallow, he wiped his mouth before he threw the manila folder across the table. The chief editor of the paper for over twenty years, Owen was a wiry, balding, acerbic man with little sense of humour and gastric reflux. A tough boss most of the time, he could be downright scathing when rattled.

He leaned across the desk with a glare. "What don't you understand about this? All you have to do is live in the house with the woman and find out what makes her tick. It isn't hard, so what's the goddamn problem? Anyone in the office would jump at the chance to be with Eleanor Godwin on a tropical island for a week, let alone two months. I want a story that unmasks that reclusive goodie two-shoes. No one is *that* perfect. You find out exactly what rocks her boat. What she likes, what she does for kicks, her vices, and most of all, who she screws."

"What about the State election? I've some important interviews lined up."

"Yeah…and that sells papers, does it? People are sick of politics. Look, my hands are tied. She specifically asked for an unattached woman in her late twenties or thirties. I didn't have a choice. It was either you or Brie."

"Then why can't Brie do it?" Her inner voice yelped *don't whine*. Sophie ignored it. "She'll jump at the chance—she *is* the social reporter, after all. You'll be handing her the Holy Grail."

A snort erupted. "Brie hardly fits the mould. Can you honestly visualize her as a domestic? Besides, I don't want to know who designed her dress, the colour of her lipstick, or how high her fucking heels are. I want something that sells papers." He scratched the side of his nose irritably. "I had to call in favours to get you a fine set of references."

"You actually sent a false CV to an employment agency? That's not right."

"So?" he said with an unconcerned shrug. "Lots of résumés have some misleading information. And it's not as though I forced them to take you. I sent it in and they picked you out of the pile. It was a long shot but it worked. The Fates are on your side."

"Why didn't they interview me?"

"Apparently, Godwin's mother did the hiring and insisted she wanted you when she was sent the short list. I fail to see why you're bellyaching anyhow. You're going to be paid by her as well as the paper. It's a windfall for you."

Though she welcomed the extra money, Sophie felt a moment of real disquiet. Eleanor Godwin would probably be within her rights to sue the paper when the article came out. Sophie hoped Owen had some contingency plan for that. She didn't want to be a sacrificial lamb in the pursuit of a scandal. "It's not ethical to spy on people in their own home," she ventured in a small voice.

"Then make sure you fulfil the terms of your employment. Do whatever the woman asks and do it properly." He squinted at her. "You know how to cook, don't you?"

"I'm half Italian…of course I do. I love it. Food's an art form in my family."

"Good. We'll cover your arse when the story's written."

Sophie picked up the folder, careful not to aggravate him further and retired sulkily to tidy her desk. An assignment of this length was a lifetime in this cutthroat business. The only hope to retain her edge would be to unearth something juicy about the film star, though the likelihood of that was slim. Eleanor Godwin was not only an excellent actor but also seemingly above reproach. She was one of the nation's favourite daughters, crème de la crème, a national treasure.

At this particular moment though, Sophie was not one of her adoring fans. Her ambition to be a top political reporter was disappearing—two months in domestic servitude sounded like a jail sentence. "A general dog's body" was the expression Owen had used. She appreciated what a coup getting the job must have been, for Eleanor was known to value her privacy, but why did she have to be the one to go? Sophie knew she hadn't a hope in Hades of wriggling out of this one.

Curious, she flipped open the folder. By nominating the age bracket, it was apparent Eleanor wanted a companion as well as help. She eyed the company logo on the front page. The employment agency was expensive and discreet, used exclusively by the rich and famous. Her enclosed application form contained a glowing manufactured curriculum vitae, with three very important referees. She recognised the names immediately—Owen's fishing cronies.

At least her alias, Sophie Ryan, was not known to the upmarket set, so she was able to keep her first name. Her photograph was flattering, though she had no idea when it was taken or by whom. It would have had to been airbrushed, for she didn't look half that good. Wincing, she scrolled down the employment criteria: *house duties, gardening, cooking, pleasant-natured, a keen reader, a good sense of humour.*

The damn woman wanted Mary Poppins.

She moved to Owen's notes on Eleanor. Born in Australia, the star had settled permanently in Hollywood after her career took off. Four years ago at the age of thirty, she had won an Oscar for her role in the acclaimed *Wings of the Hawk*, a period drama set in the American War of Independence. This year it was rumoured she would score another nomination for the grittier role of a lesbian drug addict, with a very good chance of taking out the coveted award once more.

Her working history read like a thespian Mother Teresa. She was cooperative with her fellow cast members, hardworking, never late on set and a role model for aspiring actors. Not only was she a stunning beauty, she had other starring qualities, being a noted philanthropist and humanitarian. Her personal life, however, was shrouded in mystery. Occasionally a man escorted her to a function or a show, but she had not formed any lasting attachments. She had never been seen drinking late at nightclubs or displaying herself badly in public in any way. In fact, she was always the model of decorum.

Sophie made a disparaging snort. Owen was right—no one could be *that* damn perfect. Everyone had a skeleton in a cupboard somewhere.

She flipped through to the site of her assignment. She'd never heard of the place. Eurydice was a small tropical island in the Whitsunday group in the Great Barrier Reef, a very exclusive destination with twenty-two guest villas, three privately owned. When she scanned the prices, Sophie gave an involuntary whistle. *Wow!* That was what you had to pay for complete privacy. No wonder it wasn't on the radar. Only the filthy rich would consider it. If Eleanor was hiring a live-in help, then it was a probability she was in one of the private ones. Now that would take some serious money. Given the location and the fact that there was the only one accessible point to land a boat on the island, the paparazzi wouldn't have a chance of sneaking in undetected.

At the sound of clicking heels in the corridor, she jammed the folder shut. Brie Simmons appeared around the door in an outfit that definitely did not come from Big W. Dressed in bottom-hugging pants, a low-cut top and knee-high soft leather boots she oozed panache. Her usual white smile was missing as she reached for the folder.

Sophie pulled it out of reach. "Ah, ha. No, you don't. This is mine."

"Is it true you're going to interview a movie star?" Brie screwed up her face into a frown of disapproval. "I'm the social reporter. Why was this given to you of all people?"

Sophie raised her eyebrows; the walls obviously had ears. "The news spread fast. It's not exactly an interview, *per se*. And," she said with a waggle of her finger, "it's a secret assignment, so I can't tell you any details, so don't ask. Besides," she added offhandedly, "the actor is nobody of importance."

"If it's no one famous, then why are you so tight-lipped about it? Now you've got me really curious."

"You'll just have to wear it."

"Surely you can give me a hint."

Sophie smiled at her fondly. Although totally absorbed in her appearance, Brie was warm and generous, and one of her best friends. With her elegant slim body and a passion for clothing that screamed haute couture, there was no way she would be a suitable candidate. "My lips are sealed. And what did you mean by that remark… *you of all people?*"

"Soph, have you looked in the mirror lately?"

"Why?"

"You've let yourself go. Your hair badly needs a trim, your eyebrows need work, and," she sniffed, "you have to get out of those baggy clothes you always insist on wearing. They look like they've come from Vinnies."

"For shit sake, I'm a reporter, not a model."

A slim hand reached over to finger Sophie's unruly curls. "At least take a trip to the hairdresser."

"I intend to." Sophie pulled the hand away and studied Brie's sparkling blue nails. "Manicure Monday this week?"

"Great aren't they?"

"It looks like you're cyanosed."

Brie snorted. "And you'd be the fashion expert? So…back to this film star. What did you mean it's not exactly an interview?"

"More like a position."

"What! Why did Owen give *you* that assignment?"

"He must think a lot of my reporting skills. Now no more prodding."

"Okay, but you can tell me how long you'll be away, can't you."

"I guess. It's for two months." ·

Brie stared at her, bug-eyed. "But that's a lifetime in this job."

"I know. But he gave me no choice. So much for my career as a political reporter. If I miss this election, I've lost any credibility," Sophie said bitterly.

Brie gave her arm an affectionate squeeze. "Chin up. No one can hold a candle to you, and the others will do a crap job, pissing off the readers and the pollies. Owen will welcome you back with open arms."

"I hope so."

"Well, I'm going to miss that big ol' cheery face of yours. What say I take you to the hairdresser in the morning for a new style, and then we'll buy you some clothes at that new boutique

I found in Rosalie? Afterward, we'll hit the bar with the girls for a farewell drink."

Sophie hesitated before she nodded reluctantly. Brie's idea of a hairstyle was far different from hers, but from the determined look on her friend's face, she wasn't going to wriggle out of it. And she was right about the need for a shopping expedition, though Sophie was a bit dubious that her credit card could handle the prices of any shop Brie recommended. However, if she were going to an exclusive resort, she'd need some decent gear. Most of her clothes were begging to be put out of their misery.

* * *

At the hairdresser, the trim morphed into a mod pixie look: layered at the back and short one side, while the other side feathered forward over her forehead. Sophie watched nervously as her dark curls were cut ruthlessly, while Brie directed the proceedings. Her protests were sternly ignored as the scissors snipped on. Afterward, she yelped as her eyebrows were ripped into shape with hot wax.

"There," Brie said triumphantly as they both stared into the mirror. "Isn't that simply fabulous? Wow, the style really made a difference. You look…well…rather striking now. I never realized you had such a perfectly adorable oval face. Now if you'll stop scowling at me, I might buy you lunch."

Sophie critically assessed her hair. Brie could talk rubbish sometimes, but she had to admit the style did flatter her face. Her cheekbones were accentuated, her lips fuller and her jaw not so prominent. Her brown eyes, compliments of her mother's Italian heritage, appeared as large dark pools. Who would have thought a haircut could make such an improvement?

Then it was off to the shops. She arrived home laden with parcels, with only a little time to finish packing and grab a snack before the cab arrived. Brie was already waiting at the entrance to the bar when her taxi pulled up.

Sophie self-consciously flipped back a stray bang as she trailed behind her to join the three women who sat in a corner booth. The cocktail bar was their favourite watering hole: a classic old-world bar with a warm and cosy atmosphere, subdued lighting and a dark sexy decor. It was busy with the usual professional crowd, some still in suits although it was nearly eight.

"Well, well, the *Globe* gals have arrived," murmured a petite auburn-haired woman, who moved up to make room in the booth.

"Hi, Janet," said Brie as she gracefully spread her very slim body along the padded chair. Somehow, she made it a statement of elegance. She nodded to the other two women. "Hello, Alice. Vera darling, where did you get those perfectly awesome earrings?" As Sophie plopped in beside her, Brie waggled a blue nail at her head. "What do you think of the hair?"

"Wow!"

"Fantastic!"

"Foxy!"

After accepting the A1 approval ratings with a smug nod, Brie touched Sophie's knee. "Get the drinks will you, Soph."

Used to being the gopher, Sophie went off to the bar without a word. Once settled back in her seat, she relished the sweet tang of the Moscow Mule. She tuned out as the others chatted on, lost in her own thoughts. Fashion didn't particularly interest her, nor did discussing the attributes of the males in proximity strike any chord in her breast.

After a while, she was dragged from her musings by Brie's strident voice. "Sometimes I despair about you, Sophie. You seem oblivious of every guy in the room. Haven't you noticed that gorgeous hunk at the bar has been staring at you for simply ages?"

Sophie glanced over and wished she could sink into anonymity. The *hunk* had a muscular physique, a tanned complexion that probably came from a spray can, and looked half-tanked. And he was eyeing her as if she was his next meal. She pulled up her low-cut dress self-consciously, wondering why she had allowed Brie to talk her into buying it for tonight.

Too much cleavage. It was so low she had been forced to resort to a roll of boob tape to defy gravity. She ignored his wink and pressed her lips together in disapproval. "As if. He's not my type."

"He looks familiar," said Vera. "Where have I seen him?"

They stared with renewed interest towards the bar. "I think he's a football commentator," offered Janet.

"Which program?" asked Sophie.

"Don't ask me," replied Janet. "I'm not interested in watching Neanderthal men tackle each other. I prefer the intellectual type."

"Well, I'm not a footy fan either, but he can put his shoes under my bed any day," said Alice drolly.

Sophie rolled her eyes. The poor bastard would get more than he bargained for with Alice. The solicitor was a real ball-buster.

"Well, I'm not interested. I like taller men," Sophie stated firmly.

"For Pete's sake," hissed Brie, "why are you always so effing fussy?"

"Let her alone," interrupted Janet, a thirtyish orthodontist who was newly divorced and revelling in her freedom. "She doesn't need a man in her life to enjoy herself."

Sophie smiled at her gratefully. "That's right. Anyhow, with my workload I haven't time for romance. Besides, I'm off for two months tomorrow." She caught Vera's sympathetic gaze. The quiet accountant was one of her best friends.

A "humph" sizzled out of Brie, but thankfully she went on to another subject.

Sophie knew she would have to come clean soon—her friends were getting impatient with her. She was sure Vera had already guessed, and it was only a matter of time before the others did as well. The day was coming when she would have to crawl out of the closet. But not tonight—she wanted a few drinks without drama before she headed off. Not that she was particularly worried about their reactions. They would probably find it amusing that she was no longer quite so boring and predictable. That wasn't the problem. Once it was out of the bag, there was no way her family wouldn't hear. She shut her eyes and shuddered, visualizing the news galloping like a bush fire through her myriad of relations.

Aunt Angie, the undisputed godmother of the clan, would not be amused. If only Sophie had someone special by her side to help announce her secret. Time was marching on—she would be thirty just after she got back from this wretched assignment. But it was a catch-22. No one wanted to go out with her seriously while she was hiding in there. Her love life sucked. Why was it so damn complicated?

As she was polishing off her second drink, the TV on the wall opposite caught her eye. Eleanor Godwin was being interviewed by the Channel Nine reporter, Merilee Watts. Sophie leaned forward to hear. The others stopped gossiping to follow her gaze.

"Oh, it's that gorgeous Eleanor Godwin," exclaimed Vera.

"Merilee looks smug about something," said Janet. "I can't stand the witch."

Alice sniggered. "Don't worry. Next to Godwin, she looks like a horse."

"I read Eleanor's going to be back in Australia for a few months," said Janet.

A gasp rippled into Sophie's ear. She snapped her head around to be pinned by two very angry eyes. "*She's* your assignment, isn't she?" growled Brie.

Sophie dropped her voice to a frantic whisper. "Shush! The boss will kill me if this gets out."

Brie gave her a withering look. "Okay. My lips are sealed, but I'll never forgive you. You know that, don't you?"

Sophie groaned. But if Brie thought she was going to get an argument tonight, she was sorely mistaken. "I know. Now I'm going to the bar to get myself a drink."

"Good. Don't come back for a while."

Sophie hoisted herself onto a stool and studied the shot list above the bar. Her favourite, Kick in the Crotch, was purple, sweet, and simple, but a wee bit too tame for her present mood.

The Slippery Nipple didn't have enough bite. She needed something with extra fire tonight. "Two Kamikaze shots, please."

She watched silently as the liquor splashed into the glasses, then picked one up and began singing, "Just a spoonful of sugar makes the medicine go down…"

CHAPTER TWO

The makeup artist pointed to a high-backed chair in front of the long mirror. "Take a seat, please, Ms. Godwin."

Eleanor glanced at the nametag and said softly, "Thank you, Candice. You'll have to work a minor miracle, I'm afraid. I had to lose quite a few kilos for my last film, which left me looking rather washed out. And please call me Eleanor."

The woman smiled shyly. "I don't think you need worry… um…Eleanor. You have wonderful facial bone structure. You should see some of the people I have to work with."

Eleanor closed her eyes, letting her mind drift as the artist worked on her face with assured hands. She hadn't been exaggerating about the weight loss. The addict role had required her to look gaunt, which she had achieved with determined dieting. But it had come at a cost, damaging her health in the process. She was worn out, exhausted, and her thyroid levels were out of whack.

Her doctor had sternly ordered her to take a long holiday to recuperate, and after this week, she knew she had to. All she wanted to do was to go to bed and not surface for a week. Thankfully, her mother had employed a home-help for her.

Unfortunately, she had to do one last interview to promote the film before she left for the island, something she needed like a hole in the head. But she had no hope of worming out of this contractual arrangement with the television station. And it wasn't going to be easy—Merilee Watts was a notorious bitch.

Some minutes later, Candice swivelled the chair around to face the mirror. "There, that should do it."

Eleanor had to admire the woman's talent. All traces of the last strenuous months had disappeared. Her face looked fuller, her eyes brighter. "Lovely work. Now I'd better enter the lion's den."

"Don't let her get the better of you," murmured Candice as Eleanor rose from the chair.

"I won't," she replied with a wink.

Before she stepped through the door, she plastered on a confident smile. Two lounge chairs faced each other on the studio floor, with a host of cameras and bright lights surrounding the setting. Merilee rose to shake her hand with a murmured, "Hello, Ms. Godwin," and indicated the seat opposite.

Eleanor sat down gingerly, with legs crossed to assume a relaxed pose. She studied the reporter who fiddled with her notes. Watts was perfectly groomed, dressed in a navy blue suit that fitted snugly over her tall frame. Though her face was far too long and lips too thin to be considered attractive, she did have a commanding presence.

The interview started innocuously enough. Merilee was extra pleasant, and three-quarters of the allotted time went by with no disturbing questions. In fact, the reporter had been surprisingly lighthearted as they bantered about life as a movie star. Eleanor began to relax when the director signalled five minutes to go. But then there was an imperceptible change in Merilee's demeanour and a calculating expression flickered across her face. The hairs on the back of Eleanor's neck twitched upright.

"So you play a lesbian in your latest film, *On the Edge of Life*?" asked Merilee.

"Yes, though the addiction is the main aspect of the plot."

"But a lesbian, nevertheless."

"That's right. A lesbian *drug* addict."

Merilee lowered her voice as if they were sharing secrets. "I understand in a former interview some years ago, you told a reporter you once…ah…had feelings for a woman." She drew out a long sighing breath before she announced, "And not platonic ones."

Eleanor paused as if testing the validity of the question before she gave a teasing laugh. "What a relief. I thought you were going to ask me if I've ever taken drugs."

"No. So there is truth in…"

"That I've taken drugs?"

"No. That…"

"Come now, Merilee. If I play a blood-sucking vampire, it doesn't mean I am one. So, if I play a drug addict, it doesn't mean I am one, now does it?"

"I'm not talking about drugs, I'm asking about being a les…"

Eleanor gave her a stern frown as she interjected. "Well, you should be. Drugs are a real problem in the world today. My charity supports rehabilitation programs which…" she droned on, adroitly giving no opportunity for the reporter to interrupt until, with relief, the director sliced his hand in the air.

Merilee leaned forward, her voice brittle. "I'm afraid time's up. Eleanor Godwin…many thanks from Channel Nine for sharing your thoughts with us tonight."

"My pleasure, Merilee."

Anxious not to be cornered, Eleanor rose abruptly from her chair as soon as the cameras stopped rolling. With a wave to the crew and the producer, she hurried out of the studio. When she reached the side exit door, she looked back to see Merilee leave the set with a determined expression. With a burst of speed, Eleanor walked quickly out into the laneway to her waiting limo and tumbled in.

"Drive," she ordered. As the luxury car moved off, she turned to peep out the back window. Merilee stood with her hands on her hips on the footpath outside the studio. Her body language was plain—she looked thoroughly miffed. Eleanor sank back into the leather seat with a sigh. Running away like that was not one of her finest moments. Would they never forget that dreadful interview, one of her few indiscreet moments in the last ten years? Given Merilee's reputation for hard-nosed interviews, she thought the reporter probably would bring it up, but all the same, her audacity to poke into Eleanor's personal life had hit a nerve.

Eleanor accepted that as an actor she was public property. Privacy wasn't something she could cling to, but she hated how the press invaded her life without regard. Fame had long since lost its appeal. Had it ever seduced her? Maybe when she was younger, but not now. Thank heavens she was going to the seclusion of Eurydice where no newspaper hound or paparazzi could get close. One thing was certain—if any of them did, then she wasn't going to take it lying down.

As the city whizzed by in a blur of colour, she began to feel fragile. Her mood sank lower, precarious enough to shatter by the time she reached her hotel. The feeling of displacement was acute today—it was as if she belonged nowhere. Her home was in America, yet lately she yearned to be back with her roots. Born in Brisbane, she had lived there with her parents until she finished high school and then moved to Sydney to study at the National Institute of Dramatic Art. Having to shift to the US to further her career was a wrench, though in time she came to love her life there. Now back in Brisbane, her hometown, she found she could no longer relate to the city—she had been away too many years.

Moisture welled over her eyelids and she sagged against the seat with an effort to contain the tears. Reason told her that the irrational emotions were a result of exhaustion and that her thyroid hormones were haywire, but it didn't stop the despair gnawing at her. If only she had someone to come home to, instead of having to face another night alone in a hotel room. Her life was a conundrum—the more adoring her fans, the lonelier she felt.

Her spirits lifted out of the doldrums when she found a bunch of flowers and a dinner invitation on the coffee table in the suite. Eleanor smiled as she read the scrawled handwriting.

Blade Weatherly, her old friend from NIDA days, would be a pleasant distraction for the night. Although his career hadn't taken off like hers, they had remained good friends and he always made a point of asking her to dinner when she came home. A perennial bachelor, the handsome charmer was good for a laugh, never offended by her good-natured rebuffs of his advances. She guessed it a force of habit with him. He thought she expected him to flirt.

After she swallowed her thyroxin tablet, she opened her laptop. She scrolled down to her mother's email.

Here are the particulars of your hired help, dear. A friend recommended this agency.

Eleanor clicked open the attachment, chuckling as she perused the employment criteria. Her mother had been way over the top. It read as if she wanted a superwoman rather than a simple housekeeper. Apart from that, the documentation was sketchy. No photo or particulars of the successful applicant were included, except her name, Sophie Ryan. Not that it really mattered. Help was help—domestic duties weren't rocket science. But all the same, a feeling of disquiet lingered, for the forwarded information was too bald. Her mother was holding something back.

She prayed the woman didn't look like Nanny McPhee.

She snapped down the computer lid and headed to the shower to prepare for her date. Tonight she would make a special effort with Blade even though she was tired. A good-looking man as her escort would take the heat off that ghastly interview.

It was to be televised tonight.

CHAPTER THREE

Sophie bit her bottom lip in an effort to hold back her erupting squeal. Eleanor Godwin, on the arm of a dark-haired Adonis, was walking straight toward her. Sophie galvanized into action, ducking low as she scrambled around to the other side of the bar. Instantly, she regretted the move. In her haste, she cannoned into someone, and when she turned to apologize, she groaned aloud. It was the football hunk. Now it was either an ignominious dash to the loo, or stay with him until Eleanor disappeared.

She gave him an appraising glance. He looked harmless enough, and after the vodka, she didn't feel all that picky. *Hell… why not?* It had been ages since she'd been out on the town, and the next two months were going to be a long time. At least he would be a non-judgmental drinking partner for the evening.

She swivelled until her back was to the bar, blew a stray hair from her eye and said brightly, "Hi, I'm Sophie."

He swayed forward. "I'm Jerry. You come here often?"

She wheezed sharply as a blast of beer breath whizzed up her nose. "Occasionally."

"You've got great eyes."

She stared at him for a moment. *Oh please, not that pick-up line.* "Whatever."

"You wanna drink?"

She snagged a peanut from the bowl on the bar and popped it in her mouth. "Okay. Anything with vodka, a swizzel stick and a tiny umbrella will do."

"Gotcha."

As Jerry placed the order with the bartender, Sophie watched Eleanor and her escort disappear into the dining room. She looked over to her friends. Brie raised her glass of champagne in a salute, while the others gave little waves of encouragement. With a shrug, she turned back to the bar—she hoped they were happy now.

When three hours later she checked her watch, she couldn't believe how the time had flown. Jerry was sozzled, and she wasn't much better. One last drink and she had better go home, for she'd be flat out catching the noon flight if she were any later. Surprisingly, he had been good company after she had made it clear she wasn't interested in being horizontal with him. He turned out to be a sports commentator as well as a regular on *The Footy Show*. Though not interested in football except for the State of Origin, she had to concede his anecdotes were amusing. And with alcohol running riot through her veins, everything seemed super hilarious.

She was laughing uproariously at one of his quips, when he suddenly peered at something over her shoulder. She pivoted to see Eleanor Godwin climb onto a stool on the opposite side of the bar. In the flesh, the film star looked even lovelier. She had a beauty that was graceful and natural. Her face was soft and her honey-coloured hair fell in shining waves onto her shoulders. A silky green dress showed off her slim figure, although she looked to Sophie to be unhealthily thin.

Their eyes met. Immediately, Sophie bit back the laughter under the scrutiny.

Then to her horror, Jerry said loudly, "She's got great tits." He draped his arm over Sophie's shoulder, holding her in place. "Whatcha think, babe?"

She blinked, unable to construct a pithy reply.

"Great arse too," he burbled.

Even in her befuddled state, the ramifications of his tactless remarks about her future employer sent Sophie into survival mode. "Shush," she whispered urgently. She tried to shake him off, but he clung like a limpet. It was more for support than a come-on, but it still irritated her that he took the liberty. Aware she probably looked like a happy hooker, Sophie flashed Eleanor an apologetic smile. Her effort was met with a frosty glare.

Suddenly, a camera flash went off. Then another.

Sophie fell forward onto the bar as Jerry pressed firmly against her back for a view. Her breath whooshed out. Though she jabbed him sharply with her elbow, he didn't flinch or move. All Sophie could do was watch with mouth agape, as a small crowd, including Brie, magically appeared with their phones. Eleanor didn't seem to bat an eyelid. With aplomb, she turned graciously for the cameras, posed for a minute and then departed into the night.

"Geroff me, you big lug," Sophie snapped.

"Aw Soph. Don't be like that."

"You're squashing me."

"Okay…okay!"

After she wriggled free, she tried to pull up her blouse, though somewhat unsuccessfully. She was all thumbs.

Brie appeared at her elbow and straightened the top. "It's time I took you home. You've had quite enough."

Sophie looked at her blearily. "I'm not drunk, just less classy and more fun. Isn't that what you want me to be?"

"Come on, sunshine. You'll thank me in the morning."

"You want me to take you, babe?" asked Jerry.

"Huh! No way." She fluttered her hands vaguely in the air. "This is Jerry, Brie?"

"Well, hi there," said Brie. "I thought I recognized you. You're Jerry Burrows from *The Footy Show*, aren't you?"

"Yep. That's me."

"Sorry about this, but I'd better get Sophie to bed. I'd love to stay, but she's got a plane to catch tomorrow."

"Maybe I'll see you around, babe," he said hopefully.

"Not likely," muttered Sophie. "I'll be away for two months."

"Here's my phone number." He pushed a beer-sodden card into her palm. "What about yours?"

She stuffed it into her purse. "I'll ring you."

Brie tapped her heels impatiently on the floor. "Give it to him, Sophie."

"I said I'll ring him."

"Make sure you do. I'd like to see you again," said Jerry and leaned over to plant a rum-tinged kiss on her lips.

She gave him a halfhearted smile of farewell, resisting the urge to wipe her mouth as they walked towards the exit. By the time the cab pulled up outside her door, she could barely stagger up the driveway to the front door. Fully dressed, she flopped into the bed, barely aware that Brie had covered her with the Doona before she passed out.

* * *

A persistent buzzing forced Sophie to raise her throbbing head from the pillow. *Far out, how much did I drink last night?* With a groan, she pressed off the alarm button and buried her head back under the covers. She drifted off again, only to be jerked awake by the shrill rings of her phone. She peered sullenly at the caller ID. *Brie…what the hell does she want?*

"Are you still in bed, Sophie?"

"Yes."

"Get up this minute."

"No. I'm too sick."

"You'll be sicker if you miss that plane."

"Plane? What plane?"

"The one that leaves at noon that you have to be on."

Sophie's eyes flew open. She struggled upright to look at the clock. *Oh, shit!* A quarter past nine—only an hour to shower, dress, and tidy the house. The trip to the airport would take another hour, which left the bare minimum of time to check in. She'd be lucky to make it. She would have to run and she didn't know if she would be capable of speed in her condition.

Brie's voice echoed in her ear. "Are you still on the end of the phone, Sophie?"

"Yes, yes. I'm getting up."

"Well, I'm outside. Let me in."

"I'm coming now." She swung her legs over the side of the bed, ignoring the sudden lurch of her stomach. *Not the time to be sick*. With as much speed as her aching head allowed, she trotted down the hallway to the front door.

Brie swept in, took one look at her and pointed to the bathroom. "Get in the shower. You look like something the cat dragged in and you smell like a brewery. I'll make the bed and tidy up."

Sophie nearly wept with gratitude. Quickly she stripped off the wrinkled outfit, wrapped it in plastic and jammed it in the suitcase. She'd wash it when she got there. Once in the shower, she let the spray sluice down her neck and over her shoulders. As she lathered on the soap, the remnants of the night gradually washed away. By the time she was dressed, the house was in order and the kettle on.

Brie pointed to a kitchen chair, a gleam of sympathy in her eye. "I'll make a cup of coffee and a piece of toast. Eat it or you'll be sick."

Sophie groaned. "You're a saviour. Strong black with one sugar, please." She rifled in the cupboard for the aspirin and swallowed two. "What did I do last night?"

"You tied a good one on, honey. I've never seen you drink like that. Three is usually your limit."

"I know. I was properly pinged off with everything. I can't even remember getting into bed."

Brie chuckled. "I can understand that. I helped you…with difficulty I might add. You weren't exactly cooperative. You were drunk as a skunk and a dead weight. How do you feel now?"

"Okay. I don't think I killed off too many grey cells…just have a bitch of a headache, but the painkillers should kick in soon and I'll be in a better zone."

"Good. You'll need to be when I tell you the news."

Sophie eyed her with unease. "What news?"

"Finish your breakfast. I'll tell you in the car, so keep your phone handy."

Ten minutes later, with her suitcase and backpack in the boot and the house left secure, they joined the line of traffic heading north. Sophie relaxed back into the seat, relieved to be feeling human again. Her headache had subsided to an annoying throb and her stomach had lost the urge to evacuate its contents. She looked at Brie enquiringly. "Now what do I have to look up?"

"You're not going to like it. Log on to Facebook."

When the screen flashed on, it took a moment to register the picture dominating the page. It was very popular from the numerous hits. The shot was snapped at the bar the night before, though Eleanor Godwin didn't really feature in it. Only her side was in view. The people in the background had obviously sent the shot viral. With the new haircut, it took a second for Sophie to recognize herself. Then she shuddered in horror. There she was, her mouth open, jammed into the bar, her breasts lying on top with one nipple exposed. *Holy smoke! I'm doing a Janet Jackson.* Worse still, Jerry was pressed against her back, leering at it.

The caption read, "Burrows burrows into a tasty morsel. *Ha! Ha!* Who is his latest squeeze?"

One thousand, five hundred and forty-two hits and rising.

She scrolled down. *Crap!* Some perv had edited the photo to show just her boob. It had even more hits. She switched off the phone with an agonising moan. "The bastards!"

Brie reached over to pat her arm. "Don't worry. It's lucky you got the new hairstyle and you're gaping like that fish Dory. And looking as stupid. Nobody has a clue it's you. My phone has been running hot…everyone wants to know the name of the mysterious woman, even Owen."

"Cripes, you didn't tell him, did you?"

"No and you owe me for that. It would have made a terrific story. But all was not lost… I did snag a good photo of Eleanor for the next edition. And with that divine dress and the goss on that gorgeous guy on her arm, it'll make an absolutely fab article." She glanced across at Sophie and winked. "Just as well you're getting out of Dodge."

"I'll say! By the time I get back, it should have long blown over. Things on Facebook have a fleeting lifespan. And I don't think Jerry will remember too much about last night."

Brie laughed. "I suggest you throw away his number."

"I already have." Sophie gave a convulsive swallow, her voice tinged with desperation. "But there is one problem. And it could be a freaking big one. With this many hits, Eleanor may see the photo. Can you just imagine what she'll think of me if she does?"

"Nah," said Brie with conviction. "It's hardly likely a woman of her stature would have any of the same friends on Facebook."

"I damn well hope not."

CHAPTER FOUR

Sighing, Eleanor settled into her seat and put on her sunglasses before she turned her head towards the window for some privacy. With minimal fuss, the Qantas staff had discreetly escorted her onto the plane before the boarding call for the rest of the passengers. She was grateful for the courtesy extended by the airline—she definitely was not up to playing the diva for fans today. Last night had exhausted her.

The doctor had warned her not to do anything stressful, that her medication might take up to four weeks to stabilize the thyroid, but she wanted to—no needed to take the opportunity to defuse that interview. Although Blade had been the perfect foil for any speculation about her sexual orientation, it had left her with a bad taste. She was fed up with having to use a beard to put the press off. It wasn't an acceptable way to live.

If it weren't for her profession, she would be out and proud long ago. But at Carol's insistence, she remained closeted, though it was getting more difficult as time went on. She wanted a permanent relationship, someone to share her life, a family. Sneaking around was demoralizing, making something that should be wonderful, cheap. Another Oscar and it wouldn't matter—she would be too marketable not to be offered plum roles. Carol would no doubt object vehemently, but she'd have to wear it. She was her agent, not her mother. And that was the ironic part of the whole scenario, for her mother was the one urging her to come out.

Eleanor pensively tapped her armrest. What was she going to do about Carol? She was not only important to her career as her agent, but was also a good friend and confidante. Lately, however, in many subtle ways, the attractive brash businesswoman was making it clear that she wanted more than friendship. As much as she liked her, Eleanor wasn't interested. For her part, there was no chemistry, no heart-pounding attraction. And she was not prepared to live closeted much longer. On the other hand, forty-year-old Carol remained content playing a double life.

Passengers were still filing onto the plane when her phone vibrated in her pocket. She dug it out and glanced at the caller ID…talk about the devil. "Hi, Carol. What's up?"

"I'm calling to see how you're going, Ellie."

"I'm fine. I'm on the plane ready to fly out."

"Bon voyage then. I've some good news. I've reworked my schedules so I can make it over to spend some time with you. I'll send you the date when I book the flight."

Eleanor pursed her lips. So much for getting away by herself. She nearly shouted into the phone, "Don't come," but instead said in a level firm tone. "There's no need. Really. It's too far to come for just a short time."

"Nonsense. It'll be no bother and I'd like a break with just the two of us. We should talk about the future."

"Look, we'll discuss it later. I have to turn off the phone. Bye." Eleanor jammed it back in her pocket. *Blow!* The last thing she wanted was to have her on an island where there was no escape. The pressure would be full-on then.

Relaxing back in the chair as the plane taxied onto the runway, she shut her eyes and let the hum of the engines soothe away the stress. The next thing she knew, the flight attendant was asking if she would like something to eat. Groggy after her nap, she straightened, took off her dark glasses and shook her head. Plane fare never appealed. "Just a cup of coffee, please. White, no sugar."

She was on the last sip, when a chuckle exploded from the passenger in the next seat. Eleanor turned at the sound and they shared a polite smile before the young woman's eyes widened as recognition dawned. "Oh gosh…you're Eleanor Godwin. Wow! I'm such a fan. I've just been looking at you on Facebook." She blushed and stuttered, "Sorry. That sounded rude. I wasn't laughing at your photo. The funny one is of the couple across the bar from you." She held out the phone. "Would you like a look?"

Interested now, Eleanor took the phone. She remembered it very well. How could she forget them—the man had been lecherous and offensive, the woman had laughed raucously like a hyena. Both had been very drunk. She studied the snapshot. Her eyes roved from woman's open mouth to her chest, and focused on the brown spot above the sagging top. Was that a nipple? Quickly she enlarged the photograph with her fingertips. It definitely was. Good God, the woman had no shame. She passed it back with distaste. "Who on earth are they?"

"He's Jerry Burrows, a regular on *The Footy Show*. No one seems to know who the boob chick is, but Twitter is running hot trying to find out her name."

"So she hasn't been seen with him before?"

"Apparently not. She's a newbie. He changes girlfriends as often as his socks."

"Humph. Then they deserve each other. I imagine no self-respecting man would want her after that exhibition."

Eleanor sank back into her seat. When she opened her eyes again, the plane was descending through a few wispy clouds to Mackay airport. As soon as she stepped inside the terminal, she was greeted by a portly grey-haired man who introduced himself as the Airport Personnel Officer. Dressed in a suit, a little too formal for the hot climate, he looked uncomfortable. She wished people wouldn't make such a fuss when they met her. After the introduction, he didn't stop to chat, but whisked her away immediately to a waiting car, leaving a staff member to collect her luggage. It gave her no time to peruse the other passengers. She would have liked to meet her new employee at once, but the man seemed to be paranoid about her safety, so she didn't insist.

The ride to the hangars at the end of the airport took only a few minutes, and she was happy to see a sleek blue helicopter ready on the tarmac.

The pilot, a tall fit man with an engaging grin, tipped his hat. "Captain Liam Edwards at you service, Ms. Godwin."

"Hi, Captain. Is everything ready?"

"Your luggage will be here in a minute. We've cold goods that need to go as soon as possible to the island. As some of them are sizable, would it be possible for Ms. Ryan to come over on a later flight?"

"That won't be any problem."

"Good. Then I'll arrange someone to meet her. Thank you for that. Now climb aboard. It's an ideal day for an island hop."

The inside smelt of leather and a whiff of something pleasant, a lingering perfume from a previous passenger or a particularly nice air-freshener, Eleanor surmised. She strapped on her seat belt, surprised how comfortable the cabin was, and how large the windows were for easy viewing.

Liam was right—it was a glorious day, the view spectacular as they soared north. She gazed out enthralled, marvelling at the artistry of nature. The ocean was a vast mosaic of reefs, islands, and coral cays, coloured by every shade of blue and green imaginable.

After half an hour, at a particular pretty spot where the reef was clearly reflected in the water and a small white atoll rose out of the sea, the pilot pointed toward two islands on the horizon. "She's one of those," he called out.

He circled them to give Eleanor a full view before he brought the helicopter into the flight path for the descent. She craned her head to gaze at her home for the next two months. The larger isle was uninhabited. The smaller was covered with vegetation except for a cleared strip along the front of a cove. Rugged cliffs circled the rest of the island, which meant that this bay was the only access point by boat. The one jetty jutted out into the water.

The place was as good as a fortress—the paparazzi wouldn't have a hope of sneaking in.

Eleanor felt a shimmer of excitement. Even though initially reluctant, she was very happy now that Nigel had persuaded her to use his holiday villa to recuperate. This looked like paradise. When the film finished, he had been concerned she had overdone it. And in a way, it *was* partly his fault. As the director, he had insisted she lose those extra few kilos for the last scenes, and it had wrecked her health. One good thing had come out of it though. By the end of filming she had definitely looked the part of an addict.

After they passed over the snow-white sand of the beach, a concrete slab came into view on the point. With a steady roar of the engines and clanking whirl of the rotor blades, the helicopter slowly settled down on the pad. Once the engine was turned off, Eleanor unclipped her seat belt, nodded her thanks to the pilot and stepped onto the island. Not far away, two people waited next to tray-back buggies. The woman came forward to take her arm as Eleanor bent low to avoid the blades.

"Ms. Godwin…welcome to Eurydice."

Eleanor clasped the hand of the tanned middle-aged woman dressed in white tailored shorts and a colourful pastel top. Though in casual clothes, she radiated poise and style. "Mrs. Shaw I presume. This place looks wonderful. I'm so looking forward to my stay."

"And we're extremely pleased you're spending so much time on our island. Now, we're not into formalities here. I'm Deirdre and this is my husband Len. Would you like a quick tour before I take you to your accommodation?"

"Perhaps another day, Deirdre. And do call me Eleanor." She pushed a strand of hair away from her face with a tired sweep. "To be quite honest, I'm exhausted. I've been sick for the last three months, and with jet lag and promoting my new film, I really do need to go to bed."

"I'll take you to your house immediately. Len will follow with your suitcases, and I will arrange for the chef to cook you something for an early dinner. I'll have it sent over as soon as it's prepared."

"That would be wonderful."

"What would you prefer?"

"Fish and salad would be nice."

Deirdre smiled. "The fish is freshly caught so you will love it." She started the buggy along a road and pointed to a group of buildings in the distance. "It's not a big island," she said, "and only this part is occupied. The rest is in its natural state. We're laid back here, a holiday destination with no pressures. We have an entertainment centre with a restaurant if you prefer not to cook. We also have a gym, and a hairdresser who offers massages. The owners of the private villas have an arrangement with us to use our facilities."

"I have a housekeeper coming on the next flight. We'll eat at home for the time being until I regain my strength. What about the supplies I ordered?"

"The house is stocked with the groceries. Fresh fish is available daily, as well as lobsters, bugs, and prawns. There's an electric buggy in the garage for transportation." They moved on through an avenue of coconut palms and eventually stopped in the driveway of a house on the side of the hill. "This is yours. It hasn't been used for a while. Nigel's family only comes once a year, usually at Easter, and he rarely lets it out at other times. We maintain the lawn for him, and we've prepared the house for your stay. I'm sure you'll be most comfortable and it does have the prime view of the ocean."

Eleanor studied it appreciatively. It was a modern compact house with a balcony on the second floor, set into the trees to blend in with the environment. A vibrant garden of tropical plants and a lush green lawn surrounded the entrance. It looked snug and inviting.

She took the key from Deirdre with a smile. "I'll call in tomorrow. Could you give another one to my employee when she arrives, please? Her name is Sophie Ryan, and she's coming in on the next flight. I'll retire as soon as I've eaten."

"No problem. Dial nine on your phone if you require anything during the night."

Eleanor was pleased to find the inside as charming. The wall and floors were polished wood. The lounge room was decorated with spectacular photographs of the island and the long glass window gave a magnificent view out to sea.

Oh my, I could get used to this.

She glanced at her watch—just after three in the afternoon—ten p.m. in LA. A night owl, her mother would be still up. She pulled out her phone before she remembered there was no mobile coverage. After popping it in a kitchen drawer for the duration, she picked up the landline on the wall near the kitchen.

Her mother answered after the usual pause for overseas calls. "Frances Godwin speaking."

"Hi, Mum. I'm on the island and it's beautiful."

"Good dear. Did you have a smooth trip?"

"Not too bad. The helicopter ride was fun."

"What do you think of Ms. Ryan?"

"I haven't met her yet. She's coming over on a later flight. Why?"

"Just curious. Being over here, I couldn't interview her personally."

Eleanor's nose twitched. "She's not like a hundred years old is she?"

"No…no."

"So what are you hiding?"

"Nothing. She seemed very suitable for the position."

"I'll kill you if she's a crabby bossy boots. I'm here on a vacation."

Frances laughed. "I'm sure she'll be very pleasant."

"Okay. I'll ring you tomorrow when I'm settled in. Bye for now."

Eleanor chuckled fondly as she replaced the receiver. Frances Godwin was anything but an average mother. A product of the seventies' flower-power generation, she had spent her young adult years as an avant-garde artist and a rabid advocator for non-establishment causes. Finding herself pregnant at thirty-five, she had embraced the role of mother with the same enthusiasm as everything else in her life, much to the bemusement of Errol, her staid bean-counting husband. While Eleanor was here in Australia, they were taking a holiday house-sitting her home in LA, which was convenient for both parties. Her mother would be too full-on for Eleanor in her present delicate state.

When the doorbell rang, she found Len on the threshold with her luggage. No stranger to travel, she efficiently packed away her clothes before moving on to the shower. At the mirror in the bathroom, she peered at her reflection. She was sorry she bothered. With no makeup, her face looked pinched. Tiny lines had gathered around her mouth and there were noticeable bags under her eyes that seemed bruised. Not that she was ever overly conscious of her looks, but she was pleased to be out of the public eye while she recuperated. Fans demanded perfection of their box office stars.

After setting the alarm for six p.m. for a couple of hours' sleep, she sank down on the bed, exhausted.

As persistent beeps echoed from her bedside table, Eleanor opened her eyes grudgingly. Disoriented, it took her some seconds to get her bearings. The wave of happiness that came as she recalled the picture-perfect island was short-lived as the tiredness returned. She shrugged off the cloak of depression and walked out onto the balcony. With elbows on the railing, she leaned over the railing, her chin on her hands. The sky was turning from a salmon pink to a deep red as the sun sank low on the horizon. A reflection from the sunset shone on the ocean as if an artist had splashed it with a vivid wash of watercolour. A warm gust of wind brought the smell of salt and eucalyptus, and best of all, a sense of peace.

She took a moment longer to appreciate the view. The scene was sublime after the frenetic pace of LA, but it was the quiet that she noticed most of all. No traffic, no voices—nothing, except for the sound of birdcalls and the slight rustling of the leaves in the breeze. It was Eden.

She went downstairs at the sound of the doorbell. Her meal had arrived. Gratefully she took the tray, and after finishing every crumb of the superb fish, scribbled out a note for Sophie Ryan before retiring for the night.

As she dropped off to sleep, she was vaguely aware of the sound of a helicopter in the distance.

CHAPTER FIVE

Sophie kept on her sunglasses, pulled the baseball cap low over her forehead and walked through the glass doors of the airport terminal. After the automated check-in spat out her boarding pass and bag stickers, she deposited the suitcases onto the conveyor belt and proceeded through security. She picked up the pace, conscious her flight was due to leave shortly.

When she arrived at the rows of seats occupied by the waiting passengers at gate five, she glanced furtively around for Eleanor Godwin. The star was nowhere in sight. Though it only delayed the inevitable, still Sophie was relieved. She wasn't in the mood for a confrontation in her present state. Later she should be more composed.

When the intercom blared out their boarding call a moment later, she shuffled with bowed head into the line of people. Entering by the rear steps, she saw the flight was nearly full. No one looked up as she made her way up the aisle to the fourth row of seats. Most were busy flicking fingers on phones, or making a last-minute call. As soon as slipped into her window seat and clipped on her seat belt, her eyes began to droop. In the middle of the safety briefing, she drifted off to sleep.

It seemed only a few seconds before her eyes blinked open at sound of the flight attendant's voice. "Ma'am. Ma'am. Wake up."

"Wha…what's the matter," she mumbled.

"It's time to disembark."

Sophie jerked upright and glanced around the cabin. *Damn.* She was the only passenger left on the plane. With a murmur of apology, she hurried out the door. Tired, hungry, and frazzled, she looked around for someone to report to inside the terminal. Eleanor was not there. From the snippets of conversation she caught around her, it seemed the actor had been taken away as soon she had entered the building. When no one approached Sophie, she collected her bags from the carousel and stood forlornly to the side while, one by one, the other passengers vanished out the door.

After ten minutes, she looked anxiously around. Had she been forgotten? To her relief, a large man in a suit appeared at the bag depot, his gaze sharpening when he caught her eye. "Ms. Ryan?"

Sophie nodded. "That's me."

"I'm sorry I wasn't here to greet you. Ms. Godwin has already flown out—we've put you on the next flight. It leaves in three hours."

With a resigned slump of her shoulders, she watched him signal a porter to take her suitcases before she wandered over to the café for a meal. Though she cursed the long wait, she couldn't help feeling a twinge of relief. Her unenviable meeting with Eleanor Godwin was again postponed—with any luck, the woman might be in bed by the time she arrived.

There was no doubt in Sophie's mind that even if she hadn't seen the photo on Facebook, Eleanor was sure to remember her at the bar. In the morning, she would be in a better frame of mind, and body, to meet the star. And she would have to put her best foot forward. Owen would be furious if she was fired on the first day.

By the time an attendant arrived to take her on the next leg of her journey, Sophie was fighting to keep her eyes open. Her fatigue vanished when they drove round to the hangars on the far side of the airport and she caught sight of the helicopter on the tarmac. Her stomach gave a sickening lurch. Being contained in a tube with rotor blades was not a happy experience in her book. Why hadn't she been told? She had presumed it would have been a light plane or a boat.

Sensing her reluctance, the pilot, who had been standing beside the step, came forward with a reassuring smile. "If you'd like to board, Ms. Ryan, we can be off."

She quashed down the urge to flee as she climbed stiffly into the machine. A woman dressed casually in blue cargo pants and a white tank top, was seated inside. Sophie flopped down into the seat beside her, then pressed her hands firmly on her knees to stop the tremble in her legs. A ghost of a grin curled at the corner of the woman's mouth as she glanced at the jittery feet. "Don't worry. I've made the trip oodles of times and we haven't crashed yet."

"Now that's a consolation," said Sophie dryly as she pulled the seat belt on as tightly as she could.

The woman thrust her hand out. "Lisa Parsons, the assistant chef on Eurydice."

"Sophie Ryan."

"On holidays?"

"Not really. I work for Eleanor Godwin."

"You lucky dog. She's gorgeous. How long are you staying?" asked Lisa.

"Two months."

"Well, it's great to have someone young on the island for that length of time. Most guests are middle-aged or older."

Sophie was in no doubt that was true. Only a certain type of person would come to the island—the wealthy to relax from stress or someone like Eleanor who needed a break from the paparazzi. Not many Gen Y fitted into that bracket. "You'd have a quota of youngish staff though, wouldn't you? How many employees on the island?" she asked.

"Twelve, apart from Deirdre and Len Shaw, the managers. They're very selective whom they employ. No backpackers or itinerants. It's a place for the rich and famous, and as most guests come for a quiet holiday without the intrusion of the press, discretion is essential." She grinned. "The wages are brilliant, so most of the staff have been there for years."

Sophie found herself liking Lisa despite her rather abrupt manner. She imagined what you saw was what you got with her. She looked to be in her late twenties, with a solid athletic body, short curly sun-bleached hair and a friendly moon-shaped face. As Lisa gave a running commentary of the islands they passed over, Sophie kept her eyes glued nervously on the floor. After a while, she found that if she kept them shut, the mesmerizing sound of the spinning blades dampened her fears.

When Lisa exclaimed, "There's Eurydice," a sense of well-being swept through her. Soon she'd be on terra firma. She now dared to peek out the window. The sun had all but dipped behind the horizon and the sky was dyed red. The ocean had turned a dove grey edged with crimson. Daylight still lingered in the air, but it was failing rapidly as they flew over the beach to the landing pad. Sophie began to feel the stirrings of excitement—the setting was awesome.

A tall man, with skin tanned to the colour of light tea, was waiting beside the landing area. Lisa introduced him as Len Shaw, the manager of the island. After they off-loaded the food supplies in the kitchen, Sophie was treated to a bowl of spaghetti bolognaise before Len moved her on to the villa. At the end of the beach, he continued up a hill to halt halfway at a white-pebbled courtyard. Sophie squinted into the shadows for a view of her future home, but only the grey outline of the house was visible amongst the trees. No light came from inside. With the key in hand, she waved good-bye to Len before climbing the four steps to the landing.

Immediately, a sensor light flooded the area with a bright glow. Tentatively, she pushed open the door and walked over the threshold. Eleanor was nowhere in sight in the downstairs living area. As Sophie wandered through, she spied a note with her name written on the outside sheet, propped up on the dining table.

> *Dear Ms. Ryan,*
> *I'm sorry I didn't stay up to greet you. Your bedroom suite is the one at the end of the ground floor. I'm sure you'll be comfortable there. Bring a breakfast tray, an egg dish preferably, to my room at 8:00 in the morning, please. It's the second one on the left at the top of the stairs. If I'm asleep, please wake me up. I'm looking forward to meeting you tomorrow.*
> *Eleanor Godwin*

Sophie relaxed. It simplified things that she could settle in without any pressure. Yet conversely, she couldn't help feeling a touch of hurt. Even though this was what she had wanted, she felt she had been arbitrarily dismissed. Illogical, for she actually was an employee, but it still stung. If she were a guest, Eleanor would no doubt have stayed up to greet her. She shrugged off the ill feeling to inspect the house, though thinking being at someone's beck and call may be harder to take than she had initially thought. As a reporter she more or less worked autonomously.

The house was swanky, the décor tasteful, with a modern kitchen and a spacious combined lounge-dining room. Through the huge plate glass window, the view of the ocean was spectacular. Moonbeams danced on the water and stars twinkled in the clear sky—she couldn't wait to see it in daylight. After one last look around, she headed to her living quarters.

She was pleased to find a very roomy self-contained unit. The lounge had two butter-soft leather lounge chairs arrayed in front of a good-sized TV, while a small desk sat in the corner, complete with a pen, paper, and photocopier. Pastel blue curtains decorated the large window and two seascape oils graced the walls. After a murmur of appreciation, she unpacked, showered, and set the alarm before falling into bed. As she drifted off, she thought how much she was going to enjoy living in this luxury.

* * *

At the beeps, Sophie opened her eyes and moaned. Not a morning person, she preferred to work after dark when there were no interruptions. It took a moment to realize where she was in the unfamiliar surroundings. When it sank in, she leapt out of bed. *This was it. The day of reckoning.*

As she rifled in her wardrobe for an outfit that was neither loud nor revealing, the initial panic subsided into simmering anxiety. She settled on her brown tailored slacks and the soft cream shirt, careful to do the buttons up to the neck. After applying only a touch of makeup, she brushed her hair and made her way down the hallway.

The state-of-the-art kitchen was a delightful surprise. Every appliance imaginable was at her fingertips: from the elaborate coffee machine to the hi-tech flex duo oven. She hummed with something akin to real happiness at the sight of the set of Japanese Ikasu knives slotted in a wooden block on the shelf. They were the best money could buy. She had been honest with Owen—she loved cooking. It was one of the joys of her life.

Luckily, the fridge and pantry were well stocked, for all her culinary skills were going to be needed this morning to nullify some of the debacle from the bar. She worked efficiently, and by eight o'clock, the breakfast was on the tray: a glass of freshly squeezed orange juice, a small bowl of fruit, and eggs Benedict, poached to perfection atop a thick slice of ham on a toasted muffin. Over the hollandaise sauce that frothed off the golden yolks, she ground a dash of black pepper and sea salt. Finally, she made a pot of coffee, placing a hibiscus flower in the corner of the tray before she climbed the stairs.

Sophie rapped lightly on the closed door. When there was no answer, she gently pushed it open. Eleanor was asleep, spread out on the bed with her head nestled on an arm. Her silk top fell in delicate little folds over her breasts, the fabric thin enough to outline her nipples. Without makeup, and hair tousled, the film star looked younger and vulnerable. And incredibly sexy. Sophie swallowed as heat rushed to her face, and to other parts of her body that she tried to ignore.

Embarrassed by her reaction, she said in a low voice, "Ms. Godwin. Breakfast is here."

When only a murmur came in response, she put down the tray on the bedside table, leaned over and touched her shoulder lightly. "Ms. Godwin. It's eight o'clock. I've brought you a breakfast tray."

Eleanor's eyes fluttered open. She blinked as if straining to focus, then her eyes widened. Without warning, she raised a hand and gently ran the fingertips down Sophie's cheek. "Maria, darling," she breathed huskily. "What are you doing here?"

Sophie's jaw dropped open. "Huh?"

CHAPTER SIX

The cobwebs in Eleanor's mind cleared as she slowly lowered her hand. With an inward groan, she turned her head away, mortified. "Sorry about that," she whispered. "You took me by surprise. You…you reminded me of someone."

She shivered, realizing what she had done. She had touched her employee inappropriately. The woman probably thought she was mad. She swung her eyes back to find Sophie staring at her, mouth open. Eleanor searched her face. The resemblance to Maria, she could now see, was superficial: the hair was too short, the face not square enough or the cheeks as pronounced. And Sophie had a tiny gap between her two front teeth. But she couldn't ignore that the golden skin tone, the big brown eyes and full pouty lips were a perfect match.

She was going to kill her mother.

As she examined her, Eleanor suddenly had the feeling that she had seen Sophie Ryan somewhere recently. She pulled her mind back out of the past to refocus on the present. Why did she look so familiar? Then it came. "You're that drunken floozy at the bar in Brisbane. The one with that boorish man who made lewd remarks about me," she blurted out.

Sophie flinched, pink rose in her face. She nodded but remained silent.

"The woman with the exposed chest that's plastered all over Facebook," Eleanor continued accusingly.

"You saw the Facebook photo?"

"Who in Australia hasn't?"

"I suppose nobody," Sophie said in a resigned voice. "Except my mother and grandmother, thank goodness. They don't do social media."

Eleanor regarded her intently. "Can you give me a good reason why I should keep you on after that tasteless exhibition?"

"I can only say that I heartily regret making such a punce of myself," Sophie replied. "But I would like to point out Jerry made those crude comments, not me."

"Jerry is your boyfriend?"

"No. I was merely socializing with him that night."

"So you take no responsibility for his remarks."

"I do not. And I would also like to bring to your attention, that I hadn't begun working for you at the time I…ah… accidentally made myself a spectacle."

Eleanor raised her eyebrows at these words. She had expected her to beg, but it seemed that Ms. Ryan was made of sterner stuff. Instead, she was subtly telling her it was none of her business. "What should I do with you then?"

"I guess it's up to you if you're willing to give me a chance."

"Okay, let's nip this in the bud? If you work for me, there will no more public displays. Agreed?"

A spark flashed in Sophie's eyes, but then it faded and she nodded. "Agreed, Ms. Godwin."

"Good. Then we will put the incident behind us," Eleanor responded smoothly. She swung her legs over the side of the mattress. "I'll go to the bathroom before I eat. I've worked up quite an appetite and breakfast smells divine."

Sophie solicitously propped the pillows behind her back after she climbed back into bed. "Comfortable?" she asked.

"Very," Eleanor replied, surprised at the thoughtfulness.

Once she placed the tray across her lap, Sophie asked, "Would you like the room aired, ma'am?"

"Yes please."

Sunlight streamed into the room after the curtains were pulled back. Eleanor studied Sophie as she walked out onto the balcony. She was an attractive woman: about five foot six, an inch or so shorter than her, with full breasts, slightly flaring hips, and a nicely shaped behind. She wasn't Barbie-doll pretty, more beguiling, with her brooding eyes and stylish short hair. She oozed undeniable sexual allure. Eleanor felt a twitch of arousal, but pushed the feeling aside, confident it was only a fleeting thing. The unexpected attraction was no doubt a result of her upset hormones. Her emotions would be back on an even keel after a good rest.

Sophie turned to look at her with a cheery smile. "The view is amazing."

Eleanor gave her another tick of approval. Sophie was good-natured, which she liked in a woman. She didn't seem to harbour a grudge, as she took her medicine and moved on. It was also half the battle when dealing with staff. She gestured with a hand towards the chair in the corner. "Sit down for a minute. I'd like to lay down some of the ground rules and explain a few things."

After Sophie pulled up the chair beside the bed, Eleanor continued. "I've been sick, hence the need to rest. Not life threatening, but it has been debilitating. I've been prescribed medication, so I expect to be fully recovered in a couple of weeks. Doctor's orders are rest and relaxation, which means I'm to lounge around until my energy comes back. You'll have to take up the slack until I'm on board again."

"Very good, ma'am."

Eleanor felt a wave of frustration. And a little guilt. She had set the tone for the work relationship. Two months of *ma'am* would get very annoying. This wasn't *Downton Abbey*. "Let's not be so formal. Call me Eleanor. I'm not one for ceremony and we'll be together for two months."

Surprise flittered across Sophie's face. "I'd be pleased to."

"Good. Then that's settled, Sophie. Deirdre Shaw said they have fresh seafood every day, so could you go over later and get some? Suss out the entertainment centre too. I understand there's a buggy in the shed for our use."

"Are there any foods you don't eat, or particular preferences, Eleanor?"

"I'm not fussy. Judging by this breakfast, you're a good cook."

Sophie's face lit up. "Thanks. I love cooking."

"You haven't wanted to do it for a living? I imagine it would be more lucrative and far more rewarding than housekeeping."

When spots of red tinged Sophie's cheeks, Eleanor realized she had just overstepped her boundaries again. She didn't know what was wrong with her this morning. She rarely interfered in anyone's business, and never verbalized her thoughts without thinking. "Sorry," she said quickly. "That was tactless."

"If there's nothing else, I'll see to my duties." Sophie quickly scraped back the chair. "I'll come back in half an hour and collect the tray."

Eleanor grimaced. So much for cementing a good relationship with the help. Sophie had obviously been offended. Nothing was surer to put a damper on the holiday if her live-in companion disliked her. And she wanted to get on with her. The woman was a good cook and eye candy to boot. A very appealing combination.

Now for her mother—she had some explaining to do. She reached for the phone.

A cheerful familiar voice answered at the third ring. "Frances Godwin speaking."

"Mother," Eleanor said sternly.

"Ah. You've met her, have you?"

"Yes I have. What were you thinking?"

"You don't like her?"

"That's not the problem and you know it. Maria is in the past, seven years ago to be exact, and must be left there."

A sigh came through the receiver. "Yes I know, dear, but I'm starting to worry about you. You've had no romantic attachments since."

Eleanor kept her voice level with difficulty. "And you thought that hiring someone who looks like Maria was going to get me interested?"

"Well, she was the only one you've ever been head over heels with."

"I do date, you know," replied Eleanor testily.

"Ha! Discreetly, no doubt. So how come I haven't heard you talk about anyone for years."

"Because you are *less* than discreet," Eleanor snapped.

"I wouldn't have to hold my tongue if you were out in the open. It must be very cramped with a date in that cupboard with you."

"It's called a damn closet. I know how you feel about it, and I've decided after this new film is released, I'm coming out. Are you satisfied now?"

"There's no need to take that tone. Naturally, I'll be happy… I'll throw a party when you do. And you haven't answered my question. What do you think of Sophie Ryan?"

Eleanor paused for a fraction of a second too long before she said nonchalantly, "I haven't formed an opinion one way or other. She's a good cook which is a big plus."

"Aha! Do I detect some interest?"

Eleanor groaned. A self-proclaimed matchmaker, Frances Godwin could sniff out a libido hitch a mile away. Time to throw a spoke in her wheel. "There's no interest, so don't get too excited. By the way, Carol is talking about coming over while I'm here."

There was silence at the end of the phone. Eleanor could almost hear the crackle of ice coming through the line. She chuckled. Her mother hated Carol, a feeling that was mutual.

"Humph! What brings the black widow out of her web?"

"Just a friendly visit. How are you and Dad settling in?"

"Wonderfully well. I've already met most everyone in your street…" Eleanor turned the phone onto speaker mode, and ate her breakfast while she listened to the prattle. Once she had something interesting to talk about, her mother always hogged the conversation. She was on a roll now. Fascinated by the tabloids, she was in her element in Hollywood. In two weeks, she had found out more about the neighbourhood than Eleanor had in the six years she'd been living there. She had even managed to snag an invitation from the reclusive star two doors down.

When footsteps sounded down the hallway, she said good-bye, automatically patting her hair into place. Sophie entered the room and approached the bed to take the tray. As she leaned close, Eleanor found her musky fragrance quite distracting. Sophie gave a little gasp, just the smallest intake of breath, when Eleanor lightly touched her on the arm and said, "That was delicious. Thank you."

"Um…I'm glad you liked it."

"Did you have a look around?" Eleanor asked.

"Yes."

"Well?"

"It's a great place."

Eleanor tilted her head, waiting for more. When Sophie didn't elaborate, she added, "Okay. I'll let you get on with your work."

Sophie nodded and without another word, hurried from the room. Eleanor stared after her. If monosyllables were the only conversation she was going to get, she'd be pulling her hair out by the end of the two months. Good food and attractive looks only went so far.

CHAPTER SEVEN

"Son of a *bitch*," groaned Sophie as she ran down the stairs. Was that all she could say after being complimented? What was wrong with her? She had morphed into an idiot, barely able to string two words together. Eleanor had her tied up in knots. Somehow, she had to get a grip, but the sight of Eleanor in bed was etched into her mind as permanently as the tattoo on her hip. She was so lovely with her silken hair, her soft creamy white skin and her smooth rich dark chocolate voice. But without makeup, the smattering of freckles on her nose gave her an aura of helplessness as well. Sophie had little defence against that combination.

She forced away the self-recriminations to concentrate on her work. The house was spotless—the management had obviously spruced it up ready for their arrival. She didn't even have to dust. After a quick inventory of the kitchen, laundry and cleaning products, she headed out to the back. The yard was spectacular. Set in greyish blue flagstones, a swimming pool wandered between gardens of tropical plants and trees. A natural rock waterfall formed one end, a spa on the other, while a thatched hut with a table and cane chairs stood to one side.

So cool! She could imagine the two of them sipping cocktails there in the afternoons after a swim. After a last lingering look at the inviting water, she went in search of transportation, finding a two-seater golf buggy parked in the garage, with the key in the ignition.

On the drive down the track, she could see the rest of the villas perched along the side of the hill. They blended into the natural surroundings like internal retreats. At the bottom, the road straightened and ran parallel to the line of coconut palms on the oceanfront. Halfway along, Sophie parked the buggy under one of the trees to walk to the beach. The scene was nothing short of breathtaking—postcard perfect, white sand glistening under a sky almost too blue to be real. A reef fringed the shoreline, coral plainly visible beneath the clear water. A manta ray lazily manoeuvred between the clumps of coral, and in the distance, a pod of dolphins frolicked in the sea.

She ambled along the sand until she reached the jetty. Two yachts sat gently swaying on the water nearby, while a motorboat was moored to one of the pylons. Nearby, a larger, more elaborate yacht lay at anchor. She surmised it probably belonged to one of the guests. She poked around the jetty for a while before she moved on to the boat shed, which stood behind a cement boat ramp. When she reached the threshold of the open door of the shed, a blast of cigarette smoke and oil fumes shot up her nostrils. An involuntary cough bubbled out. The stout man with his head in a boat engine, turned quickly at the sound, ash floating off the cigarette dangling from his lips. "What can I do for you?" he asked.

"I'm having a look around," Sophie answered with a smile.

"Just arrived?"

"I flew in yesterday."

"For a long holiday?"

"We'll be here for two months. I'm actually an employee of a guest."

When he visibly relaxed at her words, she guessed he liked being on an equal footing with people. As she reached out to slide her fingertips over the smooth fibreglass hull to feel the familiar texture, he looked at her quizzically. "You know something about boats?"

"My father has a Mako 234 Centre Console. I often go out with him."

"That's a nice unit. If you're interested, I run fishing and sightseeing charters for the guests." He wiped a beefy hand on his overalls before he thrust it out. "Doug Bremer. I handle most everything to do with the sea."

"Sophie Ryan. I work for Eleanor Godwin."

"Really? Eleanor Godwin is actually here? I've seen all her movies."

Sophie peered at him in surprise. Doug didn't look the type to be hung up on a film star, especially a woman. If anything, he seemed an action-flick man. He was somewhere in his late fifties, with a grizzled face, a large bent nose, and faded blue eyes rimmed red as if he needed more sleep. Something about him, though, struck a chord with Sophie. It was the way he looked her in the eye with no apology. A refreshing change from the disingenuous politicians she encountered day to day.

"She'll be here for a while, so later on I'll introduce you."

"Crikey. I'll have to shave that day," he said with a wheezing laugh. "Since you like fishing, I go out alone sometimes. I could always use a deckhand if you're interested." He gave her a wink, "I don't give away my best spots to the guests."

"That's a date. I'll call in next week," she said with a broad smile.

Pleased with the meeting and the unexpected invitation, she wandered back through the sand to the buggy. There was something to say about being on the same level as the employees. She toyed with the idea of pumping him for information about former guests. Sometimes people had shady reasons to come to such an isolated place to relax, and if anyone knew what went on here, it would be Doug. Fishing mates shared secrets, especially if alcohol was involved. She knew that well enough crewing for her father and his friends. Not to mention Owen's buddies supplying her false references.

But she quickly discarded the idea. It went against the grain to ask the man to betray confidences. She had some integrity left, even though she was forced to spy on Eleanor. At that thought, she gave a shudder but pushed it resolutely out of her mind. She might have to play Mata Hari, but there was no reason not to enjoy paradise.

She hummed a catchy tune as she drove on ahead to the large building. The entertainment centre was built in the same style as the villas, a coordinated effort to blend in with nature. There was no reception desk in the foyer. Perhaps it was somewhere else, she mused, but then maybe in this place for the super-rich, a booking was done more discreetly. Hell, how would she know? She'd never even had a toe in so upscale a resort.

An imposing woman in pressed slacks, a white shirt, and a lilac jacket, suddenly appeared at her elbow. Sophie's heart leapt into her throat. She hadn't even heard her come in. "May I be of service, ma'am?"

"Eleanor Godwin sent me for seafood."

"Of course. Come this way."

She directed Sophie past the kitchen to where Lisa was packing fresh seafood in a freezer. "Ms. Godwin has requested some supplies, Lisa," she said, and as silently as she had popped up, stole away.

The stocky chef lifted a hand in a wave. "Hi there, Sophie. Come on in and take what you want."

"Hi, Lisa." She jerked her thumb behind her. "Who's the Ghost Who Walks?"

A chuckle erupted from Lisa. "That's Monique. She's not a bad stick, just likes to creep up on people. She thinks it adds class to the place."

"Well, she gave me a hell of a fright. I nearly swallowed my tonsils."

"I know the feeling. What seafood are you looking for?"

"Prawns and fish. What's the catch of the day?"

"Coral trout…caught this morning. Guaranteed to melt in your mouth."

Sophie picked out four medium-sized fillets and handed them across. "And a kilo of king prawns as well, please."

With a smile, Lisa passed them back wrapped. "Enjoy! Have you seen through the centre yet?"

"No."

"Then come on and I'll give you the royal tour." She stripped off her gloves before she walked to the door.

The building was quietly elegant with its pale polished floors, walls and ceiling beams. It was a multipurpose centre, having an entertainment room, a restaurant with a small dance floor and stage, a cocktail bar, a small movie theatre, a well-stocked library, and a gym. Office rooms and the medic, and masseur-hairdresser were down one side, while a swimming pool and bar were out the back.

"Very impressive," murmured Sophie as they wandered through. "Do they have much night entertainment?"

"People come here for a quiet time, not like the other resorts where it's mostly a young crowd or families. We have a pianist, and occasionally a band comes over from the mainland. It depends mainly on the guests at the time. Deirdre and Len usually play it by ear, and cater accordingly."

"Nothing else?"

"Every month is a poetry night. People come over solely for it."

Sophie looked at her in surprise. "It's popular?"

"Oh yes," said Lisa. "It's a feature of the island. And they put on a quiz night occasionally."

"Hmm…that sounds interesting," said Sophie. Trivial Pursuit was something she was good at—she seemed to have two left feet for outdoor sports. "I'll pass it on to the boss. Now I'd better be off and get her smoko."

* * *

Sophie rapped on the bedroom door, balancing the morning tea tray in the other.

"Come in."

Sophie pushed through the door, happy to see that Eleanor's cheeks held a light bloom now. Propped up in bed with a book, she wore an attractive green silk shirt that enhanced her hazel eyes. She reached for the tray with enthusiasm. "A cup of decent coffee. Just what I've been waiting for."

"Sorry…it's eleven… I'm a bit late."

"No…no. That wasn't what I meant. You're not late at all," said Eleanor gently and patted the bed. "Come. Sit down and tell me what you did this morning."

Sophie sat gingerly on the edge of the bed, careful to keep her distance. Her tongue felt useless as she tried to say something constructive. "Yes, sure, okay."

"Well?" said Eleanor with an encouraging smile.

Sophie blinked, once, twice, then found herself smiling back. Her insecurities vanished as she gazed into the soft eyes. Coherent sentences finally came. "Firstly, you're never going to believe how awesome the backyard is. There's a great pool and a tropical garden. When you're feeling better, we can go swimming to make you stronger. The beach is fantastic, the water so clear you can see the coral and fish as plain as day. I don't know if we can swim in the sea, though. I'll have to find out."

"You obviously like swimming."

"Shit, yes. Um…sorry."

Eleanor chuckled. "I think I've heard a few choice words once or twice. Do you like running as well? Or jogging?"

With a laugh, Sophie whipped up the bottom of her tank top to expose the soft swell of her stomach. "Do I look like I run ten miles a day? See…no six-packs in sight." When a blush spread over Eleanor's cheeks, Sophie quickly pulled the top back down. "Sorry. I've embarrassed you with my flab. Sometimes I don't think."

With a little ticking sound, Eleanor put a spoonful of sugar in the coffee. "It's nice to see a woman with curves."

Sophie stood up abruptly, conscious she had been tactless. The woman was ill and had to put on weight. She didn't need Sophie rubbing it in. "Yes…well, I'd better go and do something.

I'll make garlic prawns for lunch and leave the fish for dinner. I'll be back shortly and get your tray."

"I'll come down for lunch. I'm sick of the bed and I can rest on the couch."

"Okay," said Sophie. She hesitated at the door, then came back and patted Eleanor's hand. "Don't worry. After a week of my cooking you won't look back."

She berated herself all the way to the kitchen. *Damn!* Eleanor was getting under her skin. She was so darn nice. If Sophie didn't start being more objective, she'd never be able to write the article. Already she had learned something very important about the star. And it wouldn't take too much digging to substantiate. Some past lover, or lovers, would be willing to tell the truth for a price. Eleanor was a lesbian. It was obvious the instance Eleanor had run her finger down her cheek. Her expression had been one of unabashed desire, as though she had wanted to taste Sophie. It was a look no lesbian could mistake. And then she had called out a woman's name…Maria.

Sophie shuffled the information around in her mind as her inner reporter wrestled with her emotional side. Though it would probably be enough to satisfy the gossipmongers, being gay in today's society was not front-page stuff even for a person of Eleanor's stature. More and more celebrities were admitting their sexuality and if anything, it was becoming fashionable. If Sophie wanted to make a mark, she'd have to come up with a better slant to her piece than that. Her gut instinct told her what the real story would be.

It was Maria *who?*

CHAPTER EIGHT

At one o'clock, dressed in a light kaftan, Eleanor appeared at the kitchen door. "How's lunch coming along?"

Sophie looked up from the dishes, pleased to see her downstairs, though whether she was very well was debatable. Eleanor appeared sicker since she had last seen her, more peaked and tired. "I've just finished the prawns and the rice is cooked. The table's set, so you can start. There's a small bowl of berries to sharpen your palate as an entree."

"You'll eat with me?"

"If you wish. I'll only have the main course."

"I'd prefer if we shared meals. I don't stand on ceremony."

They ate in silence, Eleanor seemed to be having difficulty eating as well as carrying on a conversation. By the time coffee was served, she was deathly pale. Sophie studied her anxiously over the rim of her cup, prepared to leap up if she toppled off the chair. Instinct told her that Eleanor would be reluctant to acknowledge how ill she actually felt, so she said in a mild voice, "Would you like to go back to your room now?"

"Please." It came out as a strangled moan.

"Lean on me to negotiate the stairs."

Eleanor didn't argue. They managed the climb with difficulty, taking a step at a time, with a pause before an attempt at the next. By the time the bed was in sight, Eleanor was on the point of collapse. She took a long strained breath, barely able to stand erect while Sophie turned down the covers.

"I'll call the medic," said Sophie as she carefully edged Eleanor between the sheets.

"No, no, please don't. This will pass. I've had attacks before, though this one is very nasty. The doctor said the medication would take at least another week to work and I would have to expect this."

Sophie looked at her dubiously, not entirely convinced. "I'm not a qualified health professional, Eleanor. I would like to get you checked out, for you are my responsibility. I don't want something happening to you on my watch." She took her hand, rubbing her thumb over the silky skin. "Please."

"Okay. If you must."

A weak smile accompanied the answer, but it heartened Sophie. "Good. I'll ring immediately. Could you give me the name of your specialist? The medic is sure to ask."

"Dr. Edward Davies. His number is in the side of my purse."

The medic, Bernadette, arrived five minutes after the phone call. She was a woman in her forties, with a kindly face and an air of authority. Sophie let her in, happy to pass over the responsibility for Eleanor's well-being. She had found Dr. Davies' number and was already at the front door when the buggy pulled up. After a quick introduction, she handed over the slip of paper and led Bernadette upstairs.

After the medic completed her examination, she disappeared to phone the specialist. Eleanor immediately dropped back into a sound sleep. Sophie pushed back a strand of hair from Eleanor's forehead, and feathered the back of her hand down her cheek. Curled around a pillow, Eleanor looked so wan and helpless in the king-sized bed that Sophie's heart was filled with a wave of compassion so intense it made her chest ache.

Then Bernadette appeared on the threshold, her face creased in a reassuring smile. "Is she asleep?"

"Yes."

"Then I won't wake her. She needs the rest. I'll come back later to take blood. The specialist wants an update. Let's go downstairs to talk."

Sophie let her gaze roam again over the figure in the bed before she turned to follow. "Will you like something to drink?" she asked when they were perched on the kitchen chairs.

"Just water thanks." She waited while Sophie filled two tumblers with iced water before she continued. "I know you're anxious, so I'll fill you in. It was a relapse he was afraid might happen because Eleanor refuses to rest. Her thyroxin levels were extremely low when she presented three weeks ago to her doctor in the US. Apparently, she'd been sick for over two months before she finally sought help. Then she insisted she had contractual obligations for her new film, so the doctor allowed her to fly to Australia on the condition she rested as much as possible, and that Dr. Davies take over her care when she arrived."

"Silly woman," murmured Sophie.

"Aren't workaholics all the same?" said Bernadette with a knowing smile. "We get plenty of overworked people here. And with an underactive thyroid, it normally takes seven to ten days before the meds work, but in severe cases, it can take several weeks. Even then, only some of the symptoms will improve in the beginning. The tiredness will go shortly if she rests, but she may have occasional mood swings. Weight gain is a side effect, but he wants Eleanor to gain the kilos she lost, so feed her up well. He's sure because she's young with no prior history, once she is back looking after herself, it will heal without any lasting effects."

"That's a relief. So what do I have to do?"

"With such a debilitating episode, she'll need looking after. He says there's no need for her to be hospitalised, but ordered complete bed rest for two days, then limited mobility for at least a week. Expect that she'll be plagued with waves of anxiety, which will leave her sweaty and trembling. Make sure you keep up the fluids and keep her comfortable."

"Anything else?"

"Yes. TLC is the best nursing procedure. Try allaying her fears and make sure she takes her medication." Bernadette gave her a nod of approval as she rose to go. "I can see you care very much about her welfare. Just keep her happy and stress-free and she'll be on the mend in no time. I'll call in at four to do the blood work. The helicopter leaves at five for the mainland. See you then."

* * *

The next few days were not easy for Eleanor, or Sophie. Eleanor fretted constantly, waking up at night with sheets soaked with sweat. Her bouts of anxiety taxed even Sophie's good nature, and she became exhausted too. It was easier to spend the night on the couch beside the sickbed, which meant her sleep was repeatedly interrupted. She was kept busy helping Eleanor in and out of the bathroom, cooking her meals, and washing her bedclothes.

Thankfully, by the fourth day Eleanor was definitely on the mend. She ate rather than picked at her food, and the sweats began to abate. Except for taking time each afternoon to visit the centre to de-stress over a cup of coffee with Lisa, Sophie remained at Eleanor's side. She read to her, talked to her, cajoled her to eat, and generally kept her spirits up as best she could.

As the days passed, they talked and debated a variety of topics, and Sophie formed a deep respect for the star. She was a smart, intuitive woman who cared deeply for others.

"How easy was it to make a success in the movies?" Sophie asked as she massaged Eleanor's feet, something she had begun to do when Eleanor became restless with her forced confinement.

"It's a hard business to break into. Much like writing…once you have that first novel published, it's easy to get the second one out there. You have to have talent, but being successful in the movie industry is just as much about that first big break. I started in the Sydney Theatre Company and was lucky enough to win the Critics' Newcomer Award. From there it was bit parts in TV in Australia, and later in America. Then I auditioned for the ex-girlfriend in *Golden Moon*. Only a supporting role, but it launched my film career. A prominent director noticed me, and…bingo…a plum part in his next movie. Four years later I won the Oscar, which catapulted me into stardom."

"How come I'm getting the vibes you're not entirely happy with your success?"

Eleanor plucked at the sheet absently. "It's not that I'm unhappy…it's just that…well…with success comes a new set of restrictions."

"Such as?"

"Like my life isn't my own anymore. I'm virtually owned by my fans and I can't move without the press dogging my trail. If I become friendly with anyone, the tabloids will have me in bed with them by the afternoon. Then they'll have me in an abortion clinic the next week."

Sophie burst out laughing. "Have they had you screwing someone?"

"I make sure I keep out of the limelight. I don't want to read about myself in a magazine in the doctor's waiting room. Mind you, I can't stop them making up rubbish. But so far, I've managed to keep a low profile in the scandal stakes."

"But you must have some love life, Eleanor? Any woman who looks like you should be knocking them back in droves," Sophie said teasingly, but watched her closely, waiting for the reply intently.

Except for a slight tightening of her jaw, Eleanor didn't rise to the bait. She was very adept at evasions, Sophie noted. She merely gave a secret smile and pointed to the left foot. "This one needs some attention too."

Sophie squeezed cream on her hand and skimmed her palm under the foot in a steady rhythm. When she looked up to say something, she found Eleanor staring at her with a quiet intensity. Their eyes met. Eleanor looked quickly away. Sophie let out a huff of a breath, grateful that her hands were busy. A glint had been in those eyes that hinted of desire and longing.

Lucky Maria.

CHAPTER NINE

Eleanor woke up feeling completely well for the first time in months. It was hard to believe they had been twelve days in the villa. She stretched languidly and took a deep breath as she watched the sunlight filter in soothing beams through the sheer blue curtains. The pretty glow matched her mood. It was such a relief to be healthy again after the gruelling time, for the severe bout of exhaustion had left her feeling gutted. Now finally, the tide had turned. She'd woken up refreshed and she knew she owed Sophie a huge debt for her recovery.

Eleanor glanced at the clock on the side table—seven thirty, time to get up. Time, too, to dispense with being an invalid. Since she was so much better, she'd surprise Sophie and come downstairs early. She would no doubt be very relieved she didn't have to play Florence Nightingale any longer. Not that she had ever indicated it was a burden. On the contrary, she seemed to enjoy fussing over her. And Eleanor had let her fuss, even when she was on the mend. It felt wonderful to be taken care of after living alone for so long.

As she stood under the refreshing jets of water in the shower, her thoughts swung back again to Sophie, as they were apt to do now on a regular basis. Things had become easy and close between them, but all the same, the woman was an enigma. On the surface, she was a gem: she ran the house like clockwork and helped Eleanor through her illness with tenderness and compassion. But underneath, she seemed to be masking another persona, one that was far more interesting. Every now and then, she would catch a devilish twinkle in Sophie's eye or a hint of sly wit in her conversation. And she was remarkably well read for a woman who spent her working life in such a mundane occupation.

She was a puzzle Eleanor really wanted to solve. At that thought, an annoying voice in her head said sternly. *Don't look a gift horse in the mouth. The woman's a treasure, so accept her for what she is.*

The smell of coffee was enticing as she descended the stairs. She wandered to the kitchen, and finding it empty, went in search of Sophie. She found her folding and sorting a basket of clean clothes in the laundry. When Eleanor stepped into the room, Sophie looked up in surprise. Caught off guard, she gave a shy intimate smile, which Eleanor returned with the same warmth.

"It's really great to see you downstairs. You must be feeling better this morning," said Sophie.

"Much. I'm looking forward to getting out in the sun and I'm starved. What's for breakfast?"

Sophie chuckled. "I've created a food monster. First course, yogurt with grapes and muesli, followed by an apple and cheddar tartine with crispy bacon rashes."

"That sounds divine. Umm…what exactly is a tartine?"

"It's a French open-faced sandwich."

"That'll be perfect. Let's eat on the terrace. It's such a beautiful day it'll be a shame not to enjoy it. You haven't eaten yet, have you?"

"No. Now sit down and I'll get you a cup of coffee. The rest won't be long. Everything's prepared, so it's only a matter of popping the food under the griller."

"I'll get my own coffee while you set the table," said Eleanor with a smile. "I'm not an invalid now, so you don't have to wait on me."

"Of course I do," answered Sophie a little gruffly. "It's my job."

Eleanor felt a sharp pang of hurt at the words. Was Sophie's empathy all about payment? "Silly of me to have forgotten that," she said in a clipped voice. "You can bring the coffee out onto the terrace."

The day was bright and sunny, the ocean a turquoise blue in the distance. Eleanor moved a cane chair around to face the breathtaking scene, but couldn't gather much enthusiasm as she stared into the distance.

What price paradise if no one shared it with you?

She pinched the edge of her nose with her fingertips, her eyes clouded with frustration as she struggled to sort out her thoughts. Now she was on the mend, what she needed was a friend more than a home help. And Sophie had been so good to her when she was sick, it felt wrong now to treat her as a servant.

She accepted the cup with a nod, and sipped the coffee while the table was set behind her. Only when the first dish arrived did she turn.

On the other side of the table, Sophie murmured, "Enjoy."

"I'm sure it will be tasty," said Eleanor, though she avoided looking at her directly.

"Is everything all right?"

"Yes. Why wouldn't it be?" said Eleanor and sampled the yogurt. "Very nice." As she ate slowly, she cursed that while her body had energy, her emotions were still all over the place. Her damn thyroid was still out of whack. Why was she feeling rejected? It was ludicrous—Sophie had merely stated a fact. Her thoughts were interrupted by the sharp clatter of a spoon being dropped on a plate. She jerked her head up and their eyes met.

Sophie, who watched her with worry, whispered, "Have I done something to offend you, Eleanor?"

"Honestly, it's not you…it's me. Our arrangement…well… it was fine when I was sick, but I don't think it's going to work for weeks on end."

Sophie stiffened. "Oh? I thought I was doing a good job. I've given it my best shot."

"No…no. That wasn't a criticism. You've been wonderful. Fantastic."

"But?"

"I guess I like help in the house, but I want someone to holiday with as well. A friend to share some fun. And I don't want to be coddled. I'm quite capable of doing something, though mind you, I'm nowhere near as good a cook as you."

Sophie was silent for a long moment, and then to Eleanor's surprise, she laughed. "Really? Then why didn't you say so in the first place. I was getting bored. The housework is virtually nothing with just the two of us, and now you're on your feet again, my nursing duties have finished."

"You're not upset? The terms of employment didn't state you had to be with me all the time. They were written by my mother, not me."

"Gee. It's really going to be a trial hanging out with you."

Eleanor reached over and touched the back of her hand. "You're a fun person, Ms. Ryan."

"You don't know the half of it, Ms. Godwin. I found a cupboard full of games in the back room, and the pool is calling out to us to use it." She gave a snicker. "I'm going to whip your arse in Scrabble."

"Huh…you wish. Now bring out those tartines. I've worked up quite an appetite."

As she crunched the toasted bread, Eleanor glanced occasionally at Sophie, frankly intrigued. Why was this sweet woman still unattached? Surely, someone with her sultry good looks, cooking skills, and pleasant nature, should have been snaffled up long ago. Were all the men around her blind? She noticed Sophie glanced at her with equal curiosity, and stroked the back of her hand where she had touched it. Eleanor couldn't help visualizing the finger not just on her feet, but also on the more intimate parts of her body. When she realized she was softly humming, she rose quickly from the table. "I'll put the plates in the dishwasher and you set up the Scrabble board."

* * *

"I don't believe this," snapped Eleanor, not far off a third straight loss. "Where on earth do you find some of these words? What the hell is a zampone?"

"A stuffed pig's trotter sausage. And on a triple word too," replied Sophie smugly.

"Huh! What are you? A walking encyclopaedia?"

"Prodigious vocabulary. It comes in handy with the job."

"To be a housekeeper?"

Sophie's eyes widened into the proverbial "rabbit caught in a spotlight." She ducked her head and muttered. "Um…I…I didn't mean that."

"What? You're not a housekeeper? You could have fooled me."

"I…I write novels too. Secretly."

Eleanor stared at her. "Really? What kind of books?"

"Err…romances."

"Wow! What's your pseudonym?"

"If I tell you, then my cover is blown."

Eleanor looked at her with real interest. This made Sophie infinitely more appealing. "Upmarket or Mills and Boon?" She waggled her eyebrows. "Or maybe bodice rippers?"

"No more questions. My books are not up for discussion."

"Okay, but don't expect me to leave it alone. I love a good mystery." Eleanor glanced at her watch. "Lunchtime, so what about after we eat we have a swim."

"Don't you want to look around the island?"

"Tomorrow will do. I'd better not push things too much. This is my first full day on my feet. There are lots of DVDs in the cupboard under the TV, so we can have a movie afternoon."

"Are there any of yours?"

"If there are, we won't be watching them. Now how about you make one of your fantastic sandwiches, and a cappuccino from that fancy coffee machine and I'll pack away the Scrabble."

After the box was tucked away in the drawer, Eleanor lay back in the recliner chair on the terrace. She smiled at the sound of singing drifting through the open window. Whatever attributes Sophie possessed, holding a tune wasn't one of them. Lady Gaga's "Bad Romance", was being butchered in the kitchen. As she listened, it dawned on her that for the first time in very long time she was truly happy. Here, away from the pressures of work and city living, and back in Australia, the world seemed so much simpler.

And Sophie had become an integral part of that contentment. The next weeks promised to be fun. Eleanor chewed at her lip. When was the last time she had let her hair down and really enjoyed herself? She couldn't remember. Life in the Hollywood fast lane seemed to be rounds of obligatory parties and living in trailers on location.

Her sex life wasn't to be envied either. No one had ever matched up to Maria. Theirs had been a brief, forbidden love, but the feelings had clung to her heart like glue. Perhaps if their romance had been able to proceed past that first rush of intense passion, the story would have been different. But that month of fiery happiness had remained burning bright for years, and all else faded in comparison.

Eventually though, time dimmed the memories. But when she was finally ready to embrace love again, no one came close to engaging her heart. And the dating pool seemed to have shrunk. Coupled with the fact she was still in the closet, she had become too famous for many eligible women to consider approachable. Men didn't seem to care—she was constantly hit upon at every public engagement.

At the scrape of a chair, Eleanor swung around. "That looks good. Now while we eat, tell me about your family."

Sophie placed the plate of sandwiches and coffee mugs on the occasional table between them and sank down into the other chair. "Okay. I've three brothers and a sister. My father is an Australian-born accountant of Irish descent, and my mother is an Italian housewife."

"So your brown eyes and olive skin come from your Mediterranean heritage."

"Yep. Have you seen *My Big Fat Greek Wedding*?"

"Yes. It was very funny."

"Well, ours are Italian not Greek. They're loveable, annoying busybodies and very family-oriented. Mum is one of eight, which means at a family do the house is packed. Standing room only. Everyone has to bring a dish to feed us all."

"Lucky you. I'm an only child."

Sophie whistled. "That makes my mouth water."

"No it shouldn't," retorted Eleanor and added wistfully, "I wanted desperately to have a sister. It was a lonely childhood, so I compensated by play-acting with my dolls. I got very good at it, hence my career path. Now tell me about your younger years."

"Having so many cousins and siblings, I learnt to stand up for myself. Mind you, I had no option with the nickname Chubby Cheeks. Mum and Dad let us get away with murder, but Aunt Angie didn't. She's mum's eldest sister, and runs the show. Think Don Corleone. She's old-fashioned and strict as they come. Woe betide any of us who stray from the path of righteousness."

"Then I hope for your sake she didn't see the infamous picture on Facebook?"

"She didn't, thank God. I rang my sister and she would have mentioned it. Luckily, no one had any idea that the day before I left I got my hair cut short."

"You wore your hair longer?"

"Down past my shoulders."

"Was it was wild and curly?"

"Yes. A nightmare to keep tidy."

Eleanor suddenly understood more about her mother's choice. Sophie resembled Maria now in a fashion, but with such long hair, they would be dead ringers. "I like your new hairstyle. It's very chic," she said, and meant it. Somehow, and she didn't stop to analyse why, it was important that Sophie was her own personality and not an extension of Maria's identity.

"Thanks. My friend Brie said I had to jazz myself up."

Eleanor toyed with the handle of the cup. "Does your aunt give your boyfriends a hard time?"

Sophie's eyes flew wide as if she'd been pinched. "I've…I've never brought anyone home."

"Oh!" said Eleanor, taken aback. She looked at her, intrigued. "Why not? You're a terrific catch."

When red flushed across Sophie's cheeks, Eleanor grasped her arm quickly. "I'm sorry. That was so rude of me. I didn't mean to make you uncomfortable."

"Hell, I'm not embarrassed, I'm flattered. Nobody's ever said anything so nice to me."

"It's true, so you better believe it," said Eleanor, and released her arm reluctantly. "But I'm curious about Aunt Angie. If you brought a man home, would she put him through the third degree?"

"Is the Pope Catholic? She'd chew him up without a qualm."

Out of the blue, Eleanor felt a surge of protectiveness. "I think your aunt needs someone to put her in her place." From Sophie's sceptical look, Eleanor guessed this would be a difficult, if not an impossible feat. She didn't offer another comment, instead climbed to her feet. She took Sophie's hand and pulled her up. "Let's go swimming. You can give me the next chapter of your family saga later on."

They made their way into the house to change, their fingers still linked together until they reached the staircase. As Sophie made her way to her unit, Eleanor paused on the steps to watch her disappear through the door. She slowly relaxed, not trying to analyse why her heart had skipped a beat when Sophie announced she had never brought anyone home. Some things were better left alone.

CHAPTER TEN

The new yellow bikini Brie had insisted she buy left little to the imagination. Sophie adjusted it self-consciously, wishing she were more like Keira Knightly than Dolly Parton. But no amount of pulling and pushing changed anything. Her boobs still bulged and her bum cheeks still poked out below the scanty bottom.

Her cousin, Jolene, always said no matter how much you exercise, when you first put on a bikini, you're like, "Oh fuck. Where're my boxers."

No truer word spoken, Sophie thought as she critically assessed her body in the long mirror in the bathroom. Strangely enough though, the more she looked, the more the low-rise bikini didn't look half-bad. No fat rolls in sight and her stomach was flat. Running up and down the stairs to nurse Eleanor had done wonders. After a last fleeting glance, she fetched a beach towel from the cupboard and headed out the back.

Eleanor was standing by the pool, dressed in a one-piece swimsuit that looked spectacular. The front dipped low between her breasts, the sides were high and it was backless to the waist. Sophie couldn't stop gawking. *Hot damn!* It was a seriously sexy outfit.

As Eleanor's eyes roved over the bikini, they flared briefly with emotion. "Nice," she murmured.

"Come on…last one in is a rotten egg," yelled Sophie with a running dive.

When she surfaced, Eleanor, treading water, looked at her with a crooked grin. "You're cute. I haven't heard that expression since I was a child."

"Being in a big family makes you juvenile. You should hear how we go on at Christmas."

"I can't imagine," said Eleanor wistfully. "Now I'm going to veg out for a while under the waterfall. It looks so relaxing."

Sophie watched her swim away with sure steady strokes, as graceful as a porpoise as she sliced through the water. Wasn't there anything the woman couldn't do? Sophie swam to the other end of the pool, and propped her head on her arms on the side to gather her thoughts. Or at least to face the reality of what was happening. She knew she was getting out of her depth.

Nursing Eleanor had been intimate and unsettling. She had become enormously attracted to the stay (what red-blooded lesbian wouldn't be), but it went beyond the physical. With Eleanor's collapse and her vulnerability over the following days, Sophie had never felt so protective of anyone. If she didn't get her head around this feeling, she'd never be able to write the article. And if she couldn't, she'd be out on her arse with no job.

Crap!

Uneasy, she glanced over at Eleanor under the waterfall. She was the epitome of a successful woman: well-spoken, well-groomed, well-disciplined. Yet for all of that, there was warmth about her that set her apart from many celebrities. She had the common touch. Sophie groaned. Why couldn't Eleanor at least be a bit of a bitch? It would make her task a lot easier. And because of a brain fart, Sophie had been forced to add another role to her repertoire of lies. A secret effing author and a romance one at that. At least she could have said thrillers or horror stories.

She pushed off the side and swam toward the waterfall, determined not to dwell on her predicament until she had to. As Miss Scarlet would say, "Tomorrow is another day."

Eleanor gave a wave as she approached. "Isn't it wonderful? It's almost surreal. No people, no pressures…and in these lush gardens, it's as if we're in Eden."

"I hope you're not going to tempt me with an apple."

"Oh, I think you're the one who's the temptress in that bikini," said Eleanor with a throaty laugh and a wink.

Sophie blinked. Did Ms. Hot Hollywood Eleanor Godwin just flirt with her? *Nah. No way.* She obviously meant it was too revealing. Embarrassed, she pulled at the top. "It is a bit…um… skimpy, isn't it?"

"Don't be silly. I didn't mean that. You're lovely…I mean *it's* lovely. The bikini I mean. You look nice in it." Eleanor's eyes fixed on the yellow top and she leaned forward with an audible swallow. "Very nice. I would…" She stopped abruptly with a quick hiss of breath. "Yes…well…let's swim for a while."

She powered off down the pool in a burst of spray, leaving Sophie to stare after her. After that, Eleanor became remote, still friendly, but the real warmth had disappeared. Her playfulness vanished and in its place was a cool wariness. She kept her distance each time Sophie tried to come too close. For the first time Sophie felt awkward with her, at a loss to understand what had happened. After the familiarity of the sickbed, it felt like abandonment.

When they exited the pool some time later, she turned to Eleanor, unable to keep the bitterness out of her voice. "I'll go down to the resort and get a couple of lobsters for dinner. I won't be long."

"Yes, of course. Aren't you going to…?"

Sophie missed most of the reply as she ran around the side to the garage.

She jammed the accelerator down, scowling as the buggy lurched forward with a shower of white pebbles. Once on the downhill road, she came to her senses and slowed down. By the time she reached the entertainment centre, her temper had cooled. Only then did she realize that she was still dressed in the bikini. She slipped around to the side door to the kitchen, and found Lisa stirring a pot on the stove. Her boss, Giovanni, was nowhere in sight.

"Hi there," Lisa said with a smile.

Sophie felt immediately calmer. Lisa had been a tower of strength the last week. "I was wondering if you had any fresh lobsters."

"Hang on and I'll be with you in a sec when the sauce is finished." After a minute, Lisa pulled the saucepan off the flame and washed the wooden spoon under the tap. "A batch of lobsters was brought in on the fishing boat this morning. You want a cup of coffee first?"

"A glass of wine sounds better today."

"My shout then. Come on out to the bar at the pool. I have to work so I'll only have a Coke." She eyed Sophie's outfit. "I see you've already had a swim."

"Yes. I probably should have changed before I came."

"Why? This is a beach resort...anything goes."

The bar was deserted except for an elderly couple talking quietly in the corner. After they ordered their drinks, Sophie stretched out in a recliner by the pool. Gradually, the hurt of Eleanor's rejection ebbed away. "This is great," she murmured as she gazed over the pool fence at the rugged backdrop. Where the island rose into a peak, a granite escarpment stood like a craggy fortress at the top. The vegetation consisted mainly of native hibiscus bushes, spiky spinifex and eucalyptus trees, for Eurydice was too far south for much tropical rainforest. Light greens coloured the hill, with snatches of browns from the more hardy shrubs that grew between the rocks higher up.

"I wouldn't be anywhere else if you paid me," said Lisa with a grin.

"Can guests stay for only one or two nights?"

"Nope. Minimum booking is a week. And there's a waiting list. I take it from the glass of wine that Eleanor is much better today."

"Much. She's back to her old self."

"That's good news. Now she's better, I'd love to meet her. I think she's a fabulous actor. And one hot lady too."

Something in the way she said the words made Sophie look at her sharply. Could Lisa be gay or bi? She hadn't felt any vibes, but then Sophie's gaydar usually sucked. A smidgin of jealousy prickled, which she ruefully quashed. "She'll probably come to the centre tomorrow."

"Oh." Lisa sounded disappointed. "I'd like to meet her one-on-one. You don't suppose I could bring some groceries to your house?"

Sophie nearly rolled her eyes. "If you come around tomorrow after breakfast, we should be there. Drop off some chocolate and fruit."

"Great. I can't wait. This month is going to be exciting. As well as having Eleanor Godwin here, Austen Farleigh is coming next month. Apparently, she's working on a new album and wants to get away from the press."

Sophie sat up straight at that news. Austen was the bad girl of the music scene: talented, volatile, beautiful, and an unabashed lesbian. She was the darling of the tabloids, her name linked to many high-profile women, straight and gay. With her moody androgynous good looks and lithe tattooed body, she was the pinup poster girl for younger lesbians. Whether her sexual prowess was exaggerated was hardly the point. Her notoriety, coupled with an extremely photogenic face and body, sent the press into a feeding frenzy.

She could imagine how jealous Brie was going to be when she heard Sophie had met her. Her visit here certainly piqued Sophie's interest. She loved her music and wondered whether the superstar would actually sing one night. "Do you think she'll do a performance?" she asked.

"Maybe. Deirdre can be very persuasive."

"I hope so," said Sophie.

"Me too. I'd better get back to work. Come with me and I'll get you those lobsters."

Sophie rose to her feet. The scent of roasting lamb wafted in the corridor to the kitchen. Giovanni gave her a wave as she passed the door, his ruddy face filmed with perspiration. Lisa had introduced the large Italian chef when she arrived for supplies on the third day, and they had hit it off immediately. She figured he'd fit in very well with her family.

After Lisa packed the lobsters with ice in a small esky, Sophie made her way back to the buggy. She knew she should be getting back, but a part of her rebelled. *Blow!* The beach was calling her name and Eleanor didn't seem to want her company.

Sand tugged at her toes as she ambled down to the shoreline. She sat down and rested back on her elbows to take in the view. The water was as clear as a mirror, the coral, fish, and little sea creatures plainly visible beneath the surface. A seagull swooped overhead then glided down on the slight breeze to land a few feet away. It pecked a soldier crab out of its hole before it flew off again. The place was so pristine that Sophie could only gaze around in awe. She settled down on her back, for a while enjoying the warmth of the late afternoon sun. She wished Eleanor were here to share this wonderful scenery with her.

With a sigh, she rose to her feet. Sunset wasn't far off, time to go back.

Sophie plugged the buggy into the electric charger before she walked around to enter her apartment by the back door. After a quick shower, she took time to choose an outfit, finally deciding on her black designer jeans and red silk top. She wanted to look good—she had some pride left.

Eleanor was leaning on the railing out on the terrace when she entered the lounge. She didn't call out to her, but walked quickly into the kitchen. So intent was Sophie with the meal preparation, she didn't hear Eleanor approach until she heard her clear her throat. She looked up to see her tilted against the bench with arms crossed, her eyes swirling with emotion. "I was worried about you, Sophie."

"I had a drink with Lisa and then went for a walk on the beach. I didn't think you'd care where I was," Sophie said brusquely.

Eleanor winced, giving a wry smile. "I deserved that. Of course I care." She moved up to Sophie and stroked her arm. "I behaved badly…I'm sorry. You did nothing wrong and didn't deserve a cold shoulder from me. I...I can't explain why I was such an idiot, but it won't happen again. I hated you left me in anger. Am I forgiven?"

Any animosity Sophie harboured went up in a puff of smoke at the touch of the fingers on her arm. They felt so damn good. "I wasn't too angry, just a little hurt. I didn't know what I had done wrong." Sophie knew she was whining but the constant stroking was affecting her brain. It felt like mush.

When Eleanor dropped her hand, Sophie wanted to place it back on her arm again. "Let's put it behind us," said Eleanor. "You look very pretty tonight, by the way."

"Um...thanks."

"Now, I'll get us a glass of wine and you can tell me what you're going to do with those lobsters."

Sophie smiled, on familiar ground at last. "Lobster with thermidor butter, new potatoes, and a tossed green salad."

"Oh, my. That sounds wonderful."

Sophie beamed at her.

CHAPTER ELEVEN

Eleanor heard the doorbell, wondering who would be calling this early. She opened the door to find an athletic woman with short curly hair and a ruddy round face, a covered basket on her arm. "Hello. Can I help you?"

"Hi, Ms. Godwin, I'm Lisa Parsons, the resort's assistant chef. I'm a friend of Sophie's. I promised I'd drop these off." She flipped back the cloth cover with a flourish. "Chocolates and fruit."

"They look wonderful, Lisa. Come on in. Sophie went out the back to start the pool cleaner. She won't be long. I was about to have an orange juice. Would you like one?"

"I'd love one thanks."

"Sit out on the terrace and I'll bring the jug out. Then you can tell me all about the resort."

Eleanor sat back as Lisa talked, chipping in a question or a comment occasionally. Two things were plain: Lisa liked to gossip and she knew everything that went on in the place. Staff members were always the best source of information, and an island wasn't so much different from a movie set. It was a confined community with a hierarchical structure. She had learnt over the years that it was wise if having a long stay, to get to know the people around you. With a little subtle prodding, it wasn't hard to glean from Lisa the little undercurrents of life on Eurydice. It had its power struggles, but overall, was a very pleasant place, where a guest's welfare was a priority and staff members were happy.

After some time, she realized that though Lisa was a genuinely nice person, too much of her would become very wearing. Eleanor was interested to see how she interacted with Sophie, because Lisa seemed very fond of her, and she had a sneaking suspicion that Lisa could be gay. It wasn't obvious, however, so she reserved her judgment.

They were leaning over a map, discussing walking trails, when footsteps clicked across the lounge room floor. Sophie appeared on the terrace with a plate of biscuits, fingers tensed on the china rim. They eased off when Lisa said cheerily, "Hi, Sophie. I was showing Eleanor the best hiking tracks."

"Good. We want to do a few walks."

"If you like I can go with you tomorrow. It's my day off."

Eleanor winced and flicked a look at Sophie. Her eyes were dilated like a kitten backed into a corner. "I promised Sophie we'd go today," Eleanor said quickly. "We've been cooped up too long. She's been dying for some exercise."

"*I have?*" squeaked Sophie and then continued in a rush. "Yes…yes, of course I have. I love walking."

Lisa threw an arm around Sophie's shoulders affectionately. The muscles rippled as she squeezed. "Then we'll do a long hike around the island and across the top another day. Just you and me—it might be too much for Eleanor."

"We'll talk about it later." Sophie wriggled out from under the arm. "Did you tell Eleanor who's coming next month?"

Eleanor turned to Lisa, her interest pipped. "Someone important?"

"Austen Farleigh. It'll be awesome having her here."

Eleanor froze, her hand dropped to table, clattering the glasses. *Oh my God! Austen's coming here.*

A small frown creased Sophie's forehead as she glanced across at her. "You've met her, Eleanor?"

Eleanor pulled herself together with her best poker face. "Yes, on quite a few occasions. She's very talented. Now if we're going for that walk, we should start before it gets too hot." She stood up and smiled at their visitor. "Thank you for your help, Lisa. I'm sure we'll be seeing each other again over the coming weeks and I look forward to sampling your menu. Now, if you'll excuse me, I'll get dressed. Sophie, you might like to show our guest out."

Back in her room, Eleanor sank onto the bed. Well, that news wasn't welcome. She would just try to avoid her, but knowing Austen, it would be impossible. With a determined effort, she slipped off the end of the mattress to find something to wear. After she pulled out a long-sleeved lilac shirt and a pair of dark blue three-quarter pants, she slammed the cupboard drawer shut. A low growl grumbled out as she hauled out her favourite joggers and found a hat.

That damn oversexed vixen had better keep her hands off Sophie. If she saw her in the pool, it would be like setting off dynamite.

When Sophie had come out in the bikini, Eleanor had very nearly pulled her in her arms and kissed her there and then. Perspiration blossomed over Eleanor's top lip at the thought of what Sophie's reaction might have been. A disaster. Sophie would have been within her rights to slap a lawsuit on her. She shuddered, visualizing the headlines: *Lesbian box office star sexually harasses straight housekeeper.* And no doubt, a delighted Merilee Watts would smile sardonically as she announced the news on primetime TV.

She arrived downstairs with her emotions under control, keen to get out in the fresh air. A small backpack was propped up against the wall at the front door. Sophie appeared almost immediately, wearing a collared polo shirt and a baggy pair of cargo shorts to her knees. After she wriggled into the straps of the pack, without a word, she handed over a squeeze bottle of sunscreen and a spray can of insect spray. Eleanor slathered on the cream. Her fair skin would burn quickly. Carol would never forgive her if she turned up a nut-brown colour to the launch—Eleanor's peaches-and-cream complexion was one of her assets. After dousing herself with spray, she handed them back to Sophie who stowed them in her shorts' pockets.

From the house, they took a trail that wove across the hill for a kilometre until they reached a stony outcrop at the top of the cliff overlooking the eastern end of the bay. With the sun bright in her eyes, Eleanor perched on a rock to gaze out over the water. From this vantage point with the other island behind them, the ocean looked vast and empty. The overwhelming magnitude of the scene left her off-centre. She didn't have a clue how far away was the mainland, or if they were even pointing in the right direction. Life seemed rather insignificant out here, a little frightening. Everywhere there was colour—more colour—exaggerated colour. City streets, even with their gaudy billboards and flashy lights, couldn't compete with this awesome display of nature.

Sophie handed her a bottle of water from the pack. "Carry this. You can't afford to get dehydrated. By the map, this track leads to a small plateau around the other side of this rise, which should be a good place to have lunch. It's about two kilometres, but all uphill. Will you be able to handle the climb?"

"I'm fine. Let's go."

The trail was uneven and rough, and bushes, some thorny, crowded the edges. They were both puffing like billy trains when they eventually reached the flat clearing. A stand of trees behind looked snug and inviting after the tough hike. While Sophie struggled to pull off the knapsack, Eleanor flopped down with a grunt into the cool shade. "Whew. I'm really out of condition. That was a battle."

"You can say that again," said Sophie as she settled down beside her. "I'm definitely going to give the hike with Lisa a flick."

A giggle escaped from Eleanor, now stretched out on the ground. "We're not the quintessential hikers, are we?"

"Nope. I told you I wasn't a six-pack lady. Scrabble's more my thing." She moved up to rest her back on a rock and patted her lap. "Lay your head here. Then you can tell me about your next movie."

Eleanor didn't argue. She wriggled over and nestled her head on her offered lap. "Umm…much more comfortable. My next movie is actually going to be filmed in Australia. That's why the studio asked me to do the promotions for *On the Edge of Life* here. Somewhat early as the film is still in the final stages of editing, but they took the opportunity before I came to the island. Normally press interviews are done just before a film's release."

"Have you finished them?"

"Yes. Done and dusted, though I've agreed to do one more before the event. The red carpet is being held at the Sydney State Theatre, eight days after our holiday ends." She gave Sophie's hand a squeeze. "You'll have to come. I can arrange tickets for you…and…ah…for someone you might like to bring. You can be my guests."

"I'll think about it," Sophie replied with a distinct catch in her voice, "but I probably will have to work. So, go on. Tell me about this next film."

"You'll be sorry to hear it's not a hot and heavy love story, Ms. Romance Writer." When a snort shot out from Sophie, Eleanor chuckled. "It's a futuristic thriller. Action-packed, but it does have a good plot. I believe the producers are negotiating to set up the props somewhere in an outback desert area. It hasn't been decided exactly where yet."

"Who's the leading man?"

"Devon Ward."

"He's a great actor," said Sophie.

"Yes, I've never done a film with him and I'm looking forward to it."

Sophie pulled the brim of her hat low over her face. "What about we have a nap. It's so peaceful it would be a shame to leave too soon."

Eleanor closed her eyes. The tranquillity was so soothing, she felt herself drift off to sleep.

Fingers brushing her hair were the first thing she became aware of when she woke. She kept her eyes closed as she drank in the sensations around her. The smell of warm earth and leaves mingled with the flowery scent of Sophie's soap. The screech of some faraway bird, keened faintly on the ocean breeze. She opened her eyes to see Sophie staring into the distance, as her hand slid idly back and forth across Eleanor's hair.

Eleanor reached up and touched the hand. "I had a little snooze. Thank you for the lap."

"No probs." Sophie looked down at her with a smile. "Hungry?"

"Bring it on." Eleanor moved off and sat up.

Sophie opened the knapsack, took out two brown paper packs and passed one over. They ate in companionable silence, and when the last sandwich was eaten, Sophie rose to her feet. "I guess we better get back."

"Do we go back the same way?"

Sophie opened the map, and pointed to a line that ran at the same height of the clearing for a distance then veered downwards. "We could go back this way. It'll come out behind our house."

"Okay. Let's go."

"I'll follow you," said Sophie.

In the next half an hour, the weather changed. The bright sunlight gradually disappeared as clouds gathered and the wind picked up. The stiff sea breeze brought with it the smell of salt and seaweed, with a touch of wildness that Eleanor found unnerving. By the time they reached the bend in the track, only a glimpse of sun was visible. Shadows of the clouds stretched like black inkblots across the island.

Then it happened. Preoccupied with keeping her feet on the narrow path, Eleanor didn't realize something was amiss until after it was over. A loud grunt came from behind. "Are you all right?" she called out.

When there was no answer, she chuckled. "Can't you keep up?"

After still more silence, she swung around to find the trail empty. Her heart rapped hard against her ribs, her breath caught.

Sophie had been following minutes ago, now she wasn't. Panic swam giddily in her head. There was nothing to hide behind on the track, which meant the only place she could be was down. Horrified, Eleanor dropped to her knees, crawled to edge and scanned the hill. There was no sign of Sophie.

She called her name—screamed it out repeatedly. Eventually, a sound came from below, but caught by the blustery wind, it was only very faint. She didn't even know if it had been human. Perhaps it had been a bird. Dizzy and disoriented, she pulled on all her reserves to stay calm. What could she do? If she went back to the house for a rescue party, by the time they came back it would be dark.

She studied the slope. Could she climb down? It looked doable. The incline was steep, but not impossible to descend if she were careful. Wiry grass, small bushes, and an occasional thin stunted tree covered the area, enough to hold onto. Some way down, the slope levelled off, the trees there thicker and closer. Sophie couldn't have rolled past them. It wasn't too far. All Eleanor had to do was get there. She walked back to where she had heard Sophie grunt, then with a deep breath, she forced her limbs to move, clutched the trunk of a small sapling and gingerly backed off the path.

As she inched her way downward, her eyes darted constantly for the next toehold, the next something to grasp. The quickening wind brought misty rain. Suddenly, in a flurry of motion a huge white bird rose up out of a nearby clump of bushes. Her heart leapt into her throat. It was so close she could hear the beat of its wings. Then the bird dipped and vanished over the tops of the trees as quickly as it had appeared. She went on. Her shirt was stuck to her back with sweat and her feet felt like they were on fire. A wave of fear struck as heavier drops began to splatter her face. Water blurred her vision. She shook the trickles away, and clenched her teeth until her head cleared.

Finally a few metres above the line of trees, she heard a sharp hiss. Whatever colour was left in her face, drained away. For one of the few times in her life she was truly frightened. She froze, too petrified to look. If it was snake, she was stuffed—this wasn't a scene from one of her movies, it was real.

Then a voice floated up from below. "For shit sake, Eleanor, what on earth are you doing? I thought you'd have more sense than to follow me down. I called out I was fine and I was going to climb up."

Eleanor looked down into Sophie's frowning face.

She didn't know if she wanted to kick her, kiss her, or cry.

CHAPTER TWELVE

The moment that Sophie turned to look out to sea, her foot met empty space. She began to topple, grunting in alarm when reality struck. She waved her hands frantically for something to grasp, as momentum, irrevocably took her over the edge. It was impossible to stop the downward spiral. She flew out into space, hung there for an awful second, and then, by some miracle, missed a rock by inches, and fell flat on her back on a grassy patch. The backpack took the brunt of the impact. The breath squeezed out of her and speech became impossible. She went into a tumbling slide. Again, the pack was a saviour. As she slipped and slid down the slope, one of the straps caught on a jutting root. Only for an instant, but it was enough to slow her descent.

From there on, she was able to clutch as many things as she could reach to control her fall. Saplings, bushes, vines all helped, and the tough grass cushioned her body. When she finally stopped just short of crashing into a sturdy gum, she was hurting, but in one piece. For a long while, Sophie quietly lay prone on the ground to let the shock settle. Her legs were rubber when she attempted to rise. She rested for a few minutes before she cautiously tried again, only this time she wriggled over to a tree for support. She let out the breath she was holding when she managed to stand.

She examined her weeping cuts, finding the main trauma was an angry gravel rash down her shins and arms. When she touched her stinging jaw, congealed blood came away on her fingertips. Her body ached, but she could move well enough. She exhaled, thankful she was alive to tell the tale. From above, she heard Eleanor calling her name. It was only faint, muffled by the noise of the wind in the trees. She shouted to say she was fine, that she would climb back up.

Then she remembered the first aid kit in the backpack. Her shoulder joints protested as she wriggled out of the straps, although it was worth the effort. Painkillers and a bottle of iodine were in the box, along with Band-Aids and bandages. After swallowing two tablets with the extra water bottle in the pack, she doctored her wounds as best she could. She grimaced as rain began to fall. It would make the climb more difficult. She stashed the first aid kit back into the rucksack and put it on. But when she readied herself for the climb, she looked up and could only hiss in disbelief. Not far above her, Eleanor was dangling from the root of a scraggy tree.

More from shock than displeasure, she blurted out a stinging reprimand.

With a squeal, Eleanor let go her hold, landing without dignity on her bottom at Sophie's feet. She scrambled to her feet, steadied herself against a tree and glared. "I'll have you know I didn't hear you say anything. So what would you have had me do, pray tell? Leave you to bleed to death down here while I went for help."

To Sophie's horror, tears welled up in Eleanor's eyes. Sophie swallowed to relieve the sudden dryness in her throat and tried to speak calmly. But her voice wasn't calm and even. It was trembling as the hellish scenario became too much. "I'm sorry, I'm sorry. Of course you would have been worried."

She pulled Eleanor into her arms, ignoring her own pain as she held her tight. Eleanor clung, sniffling in her neck. Without a thought, Sophie edged her head down and kissed her on the lips. A fleeting thing, but as the soft lips fluttered under hers, she drew back, embarrassed, at a loss to understand why she had been so impulsive. "Come on. We better get going before the rain really sets in," she said.

"Do we have to climb back up?" asked Eleanor tensely.

"No. We should be able to stay on this level. Remember the track was going to fork downwards." She pointed to the west. "If we make our way that-a-way, we'll meet the trail."

They trudged off, the going tough as the trees became thicker. The rain didn't let up. Water dripped uncomfortably down the neck of her polo shirt until exasperated, Sophie hauled it over her head.

"You've got a bruise under your rib which needs ice," said Eleanor.

"The rain will cool it down until we get home. Look," she called out in relief. "There's the track."

"Thank God. I've had quite enough of hiking to last me a lifetime. All I want is to get into the spa."

"Come on then. We shouldn't be too far off the house."

* * *

After they finished soaking in the spa, Eleanor gently rubbed antibiotic cream over Sophie's abrasions. As her skin quivered under the fingers, Sophie let her imagination run riot. It was easy to pretend that this was foreplay to lovemaking and not the medical administration of a friend. Once home again, Eleanor had reverted to the elegant self-possessed woman, completely in charge of her emotions. Sophie wished she would let her hair down as she had at the base of the hill. This Eleanor was completely out of Sophie's league, but the other...oh, the other was quite attainable.

Pleasure bubbled up inside her as Eleanor turned her over in the bed and unclipped the back of her bra. "Now I'll give your back a very light massage. It'll help the aches and pains."

"That sounds wonderful. Do you want me to strip down to my knickers?"

"If you like. I'll slip the shorts off."

Sophie raised her hips to allow them to be pulled down. It was like a dream, a scene straight from her fantasies, when Eleanor began to knead her shoulders with a steady soft rhythm. She let her eyes close, wrapped up in sensations as the fingers steadily worked out the knots. The hands rubbed downwards, occasionally skimming the outside curves of her breasts. By the time Eleanor began to work on the big glute muscles in her buttocks, Sophie was on fire with arousal. She began to squirm, seeking friction to relieve the ache between her legs. The hands began to massage firmer and Sophie couldn't help herself. She groaned aloud with pleasure.

Abruptly Eleanor stopped, and with a quick movement, lightly kissed the back of her neck. "That should do it. I'll see you in the lounge with a glass of wine. You can put some ice on that bruise."

After Eleanor exited, Sophie remained spread out on the quilt. She was throbbing so intensely, she'd be flat out standing up. She could still feel the kiss on her neck…soft…sweet…silky. Geez, she'd never been so aroused and Eleanor hadn't even touched an erotic part. With an effort, she redressed and went to the lounge.

Eleanor was sitting on the long lounge chair, propped up in the corner, one leg tucked under her and a glass in her hand. "The wine's in the fridge. Will you share the bottle or would you prefer something else?"

"Wine will be fine. I'll get myself a glass. Want a top up?"

"Yes please. Put it in the ice bucket."

When she came back, Eleanor pointed to the seat opposite. "If you like you can sit there. We can put the bucket on the coffee table between us."

With a swing of her hips Sophie sank into the plush leather seat. "Well, that was a bitch of an ending to a nice day."

"Yes it was. I think we should walk on the beach for exercise from now on."

"My thought entirely."

Eleanor ran her finger round the rim of the glass, her eyes fixed on the drink. "I felt vulnerable today, more so than I have for a long time. It wasn't a pleasant experience…I like being in control."

"Sometimes that's difficult, particularly when you work for someone. What about when you're making a film? Must you do what the director orders even though you don't agree?"

"To a point. The acting is still your own talent. He's there to help you get the best out of the role. And I do have the option whether I accept the part or not."

"You've never been in chaos?" said Sophie, her attention fully caught now.

Eleanor's fingers moved restlessly from the rim to the stem of the glass. "My mother's life is one chaotic moment to the next. I've always tried hard not to be as scatterbrained as she can be sometimes. I live a quiet orderly life."

"Lucky you. Hell, everything seems to happen to me. Mum calls me a walking disaster." Sophie studied her, then couldn't help herself. She prodded a little. "What about in your love life?" When Eleanor cocked her head with raised eyebrows, heat flushed across Sophie's face. "I didn't mean when you're having…I meant…you know…don't you let your lover run your life occasionally."

"That wasn't what I was referring to about control. I don't like losing my composure. And for your information, I haven't been that attached to anyone for years to worry about it."

"What! You just love 'em and leave 'em? That's mean." As soon as the words burst out, Sophie knew she had overstepped her boundaries.

Eleanor carefully placed the glass on the table, her eyes showing her anger and hurt. "Obviously you have a preconceived notion of me as a femme fatale. You are way from the truth and you were out of line just then."

The reporter in Sophie flared to the surface. Eleanor's retort didn't irk her as much as her dismissive tone. "Sorry. The remarks were inappropriate. But I can assure you I've never had any image of you one way or another, because I've never bothered with tabloid tripe. I'd rather read something more interesting, like the political page."

Eleanor poured herself another drink, ignoring the wine that splashed over the side of the glass. "So, you're a bit above the common person. Is that what you're saying?"

"What I'm saying, I don't like being treated like a bloody two-year-old." Sophie emptied her glass in one swallow and reached for the bottle.

"Then don't act like one," Eleanor snapped back.

They locked eyes. As much as she wanted to be the one to win this encounter, Sophie knew Eleanor was right. She had said something inappropriate. "I beg your pardon, that was really rude of me. I apologize. If you'll excuse me I'll put on dinner."

CHAPTER THIRTEEN

Eleanor stared blankly out the long glass window. She dragged a hand through her hair. Never had she experienced the flood of irrational feelings that Sophie provoked. The life she had carefully constructed one meticulous layer after the other, was faltering at its foundations. She had taught herself to remain composed, not to raise her voice, and to let no one ever see her without the defensive shield of elegance and good manners. But now when she had been really challenged, she hadn't made the cut.

Why was Sophie such a threat? More sophisticated and articulate people had never been able to make even a dint in her armour. In her hearts of hearts, she knew why. She was terrified of leaving that ivory tower she had fashioned for herself and Sophie had the capacity to make her do just that. She was enormously attracted to the woman. She had woken feelings in Eleanor that refused to be ignored. It would be better to back right off, because the desire might deepen into something that would really hurt when it ended. Although she was sure now that Sophie preferred women, there was no future for them. Their lives were chalk and cheese.

But no matter how much she rationalized the situation, Eleanor knew it was too late. Her heart was already engaged past the point of logic. With a long sigh, she rose from the comfort of the leather lounge chair and went into the kitchen.

As Sophie raised her head to meet her gaze, a tear slid down her cheek. Eleanor gulped—she had made her cry. She stepped forward and with her thumb, gently wiped it away. "Oh my dear, I am so very sorry."

"Why are you apologising to me, Eleanor? I was the one who was at fault. I had a bad case of foot and mouth, and then I deliberately provoked you." A sniffle was followed by a hiccup. "You're…you're always so calm and I…I felt…well… that you were talking down to me."

Eleanor flinched. "I'd never treat you like that, Sophie. You've become a good friend and I value that. Can we please put this behind us?"

"I don't know why you would want to."

"You can cook, you're a good housekeeper, you're kind and compassionate, but most of all, it's because I like you. Is that so hard to believe?"

"Yes it is, and for what it's worth, I like you too, Eleanor. You're a special person."

"Good. Now that's cleared up, let's eat."

Sophie blew her nose loudly on a tissue. "You just want me for my cooking."

"Of course. Why else?" said Eleanor, laughing. As she trailed Sophie back out of the kitchen, she shook her head. If only it were that simple.

* * *

Eleanor rose from the bed, pleased to see the morning was bright and cloudless. She was looking forward to checking out the resort today. With renewed enthusiasm, she dressed and bustled downstairs. Sophie was humming in the kitchen as she prepared breakfast. Eleanor stood and watched her from the door, suddenly shy when Sophie looked up with a smile. Eleanor risked pecking her cheek, before she stole a piece of bacon from the plate.

"Ah, ah. Don't pick."

Eleanor gave a throaty laugh. "That's the best part. I'll make us some cappuccinos while you serve out."

The argument seemed to have lifted their relationship to another level. They were more at ease with each other than ever. As they ate in companionable silence, Eleanor glanced at Sophie and thought how good it was to breakfast with someone. She wondered what it would be like to have a lover to share the burden of decision-making. At no time had her affair with Maria ever been considered long-term. That would have been impossible. It was what it was, passionate wonderful sex. No, that wasn't strictly true—she'd always thought of it as lovemaking. But had it been really? Eleanor hadn't gotten to know her first as a friend. It had been an infatuation, madness. And then Marie had gone back to her life, her husband.

Eleanor felt something cold squeeze her heart. Had she been deluding herself all these years? Had it just been an adulterous fling for Marie, an interlude, while it had left the younger Eleanor devastated, trying to pick up the pieces of her life?

"Are you all right?" Sophie asked with concern.

Eleanor made a concerted effort to shoo the memories away. It was pointless after all these years to dwell on the past, and she wondered why she was having these thoughts now. She had put it all behind her years ago. "I'm fine. Just reminiscing," she answered with a reassuring smile. "So, what are the plans for this morning?"

"Would you like to see the building first or the beach? There's a small movie theatre. We could view a film if you like. The man at the boat shed wants to meet you. We can organize a cruise with him for another day."

"Let's go down to the beach first."

"Put on your swimsuit then. We might get a spot of sunbaking as well as a swim. Wear a shirt over the top, for the sun will burn."

Eleanor rubbed on the sunscreen with anticipation. She was a keen swimmer, having had lessons at her grandmother's insistence as soon as she could walk. Nanna Godwin had lived at Noosa, and she had spent many summer holidays with the grand old lady at her seaside cottage. Nanna would sit on her folding chair on the beach, telling stories of her life in England before the war while Eleanor ate orange cream biscuits with her feet in the water. Her fair complexion was inherited from her grandmother, who looked like a china doll with her lovely glazed porcelain skin and fine snow-white hair. In those days, her parents always seemed to be busy: her father with his number-crunching work at the Government Statistician's Office and her mother with yet another bleeding heart cause. She had grown to love the sea as a refuge from both the hurts of the outside world and loneliness.

As soon as she and Sophie stepped onto the fine white sand, Eleanor felt she was home. She ran to the edge, marvelling at the clarity of the water. Like looking into a mirror, she mused.

"There's a place near the pier where we can swim," said Sophie. "You'll be stepping on coral here. We have to be careful of stonefish. They're poisonous."

"Okay, but let's have a dip before we explore. I'm dying to get into the water."

After a vigorous lengthy swim, Eleanor floated in the sea, kissed by the sun as she marvelled at the many shades of blues and greens. With no cityscape or clouds, the sky seemed endless, climbing into infinity. She glanced across at Sophie who was also on her back. She seemed equally at home in the water, swimming with an ability that appeared to come naturally.

They stayed in the water for over an hour, until reluctantly she knew if she stayed much longer, sunscreen or no sunscreen, she would be burnt. Sophie had no such worry, with her light golden tanned complexion that seemed to glow with vitality.

They sat in silence after towelling down, happy to meditate in the peaceful surroundings.

"A dollar for them," said Eleanor after a while.

"What?"

"Your thoughts."

"Oh, I was just thinking what a wow factor this place is. It's like a dream world, just the two of us alone in paradise."

With her index finger, Eleanor absently drew a heart in the sand, adding an arrow before she self-consciously scratched the doodle out. "Yes it is. Do you have someone waiting for you at home that you would like to share this with?"

"I've good friends, but no one romantically special if that's what you mean?"

Eleanor glanced down at her hands and then across at Sophie sheepishly. "That sounded like I was prying. Sorry."

"It's fine. My love life isn't worth talking about. It pretty well sucks."

"Really? I find that hard to believe."

Sophie looked quickly away. "Yeah, well, I do get asked out, but…um…my options are limited."

"Oh, so you're fussy…is that what you're saying?"

"In a manner of speaking," she mumbled.

"That sounded like twenty questions, but you are a little mysterious. So…would you like to have dinner with me tonight at the restaurant?"

"Okay. It'll be good to eat someone else's cooking for a change. Do you want to eat after the movie?"

"No…no, you misunderstood exactly what I meant. I'd like to take you out on a proper dinner date. We'll go home and get dressed up."

Sophie turned around to stare at her. "Like a date date?"

"Yes," said Eleanor with a smile.

CHAPTER FOURTEEN

Sophie discarded yet another dress and went back to the cupboard. *Damn.* Why was this so hard? When had she ever taken so long to make up her mind? She had no idea what the date actually meant: dinner between two friends or something more. Maybe it was just to make up for their fight. Whatever it was, this was probably the only proper date she was ever going to get with Eleanor, so she'd better make an impression. Tonight called for something very sexy. And she had just the outfit hanging in the wardrobe. The infamous dress from the bar.

Stop procrastinating, girl, and put it on.

As she slipped it over her head, she wondered why she was harbouring any hope that Eleanor would think her desirable. The woman was in a class of her own, way out of Sophie's league. Just watching her interact with the staff today had been an experience in itself. She had them eating out of her hand, even Monique had been ditzy. When she entered the boat shed, Sophie thought Doug was going to wet himself. Overall, it was a fruitful day for everyone. Eleanor had made a lasting impression and Deirdre had extracted a promise from the star to do a reading on their poetry night.

Finally dressed, Sophie carefully applied more makeup than normal, arranged her hair and made her way to the lounge. Eleanor looked a million dollars in cream pants, an emerald green silk blouse and a smart cream jacket. From the exquisite cut of the suit, it was way out of Sophie's price range. She was pleased to note that Eleanor's eyes widened when she entered the room, and for a second her gaze lingered on the low scoop of fabric over Sophie's bust.

"You look lovely. Ready to go," asked Eleanor.

"Yes. Do you want to drive?"

"I do. I'm looking after *you* tonight."

She waited for Sophie to climb into the buggy before she took her seat at the wheel. When a whiff of heady tantalizing perfume misted around Sophie, she inhaled appreciatively. Then as Eleanor leaned down to turn the key, her arm brushed Sophie's breast. Her nipple hardened, and embarrassed, she pulled back.

"Away we go then," said Eleanor, her voice husky.

The clicking of cicadas and the repetitive hoot of an owl followed them down the hill. The night sea breeze blew warm as they purred past the beach, which was bathed in an ethereal light of the full moon. Sophie tipped her face to the side, relishing the magical scene. They moved on to the bright lights of the front portico and parked beside the gardens. Eleanor placed her hand on the small of her back to guide her up the small flight of stairs to the front door. The possessive gesture caused Sophie's heart to flutter.

The dining room was elegant, with its stylish décor encased in the ambient glow of soft lighting. Dining tables were set up in front of a baby grand piano, while the more intimate settings for two were discreetly hidden by half-closed flimsy curtains in bay windows. A waiter, who introduced himself as Marcello, appeared as soon as they entered the room and ushered them to a window table. Once they were seated in the comfortable high-backed chairs, he took their drinks order and vanished.

Sophie looked around in awe. "This is lovely."

"It is indeed." Eleanor moved the candlestick to the end of the table. "There…that's better. I can see you properly now."

"Perhaps you should put it back then," said Sophie with a laugh.

"I can assure you I like the view."

"You're good for a lady's ego, Eleanor."

"Ah…do I detect a hint of scepticism?"

"I'm not so naïve that I don't notice you make everyone feel special. You had Doug wrapped around your finger in two seconds flat. The old bloke has seen plenty of the privileged class in action, so isn't easily impressed."

"I liked him. I'm not so divorced from the real world that I haven't learnt to interact with men like him. There are plenty working on film sets. They are the salt of the earth," said Eleanor with a small shrug.

The waiter appeared with a plate of crusty bread and dipping oil. "What may I get you to drink, Ms. Godwin?"

"Would you prefer white or red, Sophie?" Eleanor asked.

"A dry white if that's fine with you."

"Lovely." Eleanor studied the list. "The Pepper Tree Pinot Gris, please."

Minutes later he returned, showed her bottle, uncapped it and poured a little in Eleanor's glass. After she sniffed—swirled it—nodded, he filled the glasses. Once the bottle was placed in the bucket, he asked. "May I take your order?"

"The bread will be sufficient for an entrée. I'll have the salmon for my main. What would you like, Sophie?"

"The same please."

When he vanished through the curtain, Eleanor gave her a wink. "I do love that little ritual with the wine. Now let's get back to our conversation. Why are you so hard on yourself? You're a bright woman, but you really need to work on your self-esteem. Is it because of what you do?"

Her mouth went dry as Eleanor probed. She was getting in too deep, but Sophie refused to let her eyes falter as she took a sip. "No, it's nothing to do with that."

"Can I ask you a personal question?" asked Eleanor.

"How personal?"

"Very."

Sophie stared at her, tempted to say no. Instead, she nodded. "As long as I can ask you one back."

"Umm…okay, I guess that's fair."

"So…what do you want to ask me?"

"Am I correct in thinking you are a lesbian?"

Sophie watched the light from the candles flicker over Eleanor's creamy delicate features as she tried to figure out whether to answer. There was little point in denying it. After all, she was sure Eleanor was one too. "I am."

"Are you out?"

"No, I'm not."

"Why not?"

"Because…," Sophie took a bigger sip this time, "because of my family. It's going to be a shock for them. I go into a cold sweat just thinking of their reactions."

"I can understand that. Are you going to come out in the future? You can't hide who you are forever?"

"Yes, when I meet someone who can stand with me when I tell them."

"Does that mean you have never been in a relationship?" Eleanor peered at her intently. "You have been with women, haven't you?"

Sophie propped her elbows on the table, her cool shaken. "Of course I have. I've never been in a serious relationship though. Quite frankly, I'm sick of hiding who I am."

"I suggest you take the plunge and tell your family. It'll be easier than you think."

"Then why aren't *you* out, Eleanor, if it's no big deal?"

"Am I so transparent?" It was only a whisper.

"No. I just had a feeling."

"Was that the question you were going to ask me?" Eleanor met her gaze with searching eyes.

Sophie shook her head. "No. I want to know what this night is about exactly. Is it a friendship thing, a genuine date, or a pity party to give the poor housekeeper a good time?"

Eleanor withdrew sharply back into her chair. "I'm sorry you imagine that I think you're beneath me, Sophie. For what it's worth, I don't, because there is nothing about you that deserves to be pitied. You have a zest for life I find very refreshing and I envy you. So many of my friends have forgotten how to have a good time, or to be natural. I asked you out on a date tonight because I wanted to enjoy the company of a beautiful woman. We both know it can never go any further, but why can't we be happy we can share time together."

"You're right. That was ungracious and I'm sorry I was a jerk. I guess I've become a cynic in my job."

"Why is that? Have some employers given you a hard time?"

Sophie dipped a piece of bread and popped it in her mouth, chewing slowly to give herself time to sort out an answer. Nothing came, so she said vaguely, "No…no. I was just generalizing."

"So… have you always wanted to write?"

"That's the only thing I've ever wanted to do," Sophie said, relieved she was on firmer ground. She mightn't be the mythical romance author, but she did write for a living. "Housekeeping is only a way of paying the bills until my writing makes some real money."

"Then I trust you are nearly at that stage." Eleanor gave a chuckle. "Ms. Romance Writer."

Sophie turned away from her gaze at the sound of the curtain rustling, pleased to have a respite to gather her emotions while their meals were placed on the table. Lying to this woman who was fast becoming someone special to her, was getting harder and harder. She studied Eleanor cautiously as she thanked the waiter with her usual grace. Her savoir faire was admirable.

When he left, Eleanor remarked, "This looks divine. You're a food connoisseur, so tell me what you think."

The salmon was pink and tender, arranged on a bed of roasted garlic asparagus and mushrooms, with a tangy lemon sauce that smelled delicious. Sophie sampled a mouthful. "Wow. Now this really is good. I'll just have to get the recipe." She gazed at Eleanor. "What's your verdict?"

"Umm. I second that…very tasty."

Sophie ate slowly to plan her own questions. Now that they were talking frankly, this was an ideal opportunity to learn what she could about Eleanor. What she wrote in her article would be something she would have to decide later, but even if she used none of it, Sophie wanted to know for her own sake what made her tick. Outwardly, the lovely star was composed, thoughtful, and ultra-respectable, a paragon, but was it a cameo role she played or was she completely genuine? Sure, she was a closeted lesbian, but that really meant nothing. She was hardly Robinson Crusoe there. And in her position in the box office stakes, it was understandable.

"What about *your* love life?" Sophie began as she cut off another flake of salmon. "Have you got a certain someone waiting in LA?"

A faint line appeared between Eleanor's brows and her fingers fiddled restlessly with pepper grinder. "No."

"Ha! I bet there would be oodles who'd like to be."

"Be careful, Sophie. That's what started off our argument before."

"Sorry. I can't get my head around why someone hasn't claimed you long ago."

Spots of red coloured Eleanor's cheeks. She didn't answer.

Suddenly Sophie understood. Without hesitation, she reached over to cover Eleanor's hand with hers. "You've been really hurt by someone, haven't you? Whoever it was didn't deserve you. And for what it's worth, I think she was a stupendous idiot."

Eleanor went rigid, her fingers curled into a fist under Sophie's hand. Then she relaxed and murmured, "Things aren't always black and white in life unfortunately, but thanks for the vote of support. Now enough of the skeletons in our cupboards," she gave a little laugh, "or should I say closets."

Sophie placed her knife and fork on the plate, then drank the last of her wine. "Okay, let's have a bit of self-analysis instead. What do you consider your biggest vice, Eleanor?"

"You certainly aren't in the mood for small talk tonight, are you? Okay, I'll play. I like to be in control of my life. I find it difficult to live relying on someone else's whims."

"My worst shortcoming...I hate conflict, so always end up being used. Brie, my best friend, says I have to be more assertive. Mind you, she doesn't practise what she preaches. She bosses me around."

Eleanor stared at her with an odd expression, though didn't comment.

"What? You think I'm a doormat?" groaned Sophie.

"On the contrary, I was thinking you're anything but that. I think people take advantage of your good nature. And I was thinking how very well we suit each other." She shook her head as if to clear her thoughts. "Let's have some decadent dessert."

When she raised her hand, the waiter almost immediately appeared with the menu. "Would you like another bottle of wine, Ms. Godwin?"

"Two glasses of the Château d'Yquem sauterne, Marcello, thanks."

Sophie let out a soft "whew" as she caught a glimpse of the price. At nine hundred dollars a bottle, it had better taste spectacular. She didn't comment, aware the cost was probably of no consequence to someone with Eleanor's wealth. It was, however, another example of the yawning gap in their circumstances.

Eleanor passed her the menu. "You choose the sweets— perhaps we could share."

"Let's have the crème brulee."

To Sophie's delight, sharing dessert in Eleanor's rulebook was actually feeding each other. Watching the soft sweet slide into her mouth was one of the most sensuous experiences of Sophie's life. With each mouthful, emotions washed over her as the beautiful lips seductively wrapped around her spoon. When all too soon the bowl was empty, Sophie let out a hum of disappointment.

"That was delicious," said Eleanor blissfully.

Moments later, the waiter appeared. "Would you like to adjourn to a table near the piano for your coffee, ladies? The pianist is about to begin."

With the same friendly efficiency, he ushered them to a small booth in the cocktail lounge. It was a cosy candlelit room, separated from the dining area by the stage. Eleanor slipped her hand under Sophie's elbow as they followed him to the seat. When they passed through the dining room, many of the guests acknowledged Eleanor with a smile or a nod. As Sophie moved quietly by her side, she took in the tuxedos and glittering jewellery. The place reeked of money.

"Apparently Tuesday's dinners are formal dress," whispered Eleanor.

After they slipped into the seat, Marcello appeared with two small cups of thick Turkish coffee. Sophie tilted her head to the side to look at Eleanor and felt a flush of pride. Here, with the candlelight reflected in her eyes, she was easily the most compelling woman in the building. The booth was so small and intimate their thighs pressed together. Sophie began to feel a little lightheaded, though it was not all due to the wine. Eleanor's nearness was intoxicating, her perfume potent. When Eleanor took her hand and stroked its back with her thumb to the strains of a Mozart concerto, Sophie rested her head on her shoulder.

"Would you like a brandy or port," Eleanor whispered a little later.

"A port would be nice."

Sophie didn't know how long they had sat immersed in the music, but when Eleanor whispered, "It's time to go," she realized it must have been a couple of hours. The room was nearly empty and the pianist was gathering his sheet music.

Sophie straightened up with a sense of loss so acute her chest ached. She smiled shyly. "That was wonderful."

Eleanor's eyes appeared to be swirling hazel pools as they gazed at each. "Yes it was," she whispered huskily.

They rose without another word. Outside, the night breeze that ruffled their hair, brought with it the exotic perfumes of the garden. Their breath mingled as they turned to face each other in the buggy. Eleanor leaned forward to press her lips to Sophie's forehead. "Thank you for being with me tonight."

Sophie stared at her transfixed, her breathing hitched. Something fundamental in her shifted, something she was powerless to stop. Her emotions felt red raw. She knew she had drifted too far into dangerous waters, and had reached the point of no return. Awareness of how much her heart had become involved, brought equal amounts of fear and euphoria. Her feelings for Eleanor had leapt way past a teenage crush. She was in real danger of falling in love with the woman, which would be disastrous. Not only would she be incapable of writing the article, but when Eleanor found out she was a spy for the *Globe*, she would discard her. Or take her to court for invasion of privacy.

"Let's stop at a beach for a quick walk," murmured Eleanor in her ear. "That would be a perfect ending to a wonderful evening."

When Eleanor lightly stroked her thigh to emphasise the words, all self-deprecating thoughts were banished by a blissful cloud of arousal. She couldn't think of anything past the sensations that vibrated through her body. They lodged in a whirl of erotic throbbing between her legs. God, she was so far gone it wasn't funny. The walk on the beach only made her more acutely aware of Eleanor's magnetic pull as the strolled through the sand, arm in arm. The water was bathed in a warm glow by the moon that hung low in the night sky—a lover's moon, exciting and magical.

As they made their way in the buggy back up the hill to the villa, they both fell silent. At the door, Eleanor reached up and touched Sophie's cheek, a fleeting connection that nevertheless felt like a caress.

Then in a blink of an eye, it was all over. Eleanor stepped back, her voice slipped into a neutral tone. "I guess we'd better go inside. Thank you for a wonderful night, Sophie. I hope you enjoyed it as much as I did. Perhaps we can do it again before we leave."

Sophie felt like screaming, *"You can't turn it on and off like that, Eleanor. It's not only your affections you're playing with."* But she bit back the words, instead stood stubbornly in front of the door with crossed arms. "I thought this was a date."

Eleanor looked confused. "Of course it was. Why?"

"Isn't it the usual thing to kiss your date good night?"

CHAPTER FIFTEEN

At the words, Eleanor fought to stop her resolve from crumbling. Nerves prickled along her skin as Sophie swayed close. *No…no…don't do it*, her inner voice screamed, but the full rich red mouth was a temptation she couldn't deny. In a heartbeat, Eleanor closed the gap. The arousal that had been building all night finally burst free. When their lips met, the feeling was so breathtaking her knees threatened to buckle. She closed her eyes tightly as they melded together with exquisite tenderness.

"So soft," Eleanor said. She pulled back for a fleeting moment to savour the taste that was sugar and spice and Sophie's alluring essence, and murmured, "Sweet," before she leaned forward to continue a little firmer.

"I can't resist you. You're wonderful," Sophie whispered.

Slowly they began to find a rhythm, aware how perfectly their lips fitted together. Sophie's were silky and lush, and when they opened to invite her in, Eleanor curled her arms over her shoulders to pull her in closer. She groaned as her skin quivered against the soft body, her passion so fierce it would have terrified her if she hadn't been so dazed by her need. Eleanor stepped backwards against the wall and tugged Sophie over to settle into the curves of her body. She tickled the inside of Sophie's bottom lip with her tongue, then flicked it around her warm mouth. When Sophie sucked it in and lightly licked under it, Eleanor couldn't help herself. She slipped down a hand down to grasp her bottom as she nuzzled a leg between her thighs. With a husky moan, Sophie opened her legs immediately.

Her pliancy was, to Eleanor, the ultimate seduction.

Suddenly through the fog, a warning hammered in her brain. *Consider what you're doing.* If she didn't stop right now, any reserve left would be washed away on the tide of passion. And that could never happen. To have sex with Sophie would have enormous ramifications. The woman was her employee under her care. No matter she was a willing partner, Sophie was not the type to be bedded then pushed aside. Their relationship was far past casual now. She was a genuinely good person, worthy of a lover who would look after her and be prepared to offer her a long-term commitment. A promise like that would be virtually impossible for Eleanor to give. They were socially worlds apart, as well living in different countries.

Not that she thought Sophie was beneath her. Sophie was everything she ever wanted in a woman: smart, good-natured, and caring, not to mention hot. But the overriding factor was they got on so well. Eleanor had no doubt if circumstances were different, they would be extremely happy as a couple. Frustration left her almost sobbing. This woman was the one she had been years searching for, and she could do nothing about it.

Slowly she backed out of the embrace as she struggled against the need to continue. The sound of her own heartbeat hammered until she thought it might burst out of her chest. Sophie's fingers dug into her shoulders to stop the retreat, and only released her when Eleanor said gently, "I think we should stop, darling. If we go any further, we won't be able to. And we both know this can go nowhere."

Sophie's eyes were clouded, her pulse jumped in her throat. Her voice was breathy when she answered, "I know we can't possibly be a couple, Eleanor, but does that matter? What's wrong with having a night together?"

"If only it were that easy. Lord knows we both could do with some loving, but let's act with our heads. Once we go down that path, we can't go back. You know that as well as I." Eleanor leaned forward and pressed their foreheads together. "If I were staying in Australia and didn't have such a lifestyle, I wouldn't be hesitating. We could pursue this fledgling relationship and see where it went. I think you're a lovely woman, but you deserve someone who can offer you more. I had a wonderful time with you tonight, so…please…let's leave it at that."

"But that's the problem, Eleanor. Tonight was so special you've wrecked me for anyone else. You haven't been fair." Sophie said, her eyes now awash with tears.

"Oh my dear. Can't you see you've had the same effect on me? I can't go back to the women who see me as a stepping-stone in their career, or to the Hollywood princesses. Fame doesn't interest me. Though I thoroughly enjoy my career, the public facade that goes with it depresses me. To be always on show isn't an ideal way to live."

"Okay…so please explain what we do in the coming weeks. I don't want to spend my time wanting to drag you off to bed like a caveman and making you scream out my name."

Eleanor laughed spontaneously. "Now that's an exciting thought. The mind boggles." She grasped her hand. "Come on. It's time to get some sleep. I think we can manage to be adults about this and keep our libidos in check. But it wouldn't hurt to have some time apart tomorrow. Do you want to go fishing with Doug? I heard him tell you he was going out and I know you're keen. I'll take the opportunity to catch up with my correspondence. I also have to start doing something about learning the new script."

"Okay, I'd like that. He's heading off early, so I'll walk down. There's no need for you to get up. I'll leave your breakfast on the bench."

"Don't worry…I can get my own. I'll see you tomorrow night." Eleanor watched her disappear down the corridor before she climbed the stairs, relieved that Sophie had agreed to go away for the day. It would give them both a breathing space from their raw emotions. The night had left Eleanor physically and mentally on edge. Sophie had made her feel like a girl on a first date, so anxious to please it was almost pathetic. All her blasé words about control and being adults were really a load of rot. No way would it be so easy to turn off her feelings and she envisaged it would be the same for Sophie.

After a quick shower, she slipped naked beneath the sheets. Through the open window, the night sounds drifted in—the rustling breeze in the trees, the singsong of insects, the faraway cry of a seabird. The moonlight that spilled into the room landed in a jewelled glow on the bedspread. She let her consciousness go. As she sank into her imagination, she visualized Sophie's fingertips stroking her flesh, her muscles coiling and liquid under the touch. Her head tilted back in submission as the dark shadow of desire took her to the trembling precipice. When she slid her fingers into her warm wetness, almost immediately she toppled into the abyss of pleasure.

* * *

Sophie had already left when Eleanor made her way to the kitchen the next morning. She was relieved she didn't have to face her, but conversely, wished she were there. Normally content with her own company, she felt a little lost as she poured out a bowl of muesli. Though once she adjourned to the terrace to eat the cereal, it was impossible to ignore the glorious summer's day outside. Her spirits lifted, for rarely had she been in such a perfect corner of the world where she could completely relax without the pressure to perform.

Half an hour later, she checked her watch. Four p.m. in LA—a good time to ring her mother. After she moved inside, she settled down to make the call. She made herself comfortable in a chair with a footrest—it wouldn't be a short conversation. It never was. Over half an hour after her mother's voice came on the line, she turned off the phone, wondering if her LA house would ever be the same again. It was obvious from the background laughter, there was more going on than just entertaining a few neighbours. She could only hope that her possessions and reputation would survive the onslaught. Not that there was any point worrying about it. She had to trust that her sensible father would put a brake on her mother's enthusiasm.

Eleanor made another cup of coffee to fortify her nerves before she rang Carol, also in LA. No doubt, she would be in the doghouse because she hadn't phoned since she arrived on Eurydice. It was a cert there would be a few snide remarks, for she'd learnt over the years that her agent didn't appreciate being ignored. Everything about Carol smacked of self-discipline: her sharp-featured arresting face was always meticulously made-up, no strands of her short chic hair were ever out of place, nor did any crease ever mar her immaculate suits. Though Eleanor didn't always like her aggressive tactics, nor did Carol approve of Eleanor's dislike of the limelight, a lasting friendship had begun the moment the contract had been signed. Their closeness had endured over the years.

But now that Carol had made it clear she wanted more than friendship, Eleanor found her possessiveness suffocating and annoying. She was at a loss to know how to let her down without damaging their bond. In a way, Eleanor mused, it was a shame she didn't harbour any romantic feelings for her agent. They were from the same industry, with the same social network. In this business, where love interests came and went at regular intervals, sometimes a relationship with an agent was as close to a good marriage as some people came. And their connection had already been forged, so it would be only a matter of taking it to the next level…to the bed.

At the image of a bed, her thoughts swung straight back to Sophie and she smiled. Hell, it was a no-brainer. There was no way that Carol's sophisticated good looks could compete with Sophie's allure. Cocktail parties, red carpet premieres, and intimate dinners at expensive restaurants might be perfect for Carol, but she wanted more. A lover to come home to, someone she could proudly introduce to the world, a family.

With a sigh, she dialled the number with a faint hope that the answering machine would come on. No such luck.

"Carol Barton speaking."

"Hi, it's me."

"Eleanor, are you all right? I was getting worried."

As she heard her genuine concern, she felt a flicker of guilt. "I had a small setback, but I'm fine now. How is everything with you?"

"There's been good feedback from your interviews down there. The film has finished final editing and is close to ready for the premiere. Nigel said there are no problems. What do you mean you had a setback? How sick were you?"

"I had to have complete bed rest for a while, but Sophie took good care of me."

"Who on earth is Sophie?"

"She's the housekeeper that Mum found for me."

"You didn't mention you were getting help. What's she like?"

"She's excellent and a fantastic cook. Very caring too. It's nice to have someone looking after me for a change," Eleanor replied.

Then she cursed herself for being so indiscreet when Carol said in a clipped tone, "That's good. How old is this paragon?"

Eleanor felt a flash of impatience. Sophie's age was not Carol's business. "Old enough to be a good employee. Now, did you check through the new contract?"

"Everything's okay with it. It's ready to be signed when you get back to the mainland. So, what's the place like? You sound very happy with this…ah…fabulous help, or should I say companion."

Eleanor gripped the phone tighter. *Stuff Carol!* She launched into a glowing recital of the holiday, determined to let her know she was having a good time and not pining to come home. When she finished talking, Carol said in a cold voice, "This Sophie does indeed sound a very versatile woman."

Eleanor grimaced, not realizing she had mentioned Sophie quite so much. She should have shut up. Carol would never let it go now. She was very adept at making Eleanor feel guilty. "Yes, she's fun."

"Fun? That's an interesting description. She sounds a bit more than that. Be careful, Ellie. You're recuperating from a debilitating illness, and your defences are down."

Eleanor bristled. "What exactly do you mean by that?"

"Just don't get carried away and think you owe her something. You're too generous with your money as it is."

"For heaven's sake, Carol, Sophie is not after my money. Give it a rest," Eleanor snapped. "Why do you always think the worst of people?"

"Because you're so gullible."

"That depends on your viewpoint. I give to charities because there are needy folk in the world who could do with some financial help. Now I'm going to say good-bye."

Immediately the voice on the other end of the phone became conciliatory. "I'm sorry. I worry about you...you know that. Since you've been so sick, I'll come over earlier."

Eleanor drummed her fingers sharply on the arm of the chair. A visit from Carol was the last thing she wanted. "I told you it was too far to come."

"I've a spare five days on my calendar at the end of next week. I do want to see you, Ellie."

"Really Carol, what's the point? Come over for the premiere and we can get together then."

"I told you we need to talk about our future. I want your undivided attention without any outside pressures. Besides, I have to come to Australia to sign up a new client, so I'll kill two birds with one stone."

Angry resentment threatened to derail Eleanor. How dare Carol presume she would be welcome. Wanting to talk about a future that Eleanor considered nonexistent, grated on her nerves. It was obvious they needed to have a frank talk, but not here, not in this paradise, especially not with Sophie in the house. There was no way she would expose Sophie to Carol's not-so-subtle barbs. "You don't need to come. I'm fine."

"What's the problem? You know I care about you, Ellie. I thought you'd be happy to see me."

"It's not that I don't value your company, Carol. I do. But I took this holiday to recuperate and to be away from everyone I know. It's my alone time, and if I wanted to share it with you I would have asked you to come."

"So you're really against me coming, is that what you're saying?"

Trapped, Eleanor struggled with the need to say she definitely didn't want her here, but she knew it wasn't an option. Carol would take it as a personal slight and she did have a temper. "Very well…come if you're set on it."

"Well, don't do me any favours."

"It's not as black and white as that and you know it. I wanted this break away to be about my welfare and to think about my future. I need to revalue what I want in life."

"Oh? Are you thinking about changing your future direction? What the hell does that mean?" Carol's voice had raised an octave with anger.

Eleanor shook her head, frustrated. Typically, Carol tried to put her on the defensive. Well, not this time. "When I'm ready to tell you, I shall."

"Now you've got me worried. I honestly don't know what you're talking about. Why would you want to change your life? You're at the pinnacle of your career, successful beyond your wildest dreams. You command seven figures per picture. What more could you want?" Carol made a ticking sound before she snapped, "Really, Ellie, I can't understand you sometimes."

"I didn't say it was simple. We all come to crossroads in our lives, and I feel I'm at one now. I love my job but…well…I want something more. I want a life. Can't you understand that?"

A heavy silence seemed to wrap around the phone before Carol said in a kinder voice, "I think so, sweetheart. You're burnt out. Don't worry…medication and a good rest will fix the problem. I'm glad I decided to come over now rather than later. You obviously need support and some loving."

Eleanor sank back in the chair, stymied. There was no point arguing with the woman. *There are none so blind as those that will not see.* "Whatever. I'll see you next week."

"Good-bye, Ellie. Take care. I'll email my flight details."

Eleanor clicked off the phone, trying not to dwell on Carol's upcoming visit. She needed to chill out and plan. She hurried out the back to the pool, not bothering to put on a swimsuit after she stripped off. The cool water on her naked body brought tingles of pleasure, as well as a welcome feeling of liberation. Her emotions calmed as she swam lap after lap until, finally, with a sense of peace, she floated in the water. The conversation with Carol had made her more determined to do something about her life. It was time she made something happen.

Eleanor knew the problem of Carol could be easily solved. All she had to do was find someone else, and Carol would back off. At that thought, she gave a wry groan. She'd already found the one she wanted, and that begged the question. Was a romance with Sophie so unrealistic? Had she arbitrarily flicked it into the too-hard basket? Maybe it was feasible. Not here and now, for Sophie was still her employee, but later. She would just have to keep her distance on the island, which shouldn't be a problem if she was vigilant. Once Sophie's housekeeping stint was over here, there would be no reason why they couldn't see each other. She wouldn't go back to LA immediately. Her new movie was to be made in Australia, so she could stay over until they started filming to be together.

They could see each socially—see how it panned out.

Much happier now, Eleanor floated on her back and stared into the blue sky.

CHAPTER SIXTEEN

Through the doorway, Sophie watched Eleanor returning from the helicopter pad. Since their date, everything seemed back to normal, at least on the surface. They kept to themselves: swam, read, walked on the beach, and amused themselves with the games in the cupboard.

But Eleanor hadn't been quite the same with her. It wasn't obvious, she was still gracious and warm, but any spontaneity had disappeared. She also had become very adept at avoiding physical contact between them. Sophie felt the loss acutely, for as much as she tried to be circumspect, her feelings only deepened. She was so wrapped up in her now, if Eleanor asked her to lie down to be her footstool she wouldn't have hesitated.

Although Eleanor hadn't put it into so many words, it was obvious she wasn't happy about her agent's visit. Curious, Sophie studied their visitor as she climbed the stairs. She was nothing like what Sophie expected. Somehow, she had imagined her to be the stereotypical agent, a no-nonsense person who wore a perpetual frown and glasses. Instead, she was confronted with a very attractive, stylish woman, who was looking at her with an unsmiling stare.

"Carol, this is Sophie Ryan. Sophie, this is my agent, Carol Barton," said Eleanor calmly, though Sophie could tell by the way her fingers moved restlessly, she was nervous.

Carol gave a nod. "Hello, Sophie. Can you bring my suitcase up my room? I'll have a shower before lunch."

"I've prepared the guest room at the top of the stairs. I'll take it up at once." Sophie clamped her teeth shut as she heaved up the heavy bag. The woman must have rocks in it.

Eleanor gave her a suggestion of smile before Sophie walked off with the luggage. When she turned after she deposited it beside the bed, Carol was in the doorway.

"Here," she said, passing over a five-dollar note.

Sophie nudged the hand away. "There's no need, Carol. We don't tip in Australia and Eleanor pays me a generous wage. I'm only too happy to help you."

"Oh, I bet she does." Haughtiness crept into her voice. "Household staff members do not call me Carol, so I'd appreciate if you remember that. Ms. Barton if you please."

Sophie froze, confused. She either was a gross snob or had her knickers in a knot about something. From the glare she had given Sophie when they first met, she guessed it was the latter.

"Of course, Ms. Barton. You may call me Ms. Ryan then. A fair trade-off."

Sophie watched the astonishment in the blue eyes flare into fury. "Be very careful, my girl. I'm not one to be trifled with."

"The last thing I'd want to do is trifle with you, Ms. Barton. And I am neither a girl, nor yours. Now I'd better get back to my employer."

"I haven't finished with you."

Simmering, Sophie struggled against the urge to stalk out, but waited as curiosity won out. Why was the woman so antagonistic? Then an unsettling thought came. Maybe she had found out Sophie was spying on Eleanor. *Shit!* With a deep breath, she said, "Go on. It was obvious you had a problem with me as soon as you arrived."

"You're taking advantage of Eleanor while she's in a vulnerable state."

"*What?* My job is to look after her, and I've been doing that to the best of my ability." Suddenly Sophie felt a flash of intense hurt. "Has Eleanor complained about me?"

"No, but by the way she talks about you, I'm aware how you've wormed your way into her affections. She's a very wealthy woman."

"We do get on well, though that hardly is grounds for implying that I'm after her money. It's ludicrous."

"Eleanor is a soft touch when it comes to the needy."

"Well, I'm not the person you think I am. Nor am I needy. Now if you'll excuse me I have to prepare lunch," said Sophie not bothering to wait for an answer.

She ran down the stairs, as angry as she'd been in a long time. The words had made her feel dirty, and guilty. She *was* taking advantage of Eleanor, only not in the way Carol thought. Eleanor was in the kitchen waiting for her. As much as she tried, Sophie couldn't bring herself to look her in the eye, so she slipped around her to open the fridge. She felt a hand on her arm. "What's wrong?"

She jerked her arm away, more of a reflex action than a conscious thought. "Nothing. I'll have the meal ready in half an hour."

"Look at me, please Sophie," Eleanor said.

With reluctance, Sophie turned. A very stern Eleanor faced her, her mouth pressed in a grim line, her eyes bright with anger. "What did she say to you?"

"You ask her. She's your friend."

"I'm asking you."

"It was nothing. She was just being protective of you." Sophie added with an underlying tone of reproach, "She judged me without even getting to know me."

"I'll have a talk to her. She's a guest in my house and will behave properly." The words were spoken to her, but Sophie had the idea that Eleanor had directed the statement at herself. It would seem Carol knew how to press Eleanor's buttons.

When lunch was ready, Sophie had no idea if she should join them at the table. Eleanor solved the problem. She smiled sweetly at her and said, "Aren't you going to join us? You know I like you to eat with me."

Sophie cleared her throat as she glanced nervously at Carol. The agent didn't look pleased, but she ignored her when she sat down. The conversation during lunch was mostly about people she didn't know, which suited Sophie. She was content to study how the women interacted. On the surface, they seemed the best of friends. Carol was the more dogmatic of the two, but Eleanor could hold her own if she didn't agree. After a while, it became apparent Carol was more than just fond of Eleanor. Hence, Sophie reasoned, her hostility.

Although she disliked the woman, Sophie had to concede Carol was striking. Not cute-pretty, for there was no softness in her angular features. In fact, her cheekbones were so pronounced there were hollows underneath. But she had an aristocratic grace that deserved a second look, and like a marble statue, there was nothing out of place from the top of her perfectly coiffured hair to the tip of her designer sandals.

Before long, though, Sophie's peace was at an end. The sharp eyes turned in her direction. "So, Ms. Ryan. How long have you been doing domestic duties? I trust Eleanor isn't your first client?"

"Quite a while. I've worked for many people."

"Who did…?"

"Carol," ordered Eleanor. "That's none of your business. Now come with me for a tour of the island. Have we got enough seafood for tonight, Sophie?"

"Will you pick me up three lobsters and some prawns? I'll ring Lisa to have them ready."

"No problem. Tell her we'll stop for a drink at the bar. Pop a couple of bottles of that nice pink champagne on ice." She reached over and squeezed her hand. "It's time we let our hair down again." As she watched them drive down the hill, Sophie rubbed her hand where it had been touched. She smiled. Carol's visit had done some good already. Eleanor was back to touching her again.

After she cleaned up the kitchen, she went to her room. A free afternoon shouldn't be wasted. Her project hadn't even been started. Thankfully, even though the island had no mobile coverage, Internet was available via satellite. She flipped up the computer lid, flexed her fingers and ran the tips over the black plastic keys. Damn they felt good. She hadn't realized how much she missed this. First things first though—research was needed. She typed in *Eleanor Godwin*, chose "Images" and started scrolling. She flicked through them, searching for someone next to Eleanor who looked remotely like herself.

After a while, she gave up. It was a needle in a haystack. She had to narrow down when and where they had been together, otherwise she wouldn't have a hope of finding the mysterious Maria. Eleanor was too deeply closeted to be indiscreet enough to be seen with her in public. And if the woman was someone important, which Sophie sensed she was, it was certain she had been extra careful. No, this wasn't going to be easy.

She jammed that idea away for the time being and set up a profile on Eleanor. She worked quickly for most of the afternoon, tapping away nonstop, letting her creativity soar. The words flowed as the images appeared like a newsreel in her mind. She didn't stop and it soon became more than just a profile. The text morphed into a substantial article. Finally, she settled back to read it.

Two paragraphs in, her eyes began to falter. *Crap!* It was sentimental tripe, straight out of a second-rate romance. Perhaps she should take up novel writing after all. When had she ever used terms like seductive, bewitching, breathtaking, angel-awesome. Cripes, she'd even described the island as having undulating soft hills and a beach nestled in the bosom of Athena. With an anguished groan, she imagined it on Owen's desk. He'd have a pink fit. Then she visualized Brie reading it. That was enough to make her cringe.

She deleted the lot with a stab and closed the laptop. With a sigh, she searched her wardrobe for something nicer than usual to wear at dinner. It wouldn't do for the bitchy agent to think she didn't have anything decent. Once the outfit was chosen, she headed to the shower.

When she heard voices in the lounge room an hour later, she found the two women with glasses of champagne in their hands. With a welcoming smile, Eleanor waved at the bottle in the ice bucket. "Have a drink before you start dinner." She patted the space next to her on the sofa. "Sit next to me."

Conscious that Carol wore a frosty glare on the single chair opposite, Sophie filled up a glass. "Okay. Just one, otherwise you won't get dinner."

Eleanor leaned close. "I left the seafood in the esky on ice."

"How did you enjoy the afternoon?"

"Carol was impressed. She was sorry she hadn't decided to stay longer."

"What a shame, Carol," murmured Sophie. They looked at each other directly for the first time. Sophie maintained her locked gaze as she took a sip.

"It is indeed a spectacular place. I know now why Ellie raves about it."

Eleanor draped her arm over the leather back of the chair, and dangled her fingers to fiddle with the material on Sophie's shoulder. Carol frowned. When her drink was finished, Sophie rose, at loss to understand why Eleanor was starting to touch her so much. It was certainly pissing off Carol. Dinner was a subdued affair, and after she cleaned up, Sophie excused herself for the night. The disappointed look on Eleanor's face nearly changed her mind, but after the not-so-fruitful-stint at writing, she was genuinely tired.

* * *

The morning was bright and sunny, perfect for a swim. Even Carol had been chirpy at breakfast, claiming the fresh air had made her sleep like a baby. When Eleanor suggested they adjourn to the pool, she enthusiastically agreed. Sophie tried to cry off, but Eleanor insisted she join them. Reluctantly she consented, not missing the look of intense dislike Carol shot her way.

Donned in her bikini, she joined the others poolside. It took only one glance to see that Carol's classy swimsuit came straight out of the box. She looked like a model posing as a beach babe, a very expensive one. Sophie peered at her, intrigued. What kind of woman wore diamond studs in her ears when she was swimming?

Carol turned to regard her. Her radiating antagonism hung thickly in the air. At least though, thought Sophie, they had graduated to first names.

Eleanor nudged her. "Race you to the waterfall."

Sophie, needing no second urging, dived in immediately. It was their usual challenge, and she was yet to beat Eleanor. Though she had a head start this time, she was still no match for the star. After halfway, she was left in her wake. Carol, by far the worst swimmer of the trio, certainly didn't look happy as they frolicked in the water. After a few well-placed barbs, she retired to a deckchair to sunbake. When they finally emerged from the pool, she had disappeared inside the house.

With the towel draped over her shoulders, Eleanor squeezed water out of her hair. "I'm going up to change. Meet you on the sundeck."

"Okay. I'll dress and make some coffee."

Sophie watched her depart through the back door before she made her way down the outside passageway to her room. Halfway down, with a rustling of leaves, Carol stepped out from behind a bushy hibiscus. Biting back a startled cry, Sophie said sharply. "Damn it, Carol, don't creep up on me like that. You nearly gave me a heart attack."

"What a pity I didn't."

"Excuse me?"

"I want to talk to you in private."

"Okay. Eleanor's upstairs, so say your piece. You've been spoiling for an argument all morning."

"You bet I have. I told you I thought you were taking advantage of Eleanor. Your performance in the pool proved me right. You seem to be forgetting your place."

"That's rubbish. We have become good friends. We're always in the pool."

Carol moved closer until they were only a foot apart before she lowered her voice to a cold whisper. "We're both women of the world, so don't take me for a fool. You've been waggling that cute little bottom and those big tits in front of her nonstop. Now I'm warning you to back off. Eleanor and I have an understanding. She'll be my lover when she comes home to LA. You, my little housemaid, are merely a pleasant diversion to keep her amused, no doubt in bed as well."

Sophie stepped back as hatred roiled in her stomach. "Up yours," she snapped. Without another word, she hurried to her room, aware if she stayed, she would have spat in the woman's face. Slamming the door on her way in gave a small measure of satisfaction, but Eleanor upset her more. How on earth could she be a lover of that bitch? One thing was certain—Sophie couldn't stay in the house another minute with Carol in it.

After she dressed, she put clothes and toiletries in her small backpack, then stowed it in the corner of the hall before she made her way to kitchen. Soon after she took out the tray of scones and jam to the terrace table, she heard footsteps on the stairs. She recognized the tread.

With some degree of control, Sophie turned to face her. "I'd like to take three days off, Eleanor. Lisa has offered me a bed anytime and Doug has an open invitation to go out with him on the boat. I'll leave immediately, if that's okay with you."

Surprise, followed by shock, flitted across the Eleanor's face. "You want to go *now*?"

"Yes. I haven't had any days off since I arrived."

"I...I was hoping you'd help me entertain Carol."

Sophie had to grit her teeth to hold back the snort. "She'll be delighted I'm gone."

A hiss escaped from Eleanor. "Has she said something to upset you again?"

"Enough to let me know..." she began furiously then bit her tongue. "I got the message she doesn't like me."

Visibly upset, Eleanor clasped her arm tightly. "What did she say, Sophie?"

"I don't want to repeat it."

"Was it about your work? You're my employee, so that has nothing to do with her. She doesn't have the right to order you around."

"She resents me here. You know that," said Sophie.

"Our friendship has nothing to do with her."

"She doesn't think that way. It'd be better if you two spend the time together without me."

"I can't refuse your request…you're well overdue for time off, but I'd like you to stay. Would you reconsider?"

Sophie shook her head stubbornly.

"If you're determined to go, I won't ask again," said Eleanor with an edge to her voice. "Take two days off. Be back to prepare the evening meal on Thursday. She's due to fly out Friday after lunch. If you wait until after I have morning tea, I'll drive you down."

"I'll walk down. It'll be good to stretch my legs."

CHAPTER SEVENTEEN

Doug was loading gear into the fishing boat when Sophie arrived at the wharf the next morning. She had enjoyed yesterday with Giovanni and Lisa in the kitchen. A former chef in Milan, the Italian was a first-class cook and it had been a joy to watch him work. Made her feel right at home. That night, Marcello the waiter had entered the kitchen with the news that Eleanor and Carol were in the dining room. Anguish stabbed through her at this announcement, but she refrained from peeking through the door. She hoped they hadn't gone on to the cocktail lounge afterward, but didn't ask. It would have hurt too much to know they did.

When they finally finished cleaning up the kitchen, she had bunked down on the sofa bed in Lisa's unit, too tired to dwell on the events at the villa. Whether Eleanor would welcome her back with open arms was debatable. From her expression, she had been angry at Sophie's decision to leave.

Doug gave her a wave as she approached. "Glad to have you aboard," he said with a wheezing cough.

"Thanks for letting me crew for you."

"Hell…it's my gain. Put your backpack in the cabin and we'll get going."

The ceiling in the cabin was swathed in fishing equipment, which made it clear this boat wasn't used to take guests out. The interior space was reminiscent of a World War II bomber, every available space was taken, with barely room for the three bunks. Sophie tucked her pack under the right bunk before she went outside to help get the vessel ready to sail. It was a small trawler, outfitted solely for fishing, with no luxuries. Two dinghies were tied securely to the stern, which Doug explained they would use to get over to the reef for the best fishing. Nets were useless on top of the coral.

By the time they reached his favourite spot and anchored away from the fragile reef, it was past eleven. As the day wore on, Sophie could see that nothing about the job seemed to faze Doug. His well-rounded, hunched body worked tirelessly as they hauled in, filleted, and stowed the fish on ice in the refrigerated hold. Finally, by late afternoon, they had their quota.

After Doug stripped off his gloves and apron, he reached inside the cooler. "Want a beer before we head back?"

"You bet," said Sophie. It had been fun, but she was pleased to finish. Her shoulders ached from constantly pulling in the lines, and her hands stung, for even though she'd worn sturdy gloves, the saltwater still penetrated every crack.

He twisted the top off the stubby bottle and said wistfully, "Eleanor's a great lady, isn't she?"

"You were quite taken with her, weren't you, old fella?"

"Bloody oath. You'd have to be dead if you weren't."

Sophie flopped down into the dilapidated deck chair, which protested with a creak. "I reckon."

"I imagine she's good to work for."

"Yep…the best," muttered Sophie.

"Yeah. There aren't many as nice as her around." He took a large swallow of beer then wiped the back of his hand across his mouth. "And I've seen a lot of the so-called upper class."

Sophie dragged her gaze away from the ocean to eye Doug. "Many politicians come here?"

"A few. A couple came last year for some R and R, but mostly we get celebrities and business people. Usually the guests want to get away for some peace and quiet." He chuckled. "Though it's a good place to bring the girlfriend so the wife doesn't find out."

"I bet. It's super isolated here. Another world really."

"It's not for everyone, but I like it."

"Have you been here long?"

"Five years. When my wife died, I figured I'd had enough of city living."

"Any children?"

Doug shrugged in a noncommittal way. "One son. He's backpacking in South America. I haven't seen him for a year, but no doubt he'll be back when he needs more money."

Sophie looked at him in sympathy, thinking how hard it must be not having a family network to rely on. A rush of nostalgia coursed through her—she had never known what it was like not to belong to people. Her family might be irritating sometimes, but she couldn't visualize life without them. She leaned over to touch his arm. "It'll be different when he settles down."

"I hope—"

Suddenly a distress signal blared out from the VHF radio. "Mayday. Mayday. Mayday." They exchanged concerned glances. Sophie watched Doug closely as he lumbered to his feet to make his way into the wheelhouse.

After a few minutes, he poked his head out. "Come on up." He pointed to the blinking light on the radar screen. "There's a small yacht in trouble about twenty kilometres away. They're taking on water and the bilge pumps aren't coping. I've replied we're on our way as it seems we're the only boat within reach."

"How long before we get to them?"

"Our best cruising speed is eight knots, so we should sight them in about an hour and a quarter. Put your lifejacket on… we don't know what we'll have to do when we get there and it'll be nearly dark by the time we arrive." He looked at the sky with a grimace. A line of purple clouds hung on the horizon. "We'll have to hurry. There's also a warning out for all boats in the area that a storm is due around ten tonight. I thought we'd be anchored at home well before it hit."

As they powered through the water, communication with the vessel was sketchy, the static too bad to get the full extent of the damage. After motoring at full steam for just over the hour, Doug pointed toward to the north. "There she is."

Sophie squinted into the almost dark sky. Faint lights twinkled in the distance.

"We'd better get the latest weather report," he said. After listening intently for a minute, he yanked off the headphones. "Damn. It's not good. The storm's a nasty one and we're right in its path now. We'll have to hurry."

As they neared the yacht, Doug said, "They're listing badly to starboard, and very low in the water. Not much time."

Two figures were standing on the deck of the compact yacht. When Doug eased back the throttle, the engines whined loudly as the trawler chugged to a stop upwind on the port side.

"Ahoy there," he called out. "Throw us a line."

After a rope snaked onto their deck, Sophie hauled the boats together and secured the rope to a cleat. "You want me to go aboard?" she asked.

Doug's bloodshot gaze swept down to meet hers. "I'll go. They may be hurt and need help. You take the wheel."

"Right." Sophie studied the man and woman as Doug secured an extra line. In the yellow glow shining out the cabin door, the couple, not young, clutched the railing. "The wind is really whipping up. It'll only get worse, so we'd better move ourselves," said Doug. "I'm going over now."

Without another word, he heaved over both rails in a motion surprising agile for such a large a man. A wave rolled through. The trawler tipped alarmingly then crashed down onto the side of the yacht.

"Now go," Doug yelled to the woman who was clutching the railing.

With difficulty, they heaved her over into Sophie's waiting arms. The man followed quickly. Sophie ran back to the wheel.

Doug readied to join them. Another wave hit the side of the yacht with so much force that it lurched sharply, propelling him backward. He crashed onto the deck. Sophie looked over frantically, in two minds what to do. Her first instinct was to get over there to help him but hesitated. It was all she could do to keep the trawler's bow into the wind. Thankfully, the matter was solved when Doug staggered to his feet, and, with a running jump, jockeyed his bulk over the railings. A sharp oath exploded from him as he sprawled heavily on the deck of his trawler, and slid across the slippery deck to smack into the side of the large freezer. Blood crawled down his burly arm as he raised himself up on his elbows.

He waved to Sophie impatiently. "Cut the ropes," he gasped. "We'll have to abandon the yacht or we'll go down with it."

She needed no second urging. The yacht was listing badly, half submerged into the sea. Leaving the wheel, she dashed to fetch the two fillet knives from the fishing box. She handed one to the skipper of the yacht and they began to cut. After the ropes zipped off into the air with sharp twangs, the vessels parted at once. She turned to see Doug had already taken command of the wheel and was steering the trawler away from the sinking craft. "Take the folks down below," he called out, "and get them comfortable. They look bushed."

Sophie studied them sympathetically. Both looked to be in their mid- to late-fifties and from the cut of their clothes, affluent. The man was tanned and fit, and by the way that he held his stance on the lurching deck, he was quite at home at sea. Smaller and lighter, the woman was having much more difficulty keeping her footing. She was clutching the railing to keep upright, clearly at the point of collapse. Between them both, Sophie and the man managed to get her down the steps into the cabin.

"Sorry about the mess," she said as she led them past the kitchen galley to the bunks. "We weren't expecting company."

After they eased the woman onto a bunk, Sophie gave the man a nod. "She'll be comfortable here. I'm Sophie Ryan by the way."

He brushed his hair back with a jerky sweep of his hand. "Bill Harvey and this is my wife June. We're holidaying on Hamilton Island. We hired the boat to explore and fish on the reef for a couple of days, but it certainly turned out a bloody disaster. I have to say I've never been so relieved in my life to see your trawler."

"You're lucky you caught us. We were about to head in. Look, I have to get back on deck but Doug will be down shortly to see you." She flashed them both a smile. "Don't worry, you're in capable hands. He's the best seaman in the Whitsundays."

Sophie made her way to the wheelhouse, pleased to see Doug didn't seem to have any after-effects of his fall. But he was oddly quiet, frowning as he watched the turbulent water.

She glanced at the navigational screen on the instrument panel. They were tracking the wrong way. "Aren't we going home?"

He shook his head. "Nope. We're too far north to make it safely back. We're going to find shelter to wait out the storm."

Sophie shivered as she gazed past the ship's light into the inky ocean. The sky was eerily lit up at regular intervals by forked lightning. "Where are we going?"

Doug pointed at the screen. "We'll never outrun this front. It's coming too quickly. There's an island about ten clicks away. We'll anchor on the leeward side and wait it out until morning. The open sea will be too dangerous. Who are our guests, by the way?"

"Bill Harvey and his wife June. They're on holidays, the yacht's a rental."

"I'll go down to have a word with them." He fiddled with the radio and when he'd put the receiver down, he dusted his clothes. "I won't be long. Keep her on this course."

He returned with a bottle of water, which he passed to Sophie before taking back the wheel. "I told them to stay below. They seem more than happy to be out of the wind, and they're whacked. The next hour isn't going to pleasant and I don't want anyone flapping around in the way." He glanced sideways at her. "You did well today, Sophie. Many people would have panicked, but you kept your head. You're not a bad fisherman either."

Sophie felt a warm glow—Doug rarely doled out praise. "Ha! My dad taught me well, but you did all the work. So what went wrong for Bill and June?"

"He's an experienced sailor. But when the weather turned nasty, they collided with a jutting bank of coral. Before he noticed, it was too late. The hull was breached and water ran into the lower deck. They'd inflated their life raft and were about to abandon ship when they saw us coming." He tapped the radio, flipped a switch and spoke into the handpiece. After a few tries, he gave up. "Damn!" he exclaimed. "There's too much electrical interference. We'll have a try when we get out of this wind. We aren't far off now."

By the time the dark outline of the island was visible, the wind had reached gale-force. Sophie watched nervously through the glass as the ship ploughed through the escalating waves. Even with all her boating experience, the creaking of the hull was terrifying. As Doug steered closer, there was an enormous crack, which sent sparks flying from the instrument panels.

"Bloody hell," he yelled over the screaming wind. "Lightning's struck the aerial. I'll have to bring her in blind without the depth sounder."

The next half an hour was harrowing as they circled the point. Now broadside to the wind, the vessel, battered by huge waves, dipped alarmingly. Even with the spotlights and jagged lightning, visibility went down to nil, and at one stage, the vessel foundered so badly Sophie thought they wouldn't make the turn. When they eventually sailed out of the wind, she knew it was only through Doug's immense skill that they had reached the leeward side in one piece. The change was dramatic. Sheltered from the main force of the storm, the sea was calmer, the wind quieter, though her stomach remained queasy.

"That was fucking close," said Doug, sagging against the wheel. "For a moment there, I thought the old girl wasn't going to get her nose around fast enough."

"Me too," said Sophie. "I was saying my prayers."

"I'll bring her in as close to the beach as I can. I've been here before. There are no rocks, and the channel is deep enough so we won't run aground. I'll head the bow into the wind, let the anchor go and give it a shot of reverse to set the hook. It's still going to be a little rough but we'll escape the main blow."

"Will you be able to contact Eurydice?"

"There were a lot of sparks from the radio. I'll have a go, but I doubt I'll get through. If it's damaged, I won't be able to do much until first light."

"I imagine they'll be worried about us?"

"We can't do much about it. They know I answered the mayday, and that I'd find a safe haven in this weather." He gave Sophie's shoulder a squeeze. "Go on down and take the third bunk. Tell them we're safe now."

"What about you?"

"I'll keep watch for a while, and then bunk down here in case any calls come through."

Sophie gave a long sigh. She certainly needed to lie down—she was exhausted. "Okay. Let me know if you need me. I'll see you in the morning."

CHAPTER EIGHTEEN

When Eleanor heard the knock, she glanced at the clock beside her bed with a sigh of frustration. Impatient with herself for not getting her message across last night, she called out, "Come in."

Carol appeared through the door with a breakfast tray. "I thought you would like breakfast in bed."

"You shouldn't have gone to so much trouble, Carol."

Seemingly unconcerned at the lacklustre welcome, she crossed the room and settled the tray on Eleanor's lap before sitting on the end of the bed. "Nonsense. It's my pleasure." She broke a croissant, buttered it and handed it to Eleanor. "I'd like to talk about us, Ellie. You were avoiding the subject yesterday, but it's time we had a frank discussion."

"I wasn't evading the issue. I told you how I felt."

"I heard what you were trying to tell me last night, but you never really explained why you don't want to take our relationship that final step? We're great friends and you know I think the world of you, so why can't we become lovers? It would suit us both."

Eleanor met her gaze without flinching. "You forget to mention the main ingredient, Carol. Love. It wouldn't work. You must understand that while I like you very much, I haven't any romantic feelings for you."

"I'm in love with you, sweetheart. You must know that." She reached over and took Eleanor's hand prisoner. "Even if you don't feel the same way, you'll grow to love me. Lasting relationships are far more likely to succeed built on friendship."

With an irritated sweep, Eleanor brushed loose strands of hair off her face with her free hand. "Even if I loved you, I want more than you're willing to give. I want the full package: an open relationship and a family. I intend to announce my sexuality when I go home."

For a few long seconds Carol was silent, then said in a tight voice, "Why the sudden change of heart? I thought you were happy."

"I haven't been for quite a while. Oh, it's not my work—I love that. It's my private life I'm dissatisfied with."

"It hasn't anything to do with that tramp here in the house with you, has it?"

Eleanor stared at her, tiny shivers of cold shimmering over her skin. Carol was angry, but the way she spat out the words was also a little frightening. She realized now why Sophie had left. Carol had obviously said something vindictive. She took the coffee cup in both hands to cover the tremor she couldn't control. "Sophie has nothing to do with this, so leave her out of it. This is between you and me."

"Rubbish. She's trouble with a capital T. I'm not stupid, Ellie. I saw how she threw herself at you in the pool."

"We've become good friends," she said, then added a little white lie to defuse the situation. "I don't even know if she's a lesbian."

Carol made a scoffing sound. "Come off it. I wasn't born yesterday. You haven't stopped touching her since I arrived, and she looks at you like you're some sexual goddess."

Eleanor tingled with pleasure at that observation. She couldn't stop her lips curving into a smile at the image of Sophie dressed as a vestal virgin, worshipping her body. When she saw Carol stiffen, she wiped the smile. "You're imagining things. Now, let me eat my breakfast and afterward I'll take you down to the beach for a swim. Maybe I can persuade Doug to take us out on a short cruise."

Carol moved off the bed with reluctance. "Okay, I'll get changed, but don't think this is the end of the conversation, Ellie. I'd like us to come to some arrangement before I go. If it means I have to come out to have a relationship with you, then I will."

Eleanor stared silently into space when Carol walked out the door. *Damn!* Instead of shutting down Carol's advances, things had become more complicated. Now the woman was going to come out for her. One of Eleanor's trump cards had disappeared.

After swallowing down the last of the breakfast, she slipped a shirt and shorts over her swimsuit, conscious she had to have some plan to discourage Carol. Since the agent was definitely not a fitness junkie, a good dose of the outdoors should take the shine off any amorous advances. After a swim in the sea, they could take the long walk around to the point, then down to the entertainment centre. Doug might take them around the island in his boat, which would take care of the afternoon. Carol had met him yesterday. Dining out for dinner would eliminate a cosy intimate meal at home.

Happier now, she slathered on sunblock, picked up her sunglasses from the side table and put on her hat. Carol was waiting in the lounge, looking out of her element in her new holiday boutique wear. Her sandals seemed too flimsy for a hike, but Eleanor refrained from commenting.

"Ready?" Eleanor asked brightly.

"Do we need to take anything?"

"Get two big bottles of water from the fridge and I'll get the towels from the cupboard."

It was a bright sunny day, ideal for a dip in the ocean. After she parked the buggy under a palm tree, Eleanor led the way to the water, peeping into the boat shed on the way.

Doug was nowhere to be seen.

When over an hour later they emerged from the water, she suggested they walk along to the beach and around to the helicopter pad on the point.

Carol shrugged. "Okay, as long as it is not too far. The swim tired me out."

"No…no. It's just up a little way." She waved her hand vaguely. "When we get to those rocks over there, we shall have to climb to get around them. Leave the towels and we'll pick them up on the way back in the buggy, but take the water with you. It'll be better to walk barefoot until we get off the beach."

It was heavy going through the sand and by the time they reached the rocks, she could see Carol looked even less enthusiastic now. "Are you all right? Sophie hiked up to the point the other day and said it was a very pleasant walk."

"I'm fine," Carol said curtly. "Lead on."

Eleanor chuckled to herself. Sophie would no more think a hike was fun than a trip to the dentist. She didn't mention either that Lisa had warned them off this track.

As they plodded along, there were great views, but soon navigating the uneven path was beginning to take precedence over the novelty of the scenery. She didn't turn to see if Carol was still behind her until they had left the beach far behind. When she did swivel to look, Carol had a thin sheen of perspiration on her face and her breathing was ragged.

"Sorry," Eleanor said with a smile. "Have I been walking too fast?"

"How much fucking further?" she rasped.

"Not far." She hoped it wasn't. She was getting tired too, even though her strength had built up with swimming in the pool every day. "Perhaps I shouldn't have come this way, but you didn't look out of shape."

"I'm perfectly fit. Get on with it."

Despite the ache that had begun to creep into her back, Eleanor beamed. "Okay. Isn't it just the most glorious day for a hike?"

A grunt was the only answer.

With a brisk step, Eleanor started again, again not stopping to see if Carol was following. For the next half hour the track became even harder to negotiate, and at one stage, they had to crawl on their hands and knees along a particularly narrow place overlooking a cliff. Then the path veered up the hill, and as it became steadily steeper, every step became an effort. Finally, they began to descend, and after zigzagging between trees, the helicopter pad appeared in the distance. Eleanor's muscles were on fire, her legs leaden and her nerves quivering. With a long sigh, she sank down in the cool shade of a stand of Melaleuca trees near a strip of white sand.

She felt sticky, dirty, and tired. When Carol flopped down on the ground beside her, Eleanor could see she was in a worse way. Her hair under the wide-brimmed golf hat was sticking out at odd angles, her clothes dishevelled and grimy and her face a ruddy red. "You didn't say I had to be a damn mountain goat," she gasped.

"It was a bit…um…challenging. I think I must have misunderstood Sophie. I must have taken the wrong turn somewhere." Eleanor took a swallow from her water bottle. "We'll rest for a while before we head back."

"You're not thinking of going back that crappy way, I hope."

"Of course not. We'll walk back on the road to the centre. It's only a k and a half. We'll grab a snack there and cool off in the pool."

Carol groaned. "I can't walk another step. How far is it in miles? My new shoes are ruined and my feet hurt. Ring them to come and pick us up."

"You're forgetting there's no mobile coverage here. We'll have to walk."

"I can't," Carol whined. "I've had it."

"Nonsense. It's less than a mile. Where's your stamina?"

Carol eyed her irritably. "What's with you? Four weeks on this island and you've turned into one of those characters from *Lost*. And look at your skin. You're brown as a berry. You should be covering up more."

"I'm starting to feel as fit as I've ever been. More so actually. Fresh air and exercise has done wonders for my health. It wouldn't hurt you to go to the gym occasionally. You spend too much time cloistered in your office."

"For shit sake, give me a break. What are you now…a personal trainer? May I have a drink please?"

"Have you drunk yours already?"

"You only gave me one miserable bottle."

Eleanor quashed annoyance and eyed her with a degree of sympathy. As Carol did look distressed, it would be cruel to add to her misery. "Here, but go easy. There's not much left. We better get going soon or we'll seize up."

"Leave me here while you go. Tell them to come and get me."

Though Eleanor was tempted to do just that—Carol would only complain all the way—she scooped up her bottle and rose to her feet. "Don't talk such rot. Come on…get up."

Carol glared but scrambled upright. As they limped off down the road, Eleanor was relieved at least they didn't have the worry about losing their way. Not long down the road, she wriggled uncomfortably. The sun was directly overhead now, bright and hot. Sweat turned into stains under her armpits, which made her wish she had a roll-on deodorant in her pocket. She missed Sophie—she would have had all the essentials in her little backpack. At the thought of her, Eleanor felt a wave of anticipation. She would be at the resort. She hadn't realized how much she missed her and quickened her pace until strident words echoed from behind. "Slow down, damn you. I can hardly walk, let alone trot. My feet are killing me."

Eleanor looked over her shoulder to see Carol hunched over, her hands on her knees, breathing hard. She said more kindly, "We're nearly there. It's just around the next bend."

When Carol gazed up at her, all traces of her usual arrogance had vanished. She looked vulnerable and subdued. "Thank God. I'm stuffed."

"Me too. A long cool drink will be good."

When a few metres on, the gardens appeared at the side of the road, Carol gave a whoop. On top of the stairs, Eleanor glanced at the slim gold watch on her wrist. Two o'clock. No wonder she felt drained—they had been going solidly for six hours.

After icy drinks, they plunged into the cool water. Eleanor thought she had never felt anything quite so wonderful. From Carol's groans of pleasure, nor had she. Afterward, as she nibbled on the last of a snack at a poolside table, she studied her agent. She definitely was an attractive woman, more so now that she was not so perfectly made up. With her looks, intelligence, and money, she was an excellent catch. But as much as Eleanor knew this, her friend had never inspired one ounce of passion, or even tickled her libido.

In a way, she envied people who could be happy with a variety of partners. It had never been like that for her.

She was brought out of her musings, realizing she had been staring when Carol caught her gaze with a quizzical, "What?"

"Believe it or not, I was thinking what a wonderful catch you are. Smart, beautiful, rich. You'll make someone a terrific partner one day."

"But not you. Is that what you're saying?"

Eleanor gave a wry smile. "I am. I'm not attracted to you and I don't know why."

"So," said Carol sadly. "Now our defences are down, this is the frank conversation we should have had months ago."

"Yes it is. It's not because you're not attractive. You are. I'm my own worst enemy. Very few women have ever interested me."

"And I don't…not even a tiny bit?"

Eleanor reached over to pat her hand. "I'm sorry. I love you as a friend but that's all. Our friendship is very valuable to me and I wouldn't like to lose it."

"You won't. I guess it's time I faced facts and moved on. I'm not getting any younger." She watched her intently over her coffee cup as she continued, "You like Sophie, don't you? You're different when you're with her. I've never seen you react with anyone like that."

Eleanor felt her face heat. "I know. She does something to me that I haven't felt in years."

"Well, be careful. You've been sick and at a needy stage of your life. Take it easy with her until you're sure."

Eleanor smiled, though still reluctant to acknowledge to Carol the real depth of her feelings for Sophie. "I doubt it'll go anywhere, but it is nice to think I'm not so…well…oblivious to my hormones."

Carol chuckled. "You've never been a frozen princess, just goddamn fussy. Come on. Let's go back for a nap."

"Okay. If we want to go out to dinner again, we'll have to have a rest. I'll find someone to drive us back to the buggy. I've had enough walking for one day."

"Ha! Look who's talking. You ruined my expensive sandals on that shitty bush walk I'll have you know."

"That'll teach you for going for glamour rather than practicality." Eleanor rose from the table. "Wait here. I won't be a minute."

CHAPTER NINETEEN

"Have you picked out a dress for the premiere?"

Eleanor smiled at Carol over the dining table, distant thunder adding to the cosiness of the restaurant. "I bought a red one from the Donna Karan collection in New York a few months ago. At least I'm back to my normal weight and won't look like a refugee." She glanced around when Marcello approached. "Shall we order?"

Eleanor perused the menu, determined to indulge tonight. She felt like celebrating. Their talk had cleared the air and they were back to their easy friendship of old times. It was a load off her mind that they had reached an understanding. She had been serious when she said she didn't want to lose Carol's friendship, for not only was she always there as a confidante, she was also indispensible in Eleanor's professional life.

She studied Marcello as he took their order. He was certainly the perfect waiter: discreet, quiet, and attentive. She wondered why he had not given them the intimate setting that he had when she had brought Sophie. Had he guessed then they had been on a date and not just two friends having dinner? Were they that transparent? She shrugged it off with a blush—so much for secrets.

They had finished the entrees and were halfway through the main course when Deirdre appeared at their table. "I'm sorry to disturb you, Eleanor, but I need to speak to you privately if I may," she murmured.

Eleanor looked at her in surprise. Deirdre's usual cool confidence was replaced by a worried frown. Goosebumps prickled her skin. She nodded and rose quickly. "Of course… Excuse me, Carol."

She followed her through the dining tables, then crossed the hallway in her wake. As they progressed to the office, Eleanor's heart began to flutter. Whatever had happened must be important for her to be interrupted during dinner? Apprehension was gnawing at her by the time she took a seat at the desk.

Deirdre's fingers moved restlessly over the polished top as she said in a strained voice, "We've some news that's rather worrying. Doug's fishing boat is well overdue. The last communication with him was late this afternoon when he radioed he was answering a distress call."

Eleanor stared at her. "And you think something's happened to him?"

"They were answering a mayday, but running into the centre of this very nasty storm. Nothing has been heard from any of them since."

"They?"

"Sophie's with him, Eleanor."

"Oh dear God!" Eleanor closed her eyes, swallowing back the surge of nausea. She clamped her hands on her knees to force herself to speak calmly. "Is anyone looking for them?"

"The coast guard has been alerted, but it's impossible to do anything until the storm passes. We're only on the edge of it here, but according to the weather bureau there are gale force winds further north."

Eleanor felt the tremor again, this time up her spine. Fear and anguish roiled inside her. "Do…do you think they'll be all right?"

"Doug's an experienced sailor. He knows these islands and will find a safe place to anchor for the night." Though Deirdre spoke with authority, Eleanor caught her unease. "The search will begin at first light if they haven't radioed in before then."

"What about the boat they were helping?"

"According to the coast guard, it was a small yacht. A rental. The crew, a man and his wife, were fishing on the reef. As the distress signal was sent out in the late afternoon, our vessel was the only one left in the vicinity. Everyone else had come in because of the weather warning and they were lucky Doug hadn't left for home."

"Then it's a waiting game until morning."

Deirdre grimaced. "Yes. I'm sorry to be the bearer of such tidings, for I know you value Sophie highly. We've become very fond of her here as well. She's always so cheery when she pops in for supplies, and she even helped Giovanni in the kitchen last night. Now finish your meal—I'll keep you updated once there's news."

If only it were that simple, thought Eleanor. If only she was just a valued employee. But she wasn't, she was so much more. She stood up quickly as a wave of nausea hit. "I've lost my appetite."

Deirdre reached over to clasp her hand firmly. "It's started to rain, so you'll have to stay here until it's over. Go back to your friend and finish your meal. It won't do any good to worry."

Eleanor nearly replied fiercely that of course she was going to worry, that she was going to be off her head until there was news. But she held her tongue with a weak smile before she trudged out the door.

Carol looked at her with a frown when she sat down heavily in the chair. "What is it Ellie? From the look of you, it's something serious."

"Sophie went out with Doug on a fishing trip and they haven't returned," said Eleanor, forcing the words out.

"How long overdue are they?"

"They were due home hours ago. They answered a distress call from a boat on the reef, and neither has been heard from since. There was a severe storm coming toward that area. I guess we have the tail end of it here. The last communication with them was about seven o'clock."

"Doug's a fisherman isn't he? He's sure to know what to do. Do you want to go home?"

"It's pouring. We'll have to sit here until the weather clears." Eleanor pushed her plate away. "I can't eat any more."

On cue, Marcello appeared. "Would you like to see the dessert menu, ladies?"

"A cup of coffee for me. What about you Carol?"

"Coffee will be fine."

Marcello cleared his throat. "We've all heard about the missing boat, Ms. Godwin. I wouldn't worry too much…Doug is an excellent sailor. He'll take good care of Sophie."

"I'm sure he will, Marcello," Eleanor replied, pushing back the anxiety that was threatening to derail her. "It's going to be a long night though."

"Then I suggest you stay and listen to the piano. The time will go much quicker."

After an hour of music, Eleanor wished they had braved the weather and just gone home. The cheery tunes got on her nerves, the love songs depressed her. After a while, the notes seem to merge into each other until she felt like screaming. It must have been noticeable, for at one stage Carol said irritably, "For heaven's sake stop fidgeting."

"I can't help it," she whispered back.

"Relax."

"Okay, I'll try."

Finally, to her relief, the pianist rose to put away his music. When they arrived home after midnight, Eleanor went straight to the terrace to stare out over the ocean. Though the rain had cleared, the night sky was still shrouded in clouds, which would make it easy to detect a light out to sea. Carol's attempts at placating her only made her more agitated, until, exasperated,

Carol marched out with a sleeping tablet. "Take it," she ordered sternly.

Eleanor shook her head stubbornly. "Not yet. I want to sit out here for a while."

"Swallow it, Ellie. You're going to make yourself sick. Have some faith Doug will get them back safely."

This time Eleanor didn't argue. She was right. If she didn't get some sleep, she'd be good for nothing in the morning. Once she swallowed the tablet, Carol took her arm and propelled her up the stairs to her room.

"You're a damn mess. I wish they had waited to tell you bad news until they actually had some," snapped Carol.

"She's my employee, Carol."

"So? It was still premature. They're probably anchored off an island somewhere drinking grog. You told me the old codger was as tough as nails."

Eleanor couldn't help but chuckle. Carol was a realist, always so practical. "He is. If anyone can get them out of trouble, he can. Now I'd better get into bed before the sedative hits me. I never take anything to sleep."

She only had enough time to settle under the covers, before her eyes had drooped shut.

The phone ringing on the bedside table brought Eleanor awake with a jerk. Lost for a second, the memories came flooding back as her mind cleared. *Sophie!* She flicked a look at the clock. Twenty past eight. *Damn!* She'd slept in. After a fumble, she managed to bring the receiver to her ear. "Eleanor Godwin speaking."

"Deirdre here. I have some news."

Eleanor clutched the phone tighter. "Yes?"

"The coast guard helicopter has sighted our fishing boat. They're on their way in, but there's no sign of the other vessel. They presume it must have sunk, but the radio on the Doug's trawler isn't working so they can't be sure."

"How…how many people can they see on board?"

"Four…all accounted for."

Eleanor sagged back onto the pillows, a long breath sighed out. "How long before they get here?"

"An hour or so. I'll get Lisa to bring Sophie to your place when they dock."

"I'll drive down."

"It'll be best if you could wait at home. Our medic will want to check them over and I don't know the condition of the two passengers. It'll be very busy on the wharf for a while."

Eleanor leapt out of bed, keen to tell her news. With a spring in her step, she ran down the stairs to the kitchen. At the table with a bowl of cereal, Carol grunted in surprise when Eleanor flung her arms around her shoulders. "They're all right. Deirdre rang with the news they were on their way back."

"I told you all your worrying was for nothing."

"I know, but it's more difficult when your emotions are involved. You tend not to think too rationally."

"Umm…" said Carol. "Then all the more reason to step back a few paces. You've only known the woman for a little while, so go cautiously. Don't jump in boots and all into a commitment until you know her properly or understand what *she* wants."

"Leave it be. We've been through this."

"I'm looking out for you as a friend now. You could get hurt here. You understand that."

"Yes." Though it hadn't been a question, Eleanor answered all the same. "I realize that."

"Good, then come and have some breakfast and tell me about your next script. It sounded exciting when I read the synopsis."

As they talked through one cup of coffee to the next, Eleanor kept an ear open for the sound of footsteps on the pebbles in the courtyard. When eventually the door flung open two hours later, she was already halfway down the hallway. The sight of Sophie standing on the threshold took her breath away. She looked tired, grimy, and rumpled, but Eleanor thought she had never seen anyone so beautiful. Without another thought, she pulled her into a firm embrace, registering the arms around her were equally as tight. The urge to kiss her was so powerful that she automatically bent her head, but at the last moment, she noticed Lisa standing behind Sophie so she deftly diverted her lips to peck her on the cheek.

With a small cough, she gave Sophie a lingering stroke on the shoulder before she slipped out of the embrace. "Hi, Lisa," she said brightly and focused back on Sophie. "Well, you gave us quite a scare. How are you?"

Sophie answered with a strained smile, "Okay I guess. Dirty, sore, relieved it's over. I really need to have a shower badly, so I better get cleaned up before I tell you all about it." She looked at Lisa. "Thanks for the ride. I'll see you later to collect my gear."

Eleanor watched her disappear down the corridor before she turned back to Lisa. "Would you like a cup of something? We've been saturating ourselves with coffee while we've been waiting, so another one won't hurt."

"A quick coffee would be great. I have to get back to the kitchen to prepare lunch shortly."

Eleanor waited while Lisa filled them in, then leaving Carol to show her out, hurried to the back unit. She rapped on the door, and when the "come in" came from within, she pushed it open. Dressed in fresh clothes, Sophie stood in front of the mirror brushing her hair. Eleanor didn't hesitate, nor could she have stopped herself even if she had wanted to. In quick strides, she closed the distance between them, this time with no barriers to stop her. With eager fingers, she framed Sophie's face as she leaned in for a kiss. Sophie dropped the brush and met her halfway, her mouth just as urgently seeking hers. Eleanor felt her nerves melt away as their lips moulded together in a rush of emotion.

She didn't know how long they rocked together in the kiss, but when they eventually separated she was, quite literally, breathless. "Oh Sophie, I was so worried. If anything had happened to you…" She left the sentence hang, unsure how to put her feelings into words. As she pulled Sophie back into a long hug, Carol's words of warning drummed through her mind, even though she tried ruthlessly to silence them. Reluctantly, with a final squeeze, she stepped back until they no longer touched. It took more of an effort than she imagined possible to let her go.

Sophie closed her eyes as if struggling to deal with the situation. When she opened them, Eleanor could see they were filled with unshed tears. It took much more willpower this time for her to step back further, but she managed it somehow. "You look worn out, Soph, so go to bed. I can look after our meals today."

Sophie didn't say a word, merely gazed at her with an expression Eleanor could not read. As she left to go back upstairs, Eleanor tried to digest what had just happened. The kiss should have been only a kiss, yet it hadn't been. It had felt like a declaration of something important. In the end, she was forced to admit, though everything seemed back to normal, it wasn't.

CHAPTER TWENTY

Eleanor, dressed in a long shimmering silver gown, looked every bit the superstar as she walked down the stairs—alluring, elegant, a little distant.

"You look great," said Sophie as she self-consciously brushed at her cream slacks and teal top. *Damn!* Next to Eleanor's fabulous dress, her outfit sucked. "Ready to go?"

"As I'll ever be. You drive tonight. I need to compose myself before the recital."

Over a week had passed since Carol had left. It was hard to believe they had been on the island a month and a half, and this was going to be their biggest night since they arrived. Eleanor was going to perform. Excited, Sophie followed her out the door. The poetry night, Eurydice's signature event, usually brought many notable people to the island, but according to Lisa, because Eleanor was the star, the limited places were in very high demand. To accommodate the influx, some visitors were housed for the night on a hired luxury yacht at the pier, and there were quite a few privately owned smaller vessels anchored nearby. From their vantage point on the terrace, Eleanor and Sophie had watched the larger grand yacht arrive at noon. An impressive sight as it sailed gracefully into the bay.

The arrival of Austen Farleigh four days ago was the big news amongst the staff, but so far, Sophie hadn't sighted her. She wondered if the singer's visit was the reason Eleanor had remained exclusively in the villa. She certainly closed up when Sophie tried to discuss the singer.

But apart from Eleanor's dislike of Austen, there seemed to be something else bothering her. After the kiss, Eleanor had retreated into the persona she had played before Carol arrived— warm but distant. Surprisingly, Carol had been ultra-friendly on her return from the ill-fated boat trip, which made the last of her stay pleasant for everybody. But Sophie knew, even though it was obvious the two had reached an understanding, that Carol had somehow influenced how Eleanor interacted with Sophie.

As they sat close together in the buggy in the glow of the security light, Sophie turned to look at Eleanor. She was gazing through the windscreen with a faraway look, seemingly oblivious of Sophie's presence. A knot of rebellion formed in Sophie. How could Eleanor be so indifferent to her after that kiss in her room after the shipwreck? Frankly, she was tired of this hot and cold shit. It was about time they had a candid discussion about their feelings. If Eleanor didn't want her, then she should stop damn well kissing her. With deliberation, she pressed against her and she reached over to tuck the folds of the dress back from the edge. When Eleanor stiffened at the contact, Sophie stroked her thigh and let her hand rest there. "Are you comfortable?" she said disarmingly.

"I'm fine."

"Good. I won't disturb you then." Sophie idly began again to rub the leg, pleased when she felt the muscles quiver.

Halfway down the hill, Eleanor said abruptly, "Put both hands on the wheel, Sophie."

"Why? It's quite safe. It's only a golf buggy and we're creeping along."

"You have to drive safely."

As soon as Sophie removed her hand from the thigh, she regretted the loss of contact. "I'm sorry. Did I upset you?"

"You didn't."

Sophie stole another quick glance at her profile. Eleanor seemed frozen in the seat. "It won't happen again."

"Good. Now I can't have any distractions...I do have to prepare myself. I would appreciate if you are quiet until we get there."

Suitably chastised, Sophie didn't utter a peep until they arrived outside the entertainment centre. After she parked, she waited to see if Eleanor wanted her to walk in with her. With an absentminded nod, Eleanor swept up the stairs, which left Sophie to follow in her wake. Inside, the dining tables had been replaced by rows of comfortable chairs around the stage. The room already buzzed with anticipation and curiosity. Sophie estimated there were at least two hundred patrons casting eager eyes towards Eleanor as she entered.

The star was immediately claimed by a large woman with pink fluffy hair, dressed in a pink kaftan that blossomed out like a tent. By the warmth of the greeting, Sophie could see they were old friends.

Nobody even looked her way, and as Eleanor didn't seem to notice she was there, Sophie walked down to the resort staff congregated on the wooden benches at the back.

Lisa gave her a wave. "Sit here beside me."

"Thanks." Sophie sat down then felt a hand grasp her shoulder. Doug, spruced up to the nines for the occasion and smelling of spicy aftershave, sat behind her with a big grin on his face.

Curious, she looked around the room. She recognized quite a few, mostly a who's who of the Financial Times, a sprinkling of celebrities and a flock of arty types. She didn't spy any politicians, which would have been awkward. She would have had to feign illness and disappear. She relaxed back in her seat, confident that if anyone here read the *Globe*, the newspaper wouldn't be associated with her.

Over the tops of heads, she could see Eleanor in the front row, seated between the pink lady and a man with silver hair who looked like Richard Gere with a moustache. A podium was set up on the stage, in the place of the grand piano now relegated to the back wall. A hush fell over the gathering when Deirdre walked to the microphone. She didn't speak for long, merely gave a brief welcome and outlined the agenda.

Then when the room dimmed, a cone of light shone down on the polished wooden stage. As eight poets came and went, reciting one poem each, Sophie sat enthralled. She had only ever read poetry, but hearing it was so much better.

A brief interval was announced before the main act, so that waiters could serve drinks. She took two beers from the tray, and as she passed one over to Doug, she noticed a woman in dark glasses slip onto the chair beside him. At first, Sophie gave her only a cursory glance but refocused in disbelief. Why she bothered with the sunglasses was a mystery, for nobody could mistake that famous body covered with tattoos. Austen Farleigh flipped back the shades, winked and murmured, "Well hello there, pretty lady."

Sophie had no hope of stopping the heat of embarrassment that flushed across her cheeks. *Busted!* She gave a weak smile and a small, "Hi."

Then Austen was forgotten when Eleanor walked onto the stage. She stepped behind the podium, looked into the crowd and waited for the applause to fade. Again, she swept her eyes over the crowd, but this time with such intensity that all sound died. Quietly, she walked away from the dais to the very front of the stage and began to speak, "And why I pray you? Who might be…"

From those first words of Rosalind's monologue from Shakespeare's, *As You Like It*, Eleanor had the audience spellbound and held them captive for nearly an hour and a half. No one moved, riveted by the performance as she went from Rosalind, to Constance from *King John*, to Kate from *The Taming of the Shrew*, to Beatrice from *Much Ado About Nothing*, to Juliet from *Romeo and Juliet*, and finally to Lady Macbeth.

Sophie sat mesmerized, aware she hadn't fully understood Eleanor's extraordinary talent. The woman held the audience in the palm of her hand—she didn't just play the characters, she *was* them. The choice to finish with Lady Macbeth surprised Sophie. She thought she would end her recital on a lighter note like Juliet, but then again, greatness never took the common path. When the last lines were uttered, "Have done to this," the room erupted into clapping. When as one they rose to their feet to applaud, Eleanor smiled and bowed.

To Sophie, she looked like a painting: impressionistic, perfectly composed, unattainable, and untouchable.

She gulped back self-reproach. How arrogant she had been earlier this evening, to touch this woman without permission. Eleanor had more class in her little finger than Sophie had in her entire pathetic body. Hell, she wasn't even Sophie Ryan, faithful housekeeper and companion. She was Sophie Marsh, hack reporter, and spy. In this exalted company, she was a complete outsider. A nobody. All she had was a small flat in the burbs of Brisbane, an abundance of working class relations (some without a brass razoo), total savings of ten thousand dollars and a heap of a car she was still paying off. *What a loser!*

As for those kisses she still dreamed about—they had been pity kisses, that Sophie had conjured up into something more than they were. Eleanor had tried to tell her that, to keep a respectable distance, but she hadn't listened.

Her lip dropped as she fought to bite back the threatening tears. The only thing left for her now was to get over it, to banish the feelings that ached in her chest.

She had to forget how Eleanor's lips had tasted. How she had fitted perfectly in her arms. How her body had responded to her touch, her smallest sound, her slightest movement.

She was going to have to grow up.

A sharp series of whistles from behind made her turn around. Austen had two fingers in her mouth, enthusiastically blowing. Sophie laughed as her black mood faded. She joined with whistles of her own, a talent she'd perfected growing up with brothers. Deirdre appeared at the podium with an enormous bouquet of flowers, thanked Eleanor profusely and reminded everyone to stay for the party. When they stepped down from stage, the lights brightened.

Sophie craned her head to find Eleanor, but now people were on their feet she was lost in the crowd. It would probably be advisable to catch up with her later anyway, she figured. Her company would be in demand, and Sophie would only be in the way. She had very little in common with these people, except for her love of Shakespeare.

Then she felt someone take her arm. "What about we adjourn to the bar? I could do with a stiff drink," said Austen.

Sophie smiled. "Why not. I could do with one too." She turned to Lisa and Doug. "Want to come?"

Doug shook his head. "Count me out. I have a big charter at dawn. I'll take a rain check."

"I'll come," said Lisa eagerly.

Austen twitched her eyebrows. "Come on then. I like threesomes."

"Huh! You wish," Sophie shot back as she led the way to the bar.

Once they were seated with drinks, over the top of her glass, Sophie studied Austen as Lisa held her attention with her chatter. She definitely was one sexy woman, with her purple-tinged dark hair tousled casually in a bob over a very handsome face, startling grey-green eyes and a lithe well-formed highly desirable body. Colourful tattoos covered both arms, with an enticing hint of another just visible at the top of her very low-slung jeans. She was dressed all in black: a short tank top that left her lower abdomen showing, tight-arsed jeans and knee-high polished boots. She was so hot she looked ready to combust.

Though she was outrageously dressed for the present company, she somehow pulled it off, for there was no denying charisma oozed from every pore. Sophie wasn't overly impressed though. Political reporting had made her sceptical. She'd interviewed too many conceited clowns to be taken in by looks alone. People had to prove themselves in her book. Perhaps Ms. Sexy Boots needed to be taken down a peg—she looked like she always got her own way.

She slowly lifted her eyes up the body to find Austen looking at her with a lop-sided grin. "Like what you see?"

"Maybe."

"Only maybe? You wound me, babe."

"Yep, only maybe," answered Sophie solemnly, then she signalled the bartender for another round. "I like the cool reserved type best."

"Oh?" murmured Austen. "And who might that be? Now let me guess. It wouldn't be the Ice Queen from the stage?"

Sophie grinned. "That's for me to know and you to guess. But you have to admit the woman is flipping gorgeous."

"Look all you like, babe, but you won't get very far there." She sounded a little peevish.

"Aha. That sounds like you tried and she told you to bugger off."

"I know Eleanor and she's very charming," piped in Lisa.

Austen didn't acknowledge Lisa, but continued to eye Sophie with a frown. "Perhaps I blew *her* off."

Sophie swooped on that statement. "Really? Why would anyone blow off Eleanor? You'd have to be blind Freddy." She gave a snicker. "Perhaps you should take the shades off."

Austen's fingers tensed on the glass for a moment and then to Sophie's surprise, she chuckled. "Come on, drink up. You're starting to interest me. And I warn you, I play to win." She flexed an arm. "What do you think of my tattoos?"

Sophie lightly traced an intricate one with a fingertip. "Impressive."

"Would you ever get one?"

Sophie tilted her head and looked at her. "I've got a small flower on my hip, a lasting reminder of an all-night party when I was eighteen. You know, there's a saying—'For all the young women thinking of getting a tattoo, remember. When you get older, a butterfly on the back becomes a buzzard in the crack.'"

Austen began to laugh, big gusts rolled out of her. She threw an arm over Sophie's shoulder. "I know I'm going to like you."

Sophie opened her mouth to reply when she caught Lisa's nod to someone behind her.

She turned around, still attached to Austen's arm. She winced. This didn't look good. Accompanied by the woman who up close looked like a mass of candy pink fairy floss, Eleanor approached the bar.

And she looked furious.

CHAPTER TWENTY-ONE

Eleanor finished the last word of her recital and waited for the audience's response. Early in her career she had wanted to go into theatre, for to her, true acting was onstage. There were no endless reshoots—the first performance was it. During her stint with American TV, she'd auditioned for a play on Broadway, didn't make the cut and had to deal pragmatically with the misery of disappointment. These days, she only looked back at the stage as what might have been.

Tonight had been a trip down memory lane, something she had enjoyed immensely. She was familiar with most of Shakespeare's plays, so it had only been a matter of brushing up on the lines. When the resounding accolades came, she felt a rush of pure pleasure. No matter how big a star she was now, it was only ever about how the audience enjoyed the performance.

She had been delighted to find her mother's old friend, Ginny Babcock, had come over for the weekend. A popular author of self-help books, life for Ginny, a widow of five years, consisted of self-help classes and after-dinner speaker gigs. She was making a mint. With her outrageous pink theme, there was no mistaking she was as eccentric as Frances Godwin. Eleanor never quite understood what self-help Ginny had to offer, for she appeared to be in perpetual chaos like her mother. But whatever it was, it was a licence to print money.

"Wonderful," Ginny gushed as she gave Eleanor a smacking kiss when she came down from the stage. When she pulled her into a hug, Eleanor felt as if she was sinking into a marshmallow. "Now come," she continued in a voice that broached no argument, "and I'll introduce you to a few people."

Eleanor would have preferred to go home. The performance had left her drained and a stress headache had begun to throb behind her eyes. It would have been so nice to soak in a hot tub with a glass of red, but she knew that wasn't an option. She was expected to mix. After thirty minutes of socializing, she pointedly looked at her watch, hoping Ginny would take the hint. She didn't, instead dragged her on to yet another group.

Eleanor glanced around the room again, though the crush of people still limited visibility. Where was Sophie? Her absence was beginning to make her anxious. She should have been the first to congratulate her, not these people she didn't know and would never see again. And though she was loath to admit it, she wanted Sophie's approval. With a guilty start, she focused back on the conversation. As she listened to a tall, stooped bank executive waffle on about Shakespearean women, she held back a biting comment. Not only was he arrogant, his chauvinistic views were tedious and misogynistic.

Suddenly, loud laughter came from the direction of the bar and they all turned to look. Eleanor drew in a sharp breath. There was no mistaking that sound.

Austen was here.

Ginny must have sensed something from her stiffening stance, because she whispered, "What's wrong?"

"There's someone I know over at the bar." Eleanor drew back with an apologetic smile to the group. So far, she had avoided their meeting, but she knew she had been postponing the inevitable. Better to do it now, for it would be on her terms here. "Excuse me. I have to go."

As she moved off, she had no hope of losing Ginny, who clearly sensed a drama and was sticking like glue. Suddenly, a thought occurred to Eleanor. Maybe her mother had sent her friend to check up on her. It was something she would cook up without a qualm, and knowing Ginny, she would delight in the subterfuge. Talk about the witches from Macbeth—*Double, double, toil and trouble*—the two of them would stir any pot.

The sight that greeted her at the bar immediately sent her blood pressure skyrocketing. Austen, like an oversexed black-clad vampire, was hanging all over Sophie. Eleanor fought hard for control. A public altercation between two superstars wouldn't survive even Eurydice's strict privacy laws. So she said in a clipped voice, "Hello, Austen."

"Eleanor. Good to see you again. I loved your performance. It was so you, especially Lady Macbeth."

"Thank you. Coming from you, that's a great compliment."

"Come and have a drink with us." A slow smile spread across Austen's face, though her eyes remained flinty. "That is, if you don't mind slumming."

"I'd be delighted. A glass of the McArthur Park Merlot would be nice. And one for my friend," Eleanor said. Conscious that Ginny waited expectantly beside her, she introduced her reluctantly. Ginny simpered and held out her hand to be kissed, which Austen did with a flourish.

"And these two sexy girls are Lisa and Sophie," announced Austen.

Eleanor smiled at Lisa, then for the first time directly faced Sophie. "I can see now why you haven't come over, Sophie," she said.

Sophie looked more annoyed than remorseful. She slipped out from under the tattooed arm, and raised her eyebrows. "Oh? Were you expecting me to?"

"I thought you would at least have come to tell me what you thought."

"You didn't give me that impression when we came in. I thought you didn't want me hanging around, so I kept out of your way."

"I'm sorry you felt like that. I was preoccupied."

"I accept your apology then."

"I wasn't apologising, Sophie," said Eleanor sharply.

"I thought you said sorry. That sounds like an apology to me."

Eleanor gave an involuntary chuckle. "I should know better than to bandy words with you."

She looked over to find Austen staring at her. "You know Sophie?" she asked.

"She's her housekeeper," offered Lisa. "You were fantastic tonight, Eleanor."

"Thank you, Lisa. That means a lot to me. Was Doug here?"

"You bet. He wouldn't have missed it. He was wrapped in your performance."

Eleanor felt a flush of pleasure. "Well, there you go. If I can win that crusty old fellow over, I must have passed muster." She took a sip of wine and glanced at Austen, who watched with narrowed eyes. "Why are you here, Austen? This is hardly your ideal holiday destination."

"Believe it or not, I do require peace and quiet sometimes. I'm working on an album I'm bringing out early next year."

"Are you here alone?"

"Yep. Just me. I wanted to get away by myself. We've just finished a UK tour and the band is on holidays." She sidled over to Sophie and placed a hand around her waist. "So Soph here is your housekeeper? Maybe you could lend her to me occasionally. I could do with a bit of…ah…help."

Although Eleanor was well aware she was being baited, anger still came in a haze of red. She shot her a look of intense dislike. "Sophie's not a slave, Austen. She's a valued employee and I expect you to treat her like one. If she wants to help you on her time off, then ask her, not me."

Sophie stepped away from Austen and moved over to a goggle-eyed Lisa, who made room next to her at the bar. There was an awkward silence before Ginny announced in a jolly voice, "The wine is superb. Shall we have one more, Eleanor?"

"No, I'm tired…I'd like to go home. We can have another there." She looked at Lisa. "Ginny is staying with us tonight, so could you give Sophie a lift home, please, if it's not too much trouble?"

"No worries. Do you want to go now, Soph?"

"No hurry. Let's have a few more before we go." She fished in her pocket for the buggy key, which she passed over to Eleanor. "Here. I'll see you both in the morning. What time do you want breakfast?"

Eleanor bit back the flash of hurt. She slipped on her cool professional mask and said in a mild voice, "We'll get our own. You have a good time." With a last smile at Lisa, she threaded her arm through Ginny's to walk out the door.

Outside, the night was warm and balmy, the air thick with the perfume of the night-scented jasmine and the perpetual hint of salt. After Ginny settled her ample behind onto the seat, she cast a sly look. "You're very friendly with the help, Ellie."

Eleanor felt the blush rise. "Sophie's a very nice person, as well as a marvellous cook."

"Hmm…a good cook, eh. So is Hanna my housekeeper, but we aren't such close…umm…pals, if you get my drift."

Eleanor's knuckles whitened on the wheel and she jammed down the accelerator, pleased to see Ginny's foot press sharply down on the floorboard as if it were a brake pedal. "You and Mum are just the damn same. Always trying to find some gossip where there's nothing."

"If you say so, dear."

"And I expect you not to mention Sophie to mum."

Ginny chuckled. "Why not? You said yourself there's nothing going on. Though mind you, if you are having a little… ah…fling, I wouldn't dream of telling her."

"I am not having a *fling* as you so crudely put it. Sophie works for me, for God's sake," Eleanor snapped.

Ginny sat up straighter and looked at her curiously. "Oh. I hadn't realized your feelings were involved."

Eleanor nearly groaned aloud. It was impossible to pull the wool over her eyes for Ginny was the master of intrigue. Maybe she should just come clean and get her advice. After all, she was the self-help guru. She must know something. "The house is just up this hill. I'd like to get out of this dress and into something more comfortable and then we can talk. You'll have to sleep in your undies…I wouldn't have anything that would fit you."

"That's no problem. I'll get someone to bring my suitcase up tomorrow morning from the boat. You do know there's a luncheon on board tomorrow?"

"Yes. Deirdre mentioned it. Now here we are."

By the time Eleanor had a quick shower and slipped into her tracksuit, Ginny had a plate of cheese and bickies and a bottle of red on the table in the lounge. "My word, this is certainly impressive. The view with the moon over the ocean is stunning." Ginny pointed to the seat opposite. "Now, sit down and tell me all about Sophie."

"There's not much to tell really. She's employed to be my home help over here, and…well…we seem to click. She's smart, caring, and a great cook, but that's not the main thing. We've become good friends. She's so easy to get on with. I really like her, but I don't know what to do. We're worlds apart, socially as well as geographically. But I know if I let her go, I'll be losing someone I'm beginning to hold dear."

Ginny plucked a piece of cheese from the plate, and regarded it thoughtfully before she popped it into her mouth. "You know…people are like cheese. There are all sorts: bland, spicy, hard, soft, cream, young, aged, matured. Not all of them suit your palate, but when you find the one that does, you always buy it again." She shot a piercing look at Eleanor. "I'm just wondering whether you like her because she reminds you of Maria."

Eleanor felt a wave of irritation. "Sophie's not anything like Maria."

"Why is that? She certainly looks like her."

"I thought so in the beginning, but then when I got to know her, I can't see it now. It's not about looks anymore." She looked at her in surprise. "You know, Ginny, I've just realized something. I'm an entirely different person now. Then I was young, impressionable, and struggling professionally. Maria was…well, the closest thing to perfection I had ever seen. Sophisticated, beautiful and so full of life."

"And very married, dear. Don't forget that little snippet. Doesn't that tell you something?"

Eleanor cleared her throat, which suddenly seemed choked. "She didn't make a secret of it. I went into the affair with my eyes wide open."

"I'm not judging you…you've done your penance. Years of hard labour. And I've no doubt she was the one who seduced you. She was a cheat, pure and simple. She cheated on her husband."

Eleanor closed her eyes, just wanting this conversation to go away. Ginny was opening up something she didn't want to hear. "She loved me," she ground out.

"You were just a good fuck to her."

Eleanor blinked. She'd never heard Ginny say that word. "That's not true."

"Isn't it? Has she ever contacted you again…ever acknowledged you're still alive."

"You know that would have been impossible in her position."

"Rubbish. It wouldn't have hurt to at least congratulate you for winning the Oscar." Ginny reached over and took her hand. Eleanor let her, too upset to pull away. "I'm not doing this to hurt you. I'm trying to get you to help yourself. You've been emotionally crippled ever since Maria. Now you've found this lovely woman, you'll have to decide what you're going to do about her."

"What should I do?" asked Eleanor, unable to hold back her tears.

"You have to decide that and I wouldn't be too slow about it. That Austen is a very sexy woman and she's got her eye on Sophie." Ginny fanned her face with the napkin. "Whew! She put *my* heart into a flutter and I'm old and straight."

CHAPTER TWENTY-TWO

With some misgivings Sophie watched Eleanor walk away. She knew she was hurt because Sophie had decided to stay in the bar, but this was an opportunity to get to know Austen. If she found out something sensational about the singer, then maybe the article could be about her and not Eleanor. Owen wouldn't give a fig who she wrote about, so long as it sold.

After she finished her beer, she took one of the delicate little caviar nibbles from the plate on the bar. "Oh this is so good," she moaned.

"You wanna do something *really* good, babe?" Austen whispered into her ear. Her hot breath on Sophie's earlobe sent shivers down her spine. Hell, the woman even breathed sex.

"Back down, lover-girl. Another drink will be just fine for the moment." She signalled the bartender. "I'll have a vodka and lime. What about you?"

"A scotch on the rocks. Make it a double."

"Lisa?"

"No more for me. I want to check on Giovanni in the kitchen. I'll be back to take you home."

"Okay. See you then," said Sophie, sorry to see her go, though understanding why. Lisa wouldn't know how to say no to Austen. The staff had a strict policy about fraternizing with guests and if Austen made a play for Lisa, she could lose her job.

When she disappeared from view, Austen edged her stool closer until their thighs pressed together. "You and Eleanor seem very chummy. You're certainly a sneaky dark horse, aren't you? How'd you get into her pants? I don't think anyone's seen that sacred site for years. What's she like to shag? I can't imagine her letting out a good scream."

Sophie fought the urge to throw her drink into her face, but studied her instead. She drew back, surprised that behind the façade Austen looked upset. Now that was interesting. She slid into reporter mode. With a wriggle, she moved her stool away until they were no longer touching and murmured, "I don't kiss and tell. You'll just have to imagine what it's like." She ran her finger down the tattooed arm in a slow stroke. "I bet you've fantasized about it though. She makes you all hot and bothered, doesn't she?"

Austen stared at her then half emptied her glass. "What the fuck makes you say that?"

"Come off it. It's written all over your face. You're jealous."

"Don't get too worked up about it. You're only in her bed because you look like someone else." She signalled for another drink.

"Maria?"

"She told you about *Maria*?" Austen looked at her incredulously.

Sophie ran the same finger round the rim of her glass and said offhandedly, "So you know about Maria too? Why would she tell you? She dislikes you."

"Because we were friends. I was there in Rome when she met her," she snapped.

"Oh, she didn't tell me that. Perhaps she didn't think you were important enough to mention." At those words, Austen seemed to deflate. Moisture welled in her eyes and she looked like a little girl who had lost her favourite doll. Sophie suddenly had an urge to comfort her. "Oh, Austen. You were in love with her, weren't you?"

Instead of denying it, Austen was silent.

"Why does she hate you now?"

She shook her head. "You'll have to ask her."

"Okay, I won't pry. Come on…we'll have one more and then I have to go."

They sat there in silence after the drinks arrived and unexpectedly Austen asked, "How did you get to shag her? So many have tried but she doesn't seem to notice them."

Sophie laughed. "I'm just her housekeeper. I'm not in her bed."

Austen looked at her shrewdly. "But you'd like to be?"

"Hell yeah. I think she's wonderful. But seriously…look at me, Austen. I'm not in her league. She can have anyone she wants."

"Don't you believe it. She wants you all right. When she saw us together, she was ropable. I've never seen her so put out."

Sophie snorted. "I wish." She gave Austen a nudge with her shoulder. "You know, you're barking up the wrong tree with her. You two wouldn't last a month together."

"Why not?"

"Because you're both alpha females. Your partners need to be easygoing. And as well, you're extra-fiery and she's extra-reserved. You wouldn't suit at all. You'd stifle each other's creativity."

Austen stared at her. "What makes you an authority on love?" She ran her eye over Sophie. "What…you're like thirty? I bet you haven't been with too many women either…you have that look about you. And believe me, babe, I can tell."

"That doesn't mean anything," replied Sophie unconcerned. "I come from a very large extended family, and you haven't heard drama until you've lived amongst *them*. Cripes, I've listened to so many crappy sob stories it would make your mind boggle." She plucked a piece of fluff off Austen's sleeve. "Now you… you take them to bed, then disappear. You wouldn't have a clue about the heartache you leave behind."

"They never complain."

"No, they wouldn't because I bet you're good. But I imagine they don't get a repeat."

"Only occasionally I'll go for a second night. It's better that way. A clean break…no expectations." Austen downed the last of her drink. As she looked at Sophie, a discernable heat built in her gaze. "So what about it? It's been a long day and I want one of those hugs that turns into sex. Want to see what all the fuss is about? No strings."

Sophie had to admit it was tempting. Reflected in those sultry eyes was a promise of an amazingly hot wanton night. And Austen certainly wasn't expecting a refusal. "Hmmm…I can't say the invitation is not appealing, but no thanks."

"You're knocking me back? Why?" Austen looked more incredulous than put out.

"I might be extremely inexperienced by your standards, but I'm not an easy lay. I expect to be dated and wooed."

"Geez, what century are you from?"

"I dislike being a sure thing."

"How many dates before you come across with the goodies?"

"Don't be crass. I like to get to know someone first."

Austen shifted closer. "How many girlfriends have you had?"

"Not many."

"No wonder. They probably died of frustration."

"Very funny. Some of us live in the real world, Austen. Everyone doesn't leap into bed together at the first twitch of their hormones," Sophie muttered, exasperated. "But that's not the problem with me. It's a bit difficult to find someone when you're not out. All my good friends are straight. I've met a few nice girls online, but nobody wants to sneak around so nothing has lasted."

"So why aren't you out? It's accepted now."

Sophie moaned. "Not in my family."

"Then you'll have to change their minds."

"I've decided I'm going to when I get home. I want a life. I would have done it before this, but I haven't loved anyone enough to go through the drama. Let me rephrase that…I've never been in love, full stop."

Austen looked at her with a measure of compassion. "You're going to have difficulty after Eleanor, aren't you?"

"Yes I am," Sophie whispered. "I have never felt this way about anyone in my life. The thought of not seeing her again is starting to hurt. I almost wish she wasn't so great."

Austen patted her on the shoulder. "Come on. We'll have another one and hit the road. Run and tell Lisa I'll take you home. When we get there, ask me in for coffee. Eleanor's going to be properly pissed when she sees me there. It'll stir something up." She chuckled. "If she tosses you out, you can come and cook for me. Believe it or not, I like staying home most of the time, but I'm a damn awful cook so I eat out."

* * *

"Do you think she saw that?" said Austen in a loud stage whisper when the security light flashed on.

Sophie giggled. "Nah. Come into the kitchen and I'll get us something to eat. We'll clatter around a bit. That should wake her up."

"Got any grog in there?"

"There's some wine in the fridge." She peered at Austen. "Should you be drinking anything else? You've been guzzling doubles and you look pretty full."

"Aw Soph, you're not going to turn into a wowser, are you?"

"No. But you're not getting any more until I get some coffee and food into you. We haven't eaten all night. Those dainty little nibbles wouldn't have filled up a flea. Some good solid Italian cooking…that's what we need." Sophie propped her up against the door while she searched for the key. The fresh air had hit Sophie too. She was a bit wobbly in the legs and her face felt flushed.

Then she grimaced when the big terra-cotta pot at the side of the door, toppled over with a loud crash and rolled off the landing. "Shush. Be careful. Maybe this wasn't such a good idea. I don't want her to see us drunk. We'll sober up a bit then make a noise." She flipped open the door, dragged Austen down the hallway and dumped her in a chair at the kitchen table. After she put a strong cup of black coffee under her nose, she went to the pantry. "I'm going to make us a big bowl of pasta. That'll sop up the alcohol."

"Oh, this coffee's good," Austen said. She began to tap out a beat on the table and sing softly.

Sophie enthusiastically swayed to the tune as she chopped the vegetables. She looked in awe at Austen—the woman could really sing. And the hands that played on the table were beautiful: tanned, long-fingered, and strong. When she noticed Austen gazing at her hips as she rocked to the rhythm, she exaggerated the motion. So engrossed was she with the dinner preparation and song, she failed to hear someone come to the door.

"Can anyone join the party?"

Startled, Sophie turned to see Ginny standing at the doorway. Still dressed in her flowing pink kaftan, she seemed to float into the room as a bosomy ethereal being. She smelt wonderful, like rose petals and talcum powder. Without makeup, she seemed younger than at the recital, and despite her size, she definitely was alluring and voluptuous. She appeared to be in her early to mid-sixties, but was one of those women that never look much older when they are eighty. Sophie smiled and pointed to a chair. "Of course you can. I'm whipping up something for us to eat. We've had a bit to drink and need food. Would you like some pasta?"

"Yes please. Ellie told me about your cooking."

Austen jumped up and pulled out a chair. "Sit next to me, you gorgeous thing. Would you like a coffee or perhaps a wine?"

"There's a half a bottle of red in the cupboard. I think I'll have a glass. Would you girls like one?"

"Can't. I have been instructed by the boss over there that I have to sober up." Austen looked pleadingly at Sophie. "Can I have one? We can't have Ginny drinking alone."

"Finish your coffee first. The food's not far off." After she placed the pasta in the boiling water, she looked around to see Ginny gazing at her quizzically.

Ginny turned to Austen. "What about another song after we eat?"

She snickered. "I might wake up Her Majesty."

"Austen," said Sophie sternly. "That was rude. Ginny is Eleanor's friend."

"Oh," said Ginny, toying with her cutlery, "I think she should come down. It wouldn't do to miss this action. I saw some CDs in the lounge. We can adjourn there later."

The meal went down well, Sophie pleased to see that Austen and Ginny ate voraciously. She always thought the best thing about cooking was its appreciation. After finishing off seconds, Austen groaned. "I'm stuffed. That was fantastic. Now come on and I'll have a look at those CDs."

While Austen rifled through the collection in the other room, Ginny, ignoring Sophie's protest, offered to help her clean up. "Nonsense. Two hands are better than one. You wash, I'll wipe. What did you think of Ellie's performance tonight?"

"It was wonderful." Sophie skimmed the dishcloth over a plate and caught her eye when she passed it over. "I hadn't realized she was so good. I've seen a lot of Shakespeare onstage, but she brought his words to another level."

"Yes she did. And I think she'll only improve. She has the capacity to be one of the great actors of modern times. Hers is a rare talent, which needs to be nurtured. Her mother wants her to settle down with someone who'll help her achieve that, and keep her happy when she needs pleasuring." She punctuated the last words with air quotes.

Sophie gave a little gasp. Ginny would make anyone blush. She felt the heat rise in her cheeks as erotic images of languidly pleasuring Eleanor with her tongue, flickered through her brain like a porn video. "Does she?" she wheezed out.

"Yes. We're on the lookout for the right woman."

"Oh. I wouldn't bother too much. I bet there'd be a big lineup," Sophie said a little bitterly.

"I imagine there will be. And talk about talent. Austen has her share too. You seem to be getting on well with her."

Sophie chuckled. "She's fun. And not what I expected. She's actually rather sweet and quite sensitive."

"She's got a reputation though. She's one of the sexiest creatures I've ever seen. She'd be hard to resist if you were a lesbian."

"Yes, she is. She has the knack of not being offensive when she asks. Even though you know she's been with truckloads of women, she makes you feel special. Does that make sense?"

"Ah," murmured Ginny. "That sounds like she's already popped the question."

"What do you think?" said Sophie, letting out a guffaw. "Anything with breasts is fair game to Austen."

"And what did—?" Her words were interrupted by a blast of music from the lounge.

Sophie gave a cry of delight. "It's one of Austen's. Go on in and take the glasses. I'll get another bottle of wine. Maybe she'll sing along with the recording."

Out of the corner of her eye, Sophie didn't miss Ginny's chagrin at having had her question cut off. She felt a spurt of satisfaction. It was none of her business if Austen wanted to sleep with her, and Sophie wasn't a child who needed to be warned about the singer. Choosing a Shiraz, she screwed off the lid and filled the glasses.

Austen gave her a wink as she took a glass. "Ah, nectar of the gods. Now dance with Ginny and I'll sing along. It's one of my favourites."

After a halfhearted protest, Ginny allowed herself to be pulled out onto the floor. She was surprisingly light on her feet, with quite a few good moves as they gyrated to the beat. Austen looked like the superstar she was as she belted out the words. After two songs, Ginny flopped into a chair, wheezing. Sophie, in the zone now, danced on, and then felt Austen slide up behind her, mirroring her movements. With an arm around Sophie's waist, she pressed more firmly against her and crooned in her ear as they twisted in harmony.

Sophie didn't pull away, mesmerized by the way Austen led her through the dance. She closed her eyes, enjoying the sensation. It was intoxicating. But when she opened her them again, she found herself staring into two hooded hazel eyes. Eleanor, dressed in a grey tracksuit, stood against the doorframe, watching her with an expression that Sophie couldn't read. Sophie smiled widely at her.

From behind, Austen called out, "I was wondering if you were going to join us, Eleanor. Ask Ginny for the next dance. It's a slow one."

Sophie stepped forward slightly so they weren't touching, embarrassed. Nobody could have mistaken the hint of swagger and possessiveness in Austen's voice.

Eleanor's gaze remained centred on Sophie. "No, Austen. I'm sure Ginny would love to dance with you. I'm cutting in."

Without another word, she strode forward, reached for Sophie's hand and pulled her into her arms.

CHAPTER TWENTY-THREE

Eleanor lay on the bed as she listened to the music, at odds with what to do. She desperately wanted to go downstairs, although she knew she probably wouldn't like what she'd see. She had heard them come in, hurt that Sophie would have been so unfeeling as to bring Austen into their home. As the sounds died down, her hurt turned to anguish. Had they gone to Sophie's room? When Ginny's voice floated up the stairs, some of her anxiety faded. At least they weren't there yet. From the muted sounds from the kitchen, she presumed they were having something to eat. Then the music started in the lounge.

Finally, Eleanor couldn't stand it any longer. But she wasn't going to change her clothes. She wouldn't give them that satisfaction. With a last longing look at her wardrobe, she sailed off down the stairs, ready for battle. When she arrived at the threshold of the lounge, she could only remain there in silent misery. Austen was pressed against Sophie's back, her arm around her waist, dancing with a slow seductive rhythm. Sophie had her eyes closed, obviously enjoying the connection. All emotion drained out of Eleanor's body. Completely swamped, she couldn't even force her legs to move.

Barely able to hold herself together, she half turned to walk back to her room, but stopped when she caught Ginny's eye. With a sharp shake of her head, the older woman twiddled her fingers around in some elaborate sign language that Eleanor strained to decipher. She peered at the hands, figuring it must be some obscure self-help thing. In the end, Ginny shot a frustrated glare, curled her lips and mouthed, "Go. Get. Her."

She swung back to Sophie. Her eyes opened and their gazes locked. Eleanor's heart gave a lurch when Sophie's face transformed into a wide happy smile. With no more hesitation, Eleanor brushed off Austen with a few empowered words, strode forward and tugged Sophie into her arms. Immediately, Sophie threw her arm around her neck and sank into her. At the feel of the soft body, an intense wave of sensation swirled across Eleanor's skin. With slow sensuous movements, they began to sway together to the beat, Eleanor's face buried in the dark hair, Sophie's head in the crook of her shoulder.

Eleanor became oblivious to the surroundings, her world centred on the woman against her. When Sophie trembled in her arms, it was more of an aphrodisiac than she even imagined possible. The ache in Eleanor's chest turned into a deeper, richer one that lodged between her legs. She couldn't contain herself. She bent her head and sucked lightly on her earlobe, then feathered kisses up and down her neck. Sophie nestled her head further into her shoulder to expose more skin to the kiss. A cough from Ginny brought them back to earth. Eleanor straightened up a little guiltily, but kept a tight hold on Sophie.

Ginny heaved herself out of the chair. "I'm off to bed. I think that's our cue, Austen. Two's company, three's a crowd. And four definitely is."

Austen nodded ruefully. "Yep. I guess that's our call. See you tomorrow, Soph. Thanks for the pasta."

"See you."

When they had gone, Eleanor turned and ruffled Sophie's hair. "Come on, I'll walk you to your room."

Sophie looked at her questioningly, though didn't argue. Fingers entwined, they silently made their way to the unit. When Sophie dropped her hand and walked through the door, Eleanor didn't hesitate on the brink but followed her in.

"Goodni—" Sophie's words were lost in Eleanor's mouth.

With an urgent pull, she hauled Sophie closer until they were pressed together, their breath mingling. The vibration of her own heartbeat blocked out all other sounds in Eleanor's head. With slow deliberation, she kissed the soft full lips, slowly, sweetly until her mind reeled with desire, hungering to claim the woman in her arms. As the heat grew between them, Eleanor's kisses became more demanding—this time she wanted to make Sophie forget every other woman she'd ever met, especially Austen.

A current ran between them, potent and electrifying, becoming a living thing as it twirled and writhed. Licks of fire screamed down her nerve ends as their tongues danced together, sucking, weaving, and tickling until all control vanished for Eleanor. She groaned aloud as the heat between her legs reached fever point.

"May I take off your shirt?" she murmured. When Sophie nodded, she quickly hauled it over her head, which left the lacy black bra encasing her full breasts. Eleanor unclipped it and lowered her head to run her cheeks over the soft flesh. Sophie arched upward, raking her hands through Eleanor's hair with urgent tugs.

Eleanor reverently filled her palms with the warm flesh. "Oh, my darling, they're beautiful. So soft."

Sophie began to squirm with little mewing sounds as Eleanor squeezed and flicked the nipples until they were jutting out from the pebbled areolas. She drew away for a moment to gaze into Sophie's face. Strands of hair curled carelessly around her forehead and her eyes were clouded and dusty. Eleanor took a nipple into her mouth. She sucked hard, drawing it in until Sophie swayed her hips hard against her as a flurry of endearments bubbled out.

Desire stripped away all reason when Sophie slid a hand under the waistband of Eleanor's pants and slipped a finger into the moisture pooled between her legs. As the tip hit the sensitive spot, such a sharp wave of pleasure vibrated through her body that Eleanor could only gasp, "Bed."

Over tripping feet they made their way to the bedroom, Eleanor barely aware of her surroundings. Dazed and trembling, she latched onto Sophie's neck and sucked the warm skin, inhaling her scent. With urgency now, they undressed and moved quickly onto the sheets. Eleanor lay Sophie down on her back then knelt over her. Sophie reached up and stroked her cheek. "What do you want from me, Eleanor?" she breathed huskily.

"Everything, my darling…everything." A pent-up need flooded through Eleanor as she gazed at the nubile body. It was ravishing and this chalice of pleasure was all hers to enjoy. With a groan, she claimed the lips again, filling up the mouth with her tongue as she moved her body lightly over Sophie. Then she reclaimed the breasts, suckled until the globes were swollen and the nipples hard. She trailed her mouth down over her abdomen, nibbling and kissing on her journey down her body. Finally, she settled herself between her legs.

With the first long stroke of the tongue, Sophie cried out, "Oh my God, that's so good…so good."

Eleanor became lost in the taste and smell of the woman. Her essence was of spring flowers, summer rains, and salty ocean air—pure, tangy, and addictive. As the scents intoxicated her, her tongue and mouth became more demanding. Finally, she circled with the tips of two fingers and waited.

"Please," Sophie whispered.

It was the invitation she needed. Slowly she pushed inside, and began to thrust in and out. She curled the fingers, searching. When Sophie jerked her hips more urgently, she knew she had found that special spot. She quickened the pace over it. They were lost now in a whirlpool of sensation as she gradually brought Sophie to the brink. When the muscle walls tightened, she knew Sophie was close to release. When she deliberately sucked the engorged nub into her mouth, the climax hit immediately. Sophie screamed out her name as she exploded. Power sang through Eleanor, and she held her hips tenderly as the orgasm rolled through in glorious waves.

Once they had shivered away, Eleanor moved up to take her in her arms. Her head pillowed in the curve of her shoulder, Sophie smiled dreamily. "That was indescribable."

Eleanor kissed her gently on the cheek. "You're so beautiful. Amazing."

Sophie gave contented sighs, caressing Eleanor's belly with her fingertips. "You're not tired are you, Ellie? I'd like to start pleasuring you now if that's all right."

Eleanor's breath hitched. *Pleasuring* sounded so hedonistic, so sexually fulfilling, so wonderful. "I'd like that, darling," she whispered.

Her body pulsated with excitement, cried out for release. She lay down on her back and watched Sophie skim her fingers up over her body.

"Shut your eyes, sweetheart, just feel me," Sophie murmured.

Eleanor did what she was told. She let her eyes close and wrapped herself into the experience. What followed was like a dream, a fantasy that had come straight from her imagination. First, it was a hot breath all over her chest and neck until goose bumps prickled her skin, sharpening the sensations. Then slowly her body was kissed and stroked, from the top of her head to the very tips of her toes. When she twitched at her most sensitive places, these were given extra attention. She knew Sophie was learning what pleased her.

Her nipples were sucked and stretched until they were so hypersensitive every touch shot to her sex. By the time Sophie's tongue was moving in random circles over her stomach, she was ready to combust. As Sophie shimmered her lips up and down her inner thighs, Eleanor whispered frantically, "Please, darling. I need you. Please."

"Patience. Just relax."

"I'm nearly there. Please." With a growl of frustration, Eleanor coiled her legs around Sophie's waist and grasped her hair with urgent fingers.

Sophie looked up with a brief smile before she sank her mouth between Eleanor's legs. She sucked wildly and then scraped the clit firmly with her tongue. A hundred tiny pulse points drummed through Eleanor's sex, and like an exploding star, her orgasm blazed into life. She cried out, all control lost as the torrent crashed through her. The waves pulsated fiercely. When finally they ebbed away, she collapsed panting on the sheets. In all her memory, she couldn't recall experiencing anything quite that breathtaking. Not even Maria had brought her to such heights.

For a long while, they stretched out on their backs, content to stare at the ceiling in silence. Words seemed inadequate to Eleanor, but finally she felt compelled to say, "We need to sleep. I should go."

"No. Stay," Sophie said quickly.

Pleased, Eleanor rolled over and gave her an open-mouthed kiss. "You want me to stay?"

"I'd love you to. That…that was wonderful." Sophie sounded teary.

"I thought it was too. Snuggle into me."

Sophie's burrowed in with a sniffle, and when her breathing slowed with sleep, Eleanor's eyes drooped shut.

The first glow of dawn was just visible through the window when Eleanor awoke. For a second she wondered where she was, before the memories of the night flooded back. She tilted her head to look at Sophie. Naked, she was curled up against her back with only her legs covered by the sheet. She looked so enticing Eleanor was tempted to initiate another round of lovemaking. But she held back, she needed to think, to get her head around everything.

Where would they go from here? There was no pretending it had just been a night of sex. They both knew that it had been so much more. But in the light of day, she had to face reality. They hadn't known each other long enough for a commitment. She had no idea how Sophie felt about it all. But then on the flip side, they had spent nearly seven weeks together twenty-four seven. Most couples who dated for months wouldn't have shared so much time with each other.

But the big question was yet to be faced. Was she prepared to come out of the closet immediately once they left the island? If she were with Sophie, their relationship would be impossible to hide—she wouldn't be able to keep her hands off her. And she wouldn't want to keep it a secret, for the last thing Eleanor wanted to do was skulk around again. She had had enough of living that way. But would Sophie be prepared to tell her family?

She dropped her eyes to the woman lying next to her. Though their night together would complicate things, Eleanor didn't want her own insecurities to spoil what had happened. It had been the best night of her life. Sophie was everything she had ever wanted in a lover. She ran her hand through her hair, trying to rationalize things. Whether they liked it or not, there would be consequences if they rushed in too hard, too fast. Maybe it would be better to cool it for a while, though it would be difficult. Now she'd had a taste she wanted more. Oh dear God, did she want more! Her body fairly hummed.

With a sigh, she slipped out of bed and pulled on her crumpled tracksuit. If she stayed in the bed, she'd have to touch Sophie, and Ginny wouldn't get her breakfast. After one last look at the sleeping, naked body, she crept out the door. Once in her own room, she stripped off and headed for the shower. The jets of water didn't banish the hankering to replicate the night. With hands spread on the tiled wall, she let the spray wash over her. She began to tremble. The lingering desire was enough to set off whistles. It felt more like love than lust. Was she on the cusp of losing her heart?

Lover. She ran the word around in head, analysed it, found she liked the sound. Someone waiting for her at home, someone in her bed, someone to call her own. But did Sophie feel the same? Would she baulk at the thought of the press following her every move? The thought triggered a flood of unease. Being a private person, Sophie would hate the scrutiny of reporters, hate Merilee Watts poking into her life. Would she run away at the constant public exposure?

They had better talk about it before their romance went any further.

Sophie was at the kitchen stove when Eleanor wandered down an hour later. She looked up with a smile. "Hi, Ellie."

At the sight of Sophie, all her intentions of cooling it flew out the window. "Hello there," she said with an answering smile, then leaned forward and kissed her. The scent of a fragrant deodorant and the taste of mint toothpaste tickled her senses.

When she lifted her head to pull away, Sophie held her in place. "Kiss me again."

Eleanor groaned. She had no more hope of refusing than flying to the moon. She did as she was asked, only this time she drew Sophie into her arms and kissed her thoroughly, long and passionately. "Umm…that's better," Sophie murmured. "I wanted to do that when I woke up, but you were gone. I thought you would have woken me before you left."

Eleanor felt a flush of guilt. How stupid she had been. Of course she should have stayed—she had behaved as Austen did with her women. "I'm sorry. I…I wanted to be by myself to think things over."

"Oh? And what conclusions did you come to?" asked Sophie. She turned back to the stove, ostensibly to continue the breakfast preparation but Eleanor knew that wasn't the reason. She was hurt.

"We need to talk about last night…us."

"Is there an *us*, Ellie?"

"That's what I want to discuss. Where do we go from here? What are your expectations?"

Sophie looked confused. "My expectations? What do you mean?"

"I thought you would be wondering what my intentions are."

Sophie shot her a look that left Eleanor in no doubt that she was upset. "Damn it, Eleanor, why make it into a drama. I'm a big girl. We had a fantastic night together, but that doesn't mean I expect the ring and the white wedding. You don't have to worry that I'm going to make demands on you. I'm not that sort of person and I'm only your housekeeper for Pete's sake."

"No…no. That wasn't what I meant."

"So what did you mean?"

Eleanor could feel the situation spinning out of control. She had made a hash of it and she wasn't sure she knew how to right the ship. "I never thought you would take advantage of the situation. You might be my employee but you're my friend too. I…I really like you, Sophie."

"And I like you too. But I'm not your equal in any way. It was a fantastic night but there were no ties or promises made. I knew where I stood when you weren't next to me when I woke. So don't sweat. I know you don't do commitment, and I'm certainly no catch."

Suddenly, Eleanor had an awful sinking feeling. A quick touch of panic. She'd made a complete mess of things and hurt Sophie. Before she could say more, footsteps echoed on the staircase. "We'll have to continue this later. Ginny's coming."

"Whatever," Sophie said in a tired voice. "I'll have breakfast ready in fifteen minutes."

Eleanor felt something cold squeeze her heart. She had wanted to make it clear she was interested, but now Sophie thought she was being used. Why hadn't she stayed in the damn bed?

CHAPTER TWENTY-FOUR

Sophie brought coffee out to the terrace where Eleanor and Ginny sat chatting. Both thanked her, though Eleanor seemed too quiet. Sophie stole glances at her while she set the table. Her face, lifted to the sun, was luminescent in the light. Exquisite. Sophie was well aware how much trouble she was in after their night together. Eleanor had been everything she had dreamed she would be and more. The perfect lover—the perfect everything.

Restlessly, Sophie adjusted the cutlery as she felt a surge of self-disgust. She had known what Eleanor was trying to say before, but she had feigned ignorance. It was only to be expected that Eleanor wanted to talk, because that was how her mind worked. She liked to put everything neatly into compartments, especially her emotions. It had come as a surprise though, when she had asked Sophie's expectations. She had nearly blurted out she wanted to be in her life, to love her, to care for her.

What a pathetic fool she was even having that dream. Once Eleanor found out the truth, she was going to hate her. With a vengeance. And not only was she going to lose Eleanor's respect and friendship, she would have to farewell her position on the paper as well. There was no way now she could ever write one word, derogatory or otherwise, about her. Or Austen either for that matter. She liked the singer. Underneath the bravado was a woman who loved and bled just like the rest of them.

Sophie knew it was imperative to step back from the fledgling emotional bond with Eleanor, before both their lives were wrecked. She had to sever the thread between them that was fast becoming unbreakable.

A stray tear worked its way over her cheek before she could prevent its escape. She lifted her eyes to see Eleanor studying her with a concerned expression. Embarrassed at having lost control, she hurried to the kitchen. As she dished out the cheese and egg soufflé, she pushed away all traces of sadness and anxiety. Then resolutely, she clicked on an imaginary computer mouse and attached a smile on her face.

"This looks tasty," said Ginny as she accepted the plate handed to her. "After the pasta last night, you wouldn't think I'd be hungry again, but I'm starving. It must be the fresh air. Where did you learn to cook, Sophie?"

"I worked for a year at my uncle's restaurant when I finished school."

"You didn't want to be a chef? You've a talent there, my girl."

"No, it was only to get money to go to…um…to go overseas."

With a smile, Ginny touched her ample stomach. "A pity. As you can see, I'm appreciative of fine dining and I can say categorically, you're an excellent cook." She peered over her glasses. "You and Eleanor had a pleasant night, I trust?"

Sophie shot a quick glance across the table. Eleanor, with a flush on her cheeks, had her head down, her eyes on the plate. It was apparent by Ginny's quizzical look that had accompanied the question, that their night together hadn't been discussed. Sophie was about to pass it off with a vague throwaway line, but hesitated. This was an opportunity to put distance between Eleanor and herself. With a sinking heart, she said, "The night was terrific. Eleanor certainly knows how to give a girl a good time. But I'm well aware she doesn't want to go the next step, so that'll be it for me." She gave a sniff. "I'm a bit naïve when it comes to sex, Ginny, but I didn't want to become another notch on a bedpost."

Eleanor's head snapped up. "Sophie! What's gotten in to you? I said I was sorry for not being there when you woke up. I've never used women like that."

"You didn't stay all night?" asked Ginny with a disapproving frown.

"I wanted to think things over. What's wrong with that?"

Sophie stood up with a lurch. "It doesn't matter, Ellie. Really. I'm sorry I said anything. You needed release and I was pleased to be there for you. I don't have any regrets about last night. You gave me the best night of my life and I'll always cherish the memory."

Overwhelmed, she stumbled towards the door, aware how thoroughly she had trivialised what had been so special. Eleanor would never forgive her, and though that had been the desired effect, it stung like hell. She barely made it through the kitchen door before the tears began to fall. Hastily, she wiped her eyes with the back of her hand when she heard a footstep behind. She turned to look over her shoulder.

"Come with me. Please Sophie?" Eleanor asked softly. "We really need to talk."

For a second Sophie hesitated, but then nodded dumbly and followed her to the downstairs unit.

"Now," Eleanor said quietly. "Tell me what exactly that was all about."

"What…what do you mean?"

"You forget what I do for a living. I've played opposite many actors, good and bad, and you, my dear, are one of the worst I've ever seen. Now tell me what possessed you to say those things to Ginny after the night we spent together."

"Um…it was how I felt."

"Nonsense. I can see you've been crying. Now tell me the truth."

Sophie slumped forward. "Of course what I said was rubbish. I was trying to protect myself. I know what last night meant, but what future is there for us? I'm not in your class."

"Oh darling, we have to talk about many things, but not being my equal is certainly not one of them. Do you honestly think I'm so shallow?"

"You don't know enough about me. I've got secrets, I'm not…" She trailed off, not able to say the words.

Eleanor skimmed her hand through Sophie's hair, lacing the strands between her fingers. She gave a little tug. "We've all got secrets. You're not a convicted felon, are you? An ax murderer?"

"No, of course not."

"Good, then that's all I want to know. Now lie down and I'm going to finish what I wanted to do when I woke up."

Sophie gazed into the penetrating stare and could only stammer, "Okay."

By the time she wriggled up into the centre of the bed, Eleanor was stripped off to the buff. With a quick movement, she was on the bed, and without any lead-in, had Sophie down to her knickers. Then these too were gone, ripped off impatiently. Sophie's pulse thudded against her throat. This was a new and exciting Eleanor—a woman on a mission. Eleanor hovered over her and brought her hand down. Automatically, Sophie arched as red nails scraped down the side of her neck. Then when they began to flick her nipples, little charges of electricity rippled between her legs.

"Do you like that?" asked Eleanor.

Sophie silently nodded. The whole experience was so intense. Eleanor was everywhere on her body, nipping, scraping, kissing until Sophie was nearly at a screaming point. Then Eleanor moved on top and spread over her. A flood of feeling came in an all-consuming rush as Eleanor deftly manoeuvred their thighs so their centres were fused together. Sophie could feel the pressure, heady and arousing. Dazed with desire, she thrust against her in a steady rhythm. Sweat glistened on her skin—she was slick with it. Eleanor dug her fingers into her buttocks, urging her on.

Sophie felt the rapture rise to fever point as her orgasm neared. Eleanor moved her head to kiss her. Sophie parted her lips and Eleanor's tongue joined hers, slipping into the moistness, until finally, with a long last thrust, they climaxed together. A storm of pleasure barrelled through Sophie, so intense she couldn't stop a scream erupting. Only after their bodies settled did Eleanor roll off. When she did, she turned towards Sophie and held her firmly against her. She didn't say anything, but Sophie could feel her tremble, and when she looked up, she could see tears fluttering off her lashes.

"Are you all right?" Sophie whispered.

"Oh yes, my darling."

For a while, they lay still, just listening to the silence. Then Eleanor ran her hand down over her hip with a possessive sweep. "You're mine."

Sophie tilted her head enough to catch her eye. "I won't be owned, Ellie. If we're together, we're a partnership."

"Of course. This is not about a power trip for me."

Sophie nuzzled her hair. "So, where do we go from here?"

"Let's just see where this goes. So for now, we'll just enjoy ourselves." Eleanor patted her bottom. "Come on. We'd better see what Ginny is up to."

Ginny was stretched out on a lounge chair with her legs raised on the footstool, reading a book. There was no mistaking the gleam of interest in her eye as she watched them come in. She dropped her gaze to their entwined fingers. Her gaze shifted to Sophie's face briefly, before it focused on Eleanor. "So, you made up, did you?"

"No more personal questions, Ginny. Sophie and I have come to an understanding."

The pink flossy hair fluffed out in fine tentacles as she gave a hearty chuckle. "Damn long conversation."

Sophie couldn't help but laugh—the older woman was good company once you got her sense of humour. "She was very persuasive," she offered.

"It would seem she was, young lady. By the look of you, she took you for a few turns around the cherry bush."

"Ginny!" said Eleanor sternly. "Behave yourself."

"Good lord, Ellie, it won't hurt you to let yourself go occasionally." Her grin became wicked. "I hope you put your stamp on her. Austen will be at lunch and I bet she'll be back for round two."

"Hellooo. I'm here, Ginny," said Sophie annoyed. "I'm nobody's property so back off. Just because I'm with Eleanor, I don't intend to ignore Austen. I think Ellie knows she can trust me."

"Ooooh...feisty too. I like that. Now I suppose I'd better crawl out of this chair and get ready to go. Apparently, these luncheons are a blast."

Sophie grimaced. Socializing with the hobnobs on a classy yacht was the last thing she wanted to do. "I'll stay home."

"Nonsense," said Ginny.

"No one will miss me."

"I will," said Eleanor. "Truly. I want you there with me. Please come."

Sophie had no defence against that plea. She nodded.

CHAPTER TWENTY-FIVE

As Sophie was putting the finishing touches to her outfit, a thought came to her. If she couldn't bring herself to write an exposé on Eleanor, then perhaps a series of mug shots of well-known people might be an alternative. There would be plenty of notables aboard the boat. It wasn't exactly ethical, but time was marching on and she had yet to write one line. She'd have to hurry up to come up with something.

Happier now she had a plan, she pinned the mini-camera disguised as a brooch to her top. Then she slipped the electronic control into the pocket of her slacks.

Eleanor was already waiting in the lounge, dressed in a cornflower-blue knee-high dress with a low V neckline and a pair of Gucci gold sandals. She looked every bit the star. With a glance down at her own clothes, Sophie silently blessed Brie for the trip to the Rosalie boutique. Although not top drawer, the flared pants and off-one-shoulder top wouldn't be out of place amongst the designer labels.

Ginny had been picked up earlier by one of the crew, which left them to make their way down to the yacht at their leisure. "Ready?" asked Eleanor.

"Let's go." She bumped Eleanor's shoulder. "You look very chic."

A light laugh came. "Ah...clothes do not make the woman."

"Yeah. But it certainly helps," said Sophie dryly.

A cooler change had come in through the morning, a light breeze rippling the air as they drove to the jetty. The sunlight seemed softer today, and lay like silk over the water. Their hands were clasped on the way down, but when they reached the jetty, Eleanor moved away until there was a respectable distance between them. Sophie stiffened her shoulders, irritated. Aware she was overreacting, it hurt they had to hide how they felt about each other.

The luxury vessel was huge, festivities already in full swing when they reached the top deck. Fascinated, she looked around. Not the sedate luncheon she had expected. Most of the guests were in party mode, the boat festooned with balloons and streamers. Some danced on a side deck while others stood in groups to chat. Sophie smiled as she followed Eleanor into the reception room. The star certainly knew how to make an entrance as she swept majestically into the room amidst intakes of breath. They worked their way through the crowd until they reached Ginny, who was drolly reeling off one of her jokes. Her face lit up when she spied them, and she tipped her head to kiss Eleanor's cheek. She gave Sophie a friendly pat on the arm.

Someone thrust a glass of champagne into Sophie's hand and deftly eased her aside to take her place next to Eleanor. The rest surged back around. Relegated now to the edge of the group, Sophie studied the woman who had given her the drink. She was tall and slender, somewhere in her late thirties, dressed in a stylish green pantsuit with subtle white stripes. Her shoulder-length dark hair was coiled casually around a striking face. Eyes, smoky grey, sparkled as she gazed at Eleanor. Annoyance stabbed through Sophie. She took a gulp from the flute as she watched

Eleanor's crimson lips break into a wide smile at something the woman said. Sophie snapped off a couple of shots of the woman, determined to look her up later. She hoped she was someone important and hated having her picture in the paper. It would serve her right to find herself in a half page spread.

Sophie's gaze wandered around the room, looking for more photo fodder. The rich and powerful seemed less daunting now they were letting their hair down. Being more an intellectual group rather than A-listers, few artificial boobs or spray tans were evident. She grabbed another glass of champagne from a passing waiter, took a swig and smacked her lips. *Yum!* It certainly beat the el cheapo stuff they served at her uncle's restaurant. That tasted like lolly water, though had the kick of a mule's hind leg.

"Do you know Eleanor Godwin well? I saw you come in with her," a male voice asked.

She turned to see a handsome middle-aged man in a fine Italian suit behind her. His hopeful expression belied how casual the enquiry sounded. Sophie groaned. Another damn would-be suitor. "I work for her."

"Would you like another drink?"

"No thanks. I still have one." She waved her glass.

"So, how long have you been in her employ?"

"Long enough. Why?"

He smoothed his goatee in a reflective gesture. "Forgive me. I didn't mean to pry. I was merely interested in meeting her."

Sophie eyed him with irritation. "Sorry. If you want to meet her, line up with the rest. I wouldn't presume to encroach on her privacy." With a flick of her finger, she caught a snap of him before she moved off quickly. She seethed as she headed out to the dancers to see if there were any famous faces out there. *The hide of him.* What did he think she was? Eleanor's flipping dating service?

The dancers were far more in the party mood than those chatting. In fact, some looked like they hadn't even gone to bed. Sophie recognized the CEO of an investment bank draped over a Kim Kardashian lookalike. From the way he was fondling her butt, Sophie doubted she was his wife. When they began to improvise some dirty dancing moves, she took a snap and moved on. Eventually she left that crowd to their hops, shuffles, and gyrations, to where Austen lounged with a group of bohemian-looking women.

Austen raised her eyebrows in amusement when she approached. "Ladies, meet Sophie, best known for uncovering frozen artefacts and sacred sites."

"Ah," remarked a woman in a multicoloured maxi-dress, "an archaeologist."

"She's had a very fruitful dig," Austen said with a snigger.

Sophie studied her, noting that she was again dressed in black, this time with a few chains hanging off her belt. The bad-girl look was obviously her trademark. "Yes… Lucky me. But the site is ancient history to you, Austen, isn't it? You found nothing." She turned to the other women. "I'm not an archaeologist, but I did go on a dig for two months once. I learnt that if you want to find something of value, interpreting data is just as important as the excavation. Then if you use a bulldozer instead of a trowel, you destroy the site. Isn't that so, Austen?"

The oldest woman of the group gave a hearty laugh. "I don't think you two are talking about digging up some old pots, but whatever you are referring to, this little lady has your measure, Austen." After she introduced the other four women, she wriggled an empty chair between Austen and herself. "I'm Bonnie. Sit yourself down and join us. We're all poets, or profess to be anyhow. And what do you do?"

"I work for Eleanor Godwin."

"She's the housekeeper," chipped in Austen.

Sophie shot her a look of dislike but nodded. "I am."

"I imagine she would be good to work for," remarked Bonnie.

"She's the best—dream job actually."

"So how long have you been with her?"

"I'm only here with her on this holiday."

A woman wearing glasses interjected dryly, "She'd run rings around all the wealthy here. More talent in her little toe than most of the pretentious idiots that came over on the boat with us."

"Don't be so judgmental," said Florence in the maxi-dress.

"Well she does. Have you ever heard Shakespeare performed like that?"

"I haven't," chipped in Sophie. "She made all the women so…so alive. The way she enacted the Constance 'I am not mad speech' was unreal. It gave me goose bumps."

Bonnie looked at her appraisingly. "You're remarkably versatile for a housekeeper. Going on digs and familiar with one of Shakespeare's lesser-known works. Is this a one-off or your permanent employment?"

"No pressure cleaning someone's house. Who wants to have a heart attack at fifty?" said Sophie airily.

Florence slapped her on the back. "I agree. I can see you don't give a flick about convention. Me too." She reached down to pluck a bottle from an ice bucket at her feet. She popped the champagne cork with a flourish. "Top up your glasses…it's free booze and we can't solve the woes of the world sober."

Sophie held out her flute, watching the bubbles rise. It promised to be a fun afternoon. During a heated debate about some obscure poet, Austen's arm snaked around her shoulder. Sophie rolled her eyes—she was nothing if not persistent. Then while the others were still arguing, Austen leaned over and whispered in her ear, "Did you have a good night?"

Sophie turned to study her, realizing it wasn't a casual question. Austen was fishing. "Hell yeah," she murmured back, then hummed happily, pleased to see a frown appear like a thundercloud on Austen's face. When she patted the singer's leg, it twitched under her hand. "It was so definitely worth the wait. Quality not quantity. You should try it sometime."

"Shit you're a know-all. A bitchy know-all."

"Well that was a little nasty," said Sophie unruffled. "I was merely stating a fact."

"What fact?" asked Florence, catching the last of the conversation.

"I was just suggesting to Austen that she should be a little more discriminating in her love life."

All eyes swivelled to Austen who shifted uneasily in her seat. "Don't believe all you read in the tabloids," she muttered.

"You mean you're not Ms. Don Juan," asked Florence. "How disappointing."

Austen gave her a wink. "Well, you could always test the waters."

There was no denying the sparkle of interest on Florence's face. Sophie just shook her head. As the poets launched into another contentious subject, Austen put her mouth back to Sophie's ear. "You're un-fucking-believable."

"You can't take a joke," she whispered back. "What about we bury the hatchet? I've a favour to ask."

"Oh? That's interesting. What do I get in return?"

"I'll come over and make dinner for you one night and do some baking to stock up your supplies. I do awesome cookies."

"Sounds enticing. What do I have to do?"

Sophie sucked in a breath. "One of my best friends works for a paper. I'd like to do a photo shoot of you for her. Nothing gross, just you playing and singing...stuff like that."

"Okay." She leaned forward conspiratorially. "On one condition. You don't tell Eleanor why you're cooking me a meal. Tomorrow night then."

Sophie grimaced. *Crap!* Eleanor was going to be so pissed off, but there was no other option. The photographs would go a long way to keeping her job. "All right. It's a deal."

When a sudden silence fell around her, she looked up to see a smiling Eleanor walking toward them. She gave a wave. "Hi Ellie...um...Eleanor. Come and meet these women."

After she did the introductions, Sophie stood back, proudly watching Eleanor weave her charm. It didn't take long for her to twig that she seemed to be putting in extra effort. Sophie suspected it was because of Austen's magnetic presence and Eleanor was launching a counterattack. It was evident by Austen's stiff stance that she thought so too. Then out of the corner of her eye, Sophie caught movement, and Ginny floated up in a swirl of pink silk.

She put her hand out for Austen to kiss as she took stock of her outfit. "My, my, Austen, those pants are so tight you look like you've been poured into them. You're certainly an alluring creature."

Austen grinned, mollified.

"Now you'll have to excuse us, for Eleanor and I have some business to attend to in my cabin. We'll need your help as well, Sophie."

"Of course. It was a pleasure to meet you ladies, and I'll be… ah…seeing you, Austen."

Sophie could only gawk around at the opulent fittings as they made their way through the boat to Ginny's stateroom. It was considerably larger, far more up-market than a cabin on a commercial liner, or at least the one Sophie had had on her one and only Pacific Island cruise in economy class.

As soon as they entered, Ginny went to the mirror, brushed her hair and walked back to the door. "Right, I'm off," she said briskly. "Have fun."

When the door clicked behind her, Eleanor pulled Sophie into her arms. "Now, I'm going to do what I've wanted to do since we arrived."

"You fox," said Sophie, laughing delightedly.

"I am, my sweet." When Eleanor kissed her, the intoxicating taste of champagne was on her tongue and the smell of her perfume mixed with a whiff of the sea, tickled her nose. Then the heady scent of arousal drifted up as she was led to the bed.

"I'm like a thirsty traveller in the desert who has found water," murmured Eleanor. "I want to keep drinking. I hope you do too."

CHAPTER TWENTY-SIX

Eleanor looked down lovingly at the naked figure pressed against her in the bed. Sophie's head was pillowed in the curve of her shoulder, her arm flung over her waist. Eleanor took a deep breath of her scent, enjoying the fragrance that reminded her of wildflowers and cinnamon. Sophie's breathing was slow and even, a sign she was still snoozing after their long spell of lovemaking. Eleanor tilted her head to take in the curve of the hip, then careful not to wake her, allowed herself the luxury of cuddling closer. A wave of tenderness washed through her, so overpowering that it triggered a trickle of unease. If she didn't know better, she would have said she was falling in love.

Falling in love. She ran the phrase around in her head, took it apart and put it together again with a great deal of caution. Was she ready to commit to someone? The answer sprang into her mind with no hesitation. Absolutely. She'd never been so happy in all her life. The affair with Maria might have been passionate and exciting, but what she had now was so much more. She ghosted her hand down the length of Sophie's body with a surge of love. Was Sophie ready to commit to her? She desperately hoped so.

Her thoughts wandered to Austen. What was it with the oversexed vixen? Why did she have to try to bed every woman she met? And more to the point, why would she want to? Surely, out of the myriads of women she'd slept with, someone must have caught her eye. The sad thing was, they had once been the best of friends, but now Austen's behaviour was trashy.

She glanced down when she felt Sophie stir. In the light filtering through the porthole, she looked adorable with her hair mussed, her skin flushed from sleep and her lips still plump from their kisses. Her face broke into a gentle smile when she caught Eleanor's gaze and reached up to lightly stroke her cheek. "Hello, sweetheart."

"Hello yourself," said Eleanor, and kissed her, savouring the warm sweet taste of her mouth. "Hmm…I could do that forever. I didn't know there could be such pleasure in a kiss."

With an inarticulate murmur, Sophie drew closer and claimed her mouth again. This kiss was deeper, more intoxicating and Eleanor felt the now familiar erotic ache begin between her legs. She pulled back with a gasp. "I'm nearly ready to come again. What have you done to me? You've turned me into a sexual creature I barely recognize."

Sophie didn't answer, simply slipped down to take her with her mouth and tongue. As Eleanor felt her orgasm rise, she wound her fingers around Sophie's head and arched into her. When the storm broke, her emotions shattered as the tide of pleasure barrelled through every nerve ending in her body. She screamed out a heartrending cry, "I love you, my darling."

Sophie went still and slowly withdrew until they no longer touched. With downcast eyes, she swung her legs over the side of the bed.

Eleanor swallowed hard, the euphoria of the climax changed quickly into dread. What had she done? She had made the declaration in the heat of moment, without a thought that Sophie might not reciprocate her feelings. "Oh God, I'm sorry I blurted that out. I don't expect you to feel that way about me…

our romance is too new." Nervously, she plucked at Sophie's arm. "Look at me, darling. Please. I don't expect you to say it too now, but I hope you will one day."

"I have to tell you something, Ellie."

Eleanor felt something cold squeeze her heart. "Go on."

"I promised to cook Austen dinner tomorrow night."

"Oh?" This wasn't what she had expected her to say. "You're going over to her place tomorrow? Alone?"

Sophie looked miserable when she turned around. "Yes. Um…you're not exactly invited. It…it was something I said I'd do on an impulse. I gave her my word, Ellie."

"But why would you want to go without me, Sophie. I thought…I thought we're together now."

"We are. Can't you trust me?"

"It not you I don't trust, it's Austen." Eleanor squeezed her eyes shut, remembering how much she had been hurt years ago. And now it was happening again. "She's done it before to me. You must wonder why I dislike her so much. Didn't she tell you?"

Sophie shook her head. "She said if I wanted to know I would have to ask you."

"We were once best friends," Eleanor began quietly. "Seven years ago I was in Rome on location, and she had a gig in a nightclub there, when I met a beautiful woman…um…Maria… at a dinner party. I was besotted with her, we had an affair, and to make a long story short, Austen made a no-holds-barred play for her even knowing how I felt about her."

"That would have hurt."

"It caused an irrevocable rift in our friendship. I hated her for it. Friends don't do that to each other. We had a bitter argument…things were said which couldn't be forgiven. After that, Austen made quite a name for herself with women."

Sophie watched her with a frown. "So, where is Maria now?"

"It was only an affair. She was married," Eleanor said flatly, wishing she had just trusted Sophie. Admitting to an affair with a married woman didn't put her in a favourable light.

"So," said Sophie, "I gather from your reaction when we met that I look like this woman."

"Yes."

"Well, that's a blow to my ego. I'm with you because I look like a former lover who cheated on her husband. Now that would make any girl feel valued."

Eleanor put her arms around her waist and pressed into her back. "You know perfectly well how I feel about you has nothing to do with any former lover. If you don't know that by now, I don't know what we're doing here. I said I love you Sophie and I meant it."

"Sorry, I was just being flippant because I'm jealous. I want you to like me for myself and not because of someone who, as far as I'm concerned, didn't deserve one ounce of your love. Where is she now, by the way?"

"It's complicated. She's…well…she's married to someone very important, whose name I really can't divulge."

"Fair enough, I won't pry. We all have our secrets and at least she's long since gone." Sophie moved restlessly. "I still need to tell you something."

Eleanor gave a sigh. She didn't feel she could cope with any more surprises. "Shush. Please…no more secrets today. Tell me tomorrow. Now we'd better have the bed linen changed, give the key back to Ginny and say good-bye. The party will be winding down—the boat sails in two hours."

They reached the outer deck to see Ginny seated there with the poets, watching the sunset. Austen was nowhere in sight. Ginny bounded to her feet, pulled Eleanor into a hug and whispered. "All went well I see. You've been away quite a while."

"Trust you to be counting. We're ready to head home." Then she added with a stern look, "When you're talking to Mum, you needn't elaborate on what's happening here. I'll tell her myself."

Ginny put her hand across her heart in outrage. "Really, Ellie, you know I'm the soul of discretion."

"Huh! Pigs might fly too. Just don't say too much. I don't want her interfering." Eleanor caught Sophie looking at her quizzically. "My mother is a law unto herself. She's an acquired taste and only in small doses."

Then Ginny swept Sophie into a hug with a murmured, "Look after our girl. No doubt I'll be seeing you again."

They slipped away down the gangplank, and later from their vantage point on the terrace in the villa, watched the grand yacht sail out of the bay.

When its lights could no longer be seen on the dark ocean, Eleanor entwined their fingers together. "You'll sleep in my bed for the rest of our stay here, won't you?"

Sophie looked up, her irises dark and stormy under her lashes. "If you want me to."

"I do. You belong there now."

She took Eleanor's hand, pressing the palm to her lips. "That would be perfect."

"I've never actually asked a woman to share my bedroom before," said Eleanor.

She felt herself blush as Sophie said curiously, "Haven't you had women stay over?"

"I do date, but...well..." She stopped abruptly. "Come on. I've had enough Eleanor exposés for the time being. What about you?"

"My home isn't exactly an ideal place to invite someone for an extended stay. It's a cramped duplex with leaky plumbing, and if the couple next door have an argument, every word can be heard through the thin walls. Not to mention other things they do that go bump in the night."

Laughing, Eleanor gave her hand a squeeze. "Then I'm glad you have a pokey apartment. Now let's go have something to eat and watch a soppy movie."

* * *

After Eleanor topped off a second glass of wine, her mood sank lower as she glanced again at the clock in the lounge. Eleven o'clock and Sophie still hadn't come home. *What were they doing?* She knew she shouldn't be sitting and drinking alone, but any attempt about being rational about Sophie was fruitless. As much as she knew it was soul-destroying, she was worried.

When ten minutes later she at last heard the crunch of shoes on the pebbles outside, she hurried to the front door and flung it open.

"Eleanor, what a nice surprise," said Austen.

Sophie poked her head around the doorframe. "Hi Ellie, I didn't expect you to wait up."

Eleanor gave her long relieved hug. "Would you mind if I had a word alone with Austen."

"No, I'm ready for bed. I'll pop up stairs and have a shower," said Sophie, giving her a quick kiss. "Bye, Austen."

"I won't be long," Eleanor said, and when she disappeared up the stairs, she turned to Austen. "We can talk on the terrace. It's a pleasant night."

Outside in the warm air, Eleanor could barely suppress the dislike she felt for the singer, who lounged insolently against the railing. She couldn't deny Austen looked particularly attractive tonight, with her bright hair carelessly tumbled and her tattooed skin glowing in the moonlight. "So," she began, "is this payback for the things we said to each other in Rome, or have you become so immoral that you try to have every woman you see, even if she's with someone else?"

"What do you think? When did you become such a judgmental prig?"

"At least I'm not trash."

"Damn you, Eleanor. How do you know what I am?"

"Your reputation precedes you. And to think we were once friends," Eleanor retorted.

Pale now, Austen pushed away from the railing until they were only a foot apart. "Well you certainly threw that friendship into the garbage."

"*I* threw it away? You're the one who couldn't keep her hands off Maria."

"I did it for you…to show you what she was. She used you Ellie, and you couldn't see it. She was a player. You were only one in a long line of lovers…she was screwing you in more ways than one."

Eleanor's hands began to tremble, her mouth clamped into a thin line. She fought the urge to order her from the house, or do something worse. But as she stared at her with aversion, the reality of what she had heard set in. "What did it matter to you?"

"Because…" Austen's shoulders sagged, her eyes glinted with moisture, "because I was in love with you. But you never saw me, never gave me a chance."

"You…you were *in love* with *me*?"

"Yes I was. But as soon as Princess damn Maria smiled at you, you went running to her. Dammit, Ellie, she was royalty…what did you think would happen. That she would leave her husband and her grand life for you. Now *that* was a scandal you wouldn't have survived. It would have been the end of your career."

All fight went out of Eleanor. She felt so drained, so confused. Had she been a blind fool all these years? Had she been simply one in a long succession of lovers for Maria? Not that it mattered now—it was very much in the past. But how could she not have seen how Austen felt about her. It had never occurred to her. "Why didn't you ever tell me how you felt?"

Austen turned to stare over the ocean. "There were a multitude of reasons…we were young, had different careers, both trying to make names for ourselves. I told myself it was too soon for either of us to have a serious attachment, but I wish now I had listened to my heart not logic. I should have told you then how I felt."

"It wouldn't have done you any good, I'm afraid," said Eleanor with a touch of irony. "I'm so reserved. It's not that I'm fussy, it's just that very few people interest me romantically. After that fling, I didn't seem to have much libido."

"Now you have."

"Yes, it's come back." She closed her eyes and rubbed her forehead absently. "I seem to have lost my inhibition at long last. It's frightening but wonderful."

"So, you're hooked on the ol' Soph?"

"I'm nuts about her."

"Lucky you."

"Now explain to me, Austen, when you only have to crook your little finger to get any woman you want, why are you set on taking her away from me."

Austen turned back from the ocean view and regarded her with a twinkle in her eye. "You haven't a clue about women, have you? She put me in my place as soon as we met. I haven't gotten to first base with her. As much as you think I can get any woman I want, there are some out there impervious to my charms and Sophie's one of them. So stop all your drama or you'll lose her."

"Oh!" said Eleanor, rocking back on her heels in relief. "So why did you want her to go alone tonight?"

"To piss you off. You're getting too high and mighty for your own good." She gave a knowing grin. "She's not going to bow to your every whim, Ellie, which will do you good. She has a mind of her own."

"I know and I love her for it. It'll make life interesting."

"Come on and walk me to the door. It's time I went home. I promised Deirdre I'd sing next Saturday night so I hope you'll come."

When they reached the door, Eleanor hesitated before she gave her a peck on the cheek, as much a sign of forgiveness as a good night. "I'm sorry we lost each other, Austen. You really were a dear friend." She bumped her affectionately on the shoulder. "And I'm sorry I didn't realize how you felt about me. I trust those feelings are in the past."

"Hell yeah. We've both moved on. Besides, Sophie said we never would have suited. According to her, we're both alphas. Pretty cluey for a housekeeper, isn't she?"

"Yes, she is," said Eleanor thoughtfully.

CHAPTER TWENTY-SEVEN

Sometimes it was better to follow your impulses. Sophie reasoned that if Austen was giving a concert, she should support her. So the red dress was put back in the wardrobe in favour of her low tight jeans, hot pink tank and old black boots. She spiked up her hair with gel into a punk style and applied winged eyeliner. As she gazed in the mirror, she had to admit the outfit gave her a sense of freedom that not even her old daggy wardrobe had achieved. No wonder Austen dressed as she did. It must be satisfying for someone as talented and volatile to snub convention and mediocrity.

Eleanor was already waiting when she walked into the lounge. She was, as usual, immaculately dressed, this time in a pretty peach silk jacket and slacks that flattered her slim frame. When she saw Sophie, she let out a wolf whistle, which brought a smile to Sophie's face. "I thought I'd get in the mood," she said.

"Wow. You can put those boots under my bed any day."

Sophie threaded their fingers together. "Ha! I might just have to do that when we get home, Ms. Godwin. Come on. I'll drive tonight."

Halfway down the hill, they stopped briefly to admire the view. The evening was drawing to a close, a reddish pink glow caught in the line of clouds on the horizon. It was always a special time, but as Sophie gazed over the seascape, a shiver walked down her spine. She felt cold, though the air was warm and balmy. Everything was too perfect. She'd have to tell Eleanor the truth tonight, for it couldn't go on much longer. Their holiday had only six days to go. She'd never been a coward, but she *had* to make Eleanor understand. It was going to be the hardest thing she'd ever had to do.

Everyone in the resort must have turned up to see Austen, for the dining room was packed. Marcello appeared as soon as they entered and directed them to a table in front of the stage. "Ms. Farleigh has requested you be seated here."

"Thank you, it's most appreciated," said Eleanor graciously.

A variety of instruments graced the stage, which meant Deirdre had hired a band rather than just having the piano as accompaniment. After an aperitif, she watched Eleanor peruse the menu with a frown of concentration, the pink tip of her tongue just visible as she scanned down the sheet. Sophie licked her own lips in fascination before she dropped her eyes guiltily. Hell, she was really whipped thinking reading a menu was erotic. She cleared her throat. "What will you have?"

"What about the seafood platter. We could share if you like."

"Uh-huh. Sounds good." Even the way Eleanor said *share*, sent little tingles across her skin. Then Sophie was lost again as she gazed into the hazel eyes that seemed flecked with soft golden highlights in the muted lighting. The dinner passed in a blur. Though unable to be affectionate in public, they still managed to brush fingers often as they reached for a delicacy on the large plate. When the lights dimmed signalling the show was about to start, Eleanor turned her chair next to hers to view the stage. With the soft thigh pressed against hers, Sophie sat back happily to enjoy the performance.

The stage lights lit up to reveal the band waiting for the singer's entrance. With a burst of pyrotechnic magic, smoke exploded with a glitter of sparks and Austen swaggered to the microphone. Her tatts were a thing of beauty in the flashing lights. They writhed down her arm like living entities, coiling and uncoiling in streams of colour. Her clothes were the usual black, though this time sparkling. The tank top was tight across her chest, her jeans cut low over slinky hips, her boots mirror-shiny. She looked exactly how she wanted to appear—sexy, charismatic, self-assured, and bad to the bone.

Music exploded with a thrashing of drums and wailing of guitars. A collective gasp echoed around the room. Hell had just erupted. With a flick of her fingers, Austen killed off the raging storm. "Not the crowd for this shit yet, boys. Ya gotta work up to it," she admonished. "Something softer, sexy to begin with. Whatcha say, folks?"

From the start, Austen had the audience eating out of her hand. She sang through a wide repertoire: metal, punk rock, old-style rock, love songs. Not all were hers, though her latest hits were included. Sophie thought her awesome in the true sense, magnetic as she bounced on the balls of her feet, tirelessly working the crowd. By the end of the performance, the sedate audience was cheering like teenagers at a pop concert. With a satisfied grin, Austen walked to the edge of the stage. "My finale will be a duet." She squatted down and held out her hand. "Sophie, will you do me the honour."

Sophie blanched. Crap, she couldn't hold a tune to save herself. "I can't sing," she squeaked.

"Oh, I'll get something out of you, babe. Come on. These folks are waiting."

Having no way out, she reluctantly climbed onto the stage.

"Well, well. You dressed for the occasion. Verrrryy hotttt." Austen signalled to the band then clutched Sophie from behind and began to sway. "All you have to do is say *oh yeah* when I nudge you. Got it?"

"Oh yeah."

She shuddered to think what Eleanor was thinking, but she had to admit it was exciting, and arousing, with Austen pressed against her back, crooning a love song into her ear. They moved fluently together, Sophie's *oh yeah* interjection, punctuated the ballad with more than a little spice. Sophie closed her eyes, swaying to the music, until another burst of glitter shot over the stage and it was all over.

Austen was panting, covered in perspiration and grinning like a Cheshire cat when she raised their clasped hands in the air. The room exploded into clapping and whistling. Sophie, with a smile equally as wide, looked down from the stage at Eleanor. She was on her feet, applauding enthusiastically with the rest of them.

"You gotta love it," shouted Austen.

"Damn right," said Sophie. "This is the biggest kick of my life." She looked over the sea of faces, savouring the moment.

Then it all came crashing down.

One moment she was in utopia, the next in hell. There was no mistaking the man staring at her, three tables behind Eleanor. The Honorable Graham Fortescue MP, Shadow Minister for the Environment. And the woman hanging over him was definitely not his wife. She looked like a high-class escort, with long blond hair, perky boobs, and a lithe body, and half his age. The Member of Parliament had every reason to dislike Sophie. Six months ago, she had interviewed him and written a scathing article on his stance, or lack of it, on coal seam gas. He was furious, had threatened legal action and would most definitely remember who she was.

Panic sliced through her when their eyes met. Sophie looked away quickly. There was no doubt he'd recognized her, or thought he did. Whatever happened next was in the lap of the gods. If she kept her head, she reasoned, not all was lost. She might be able to bluff her way through this. She was under a false name and her appearance was considerably altered since the article, especially in tonight's getup, so she must act as though she didn't have a clue who he was.

Without a blink, she brought her eyes to Eleanor, careful not to look back in his direction again. She leapt down from the stage to join her, Austen close behind.

"Did I pass, Ellie?" asked Austen.

"You were wonderful. You deserve all the accolades. The two of us have come on. Not the green young women we were seven years ago."

"I'd like it if we were friends again."

Eleanor was silent for a moment then took her hands. "We'll try again shall we? We can't turn back the clock, but it's time we moved on and forgave. Would you like to come to our place for dinner tomorrow night?" She dug Sophie in the ribs. "My girl mightn't be able to sing, but she can cook up a storm."

"I'll be there."

"Good. Are you ready for home, darling?" When Sophie nodded, Eleanor continued. "We'll leave you to your partying then."

After she walked away, Eleanor gave Sophie's hand a squeeze. "We can have our own little private party at home."

With a nervous smile, Sophie followed her to the door. Fortescue was nowhere in sight. After they stepped into the warm night air without a glimpse of him, she let out the breath she was holding, reassured the crisis was averted. Her relief was short-lived. With no warning, he stepped out from behind a buggy in the parking area and it all went downhill from there.

"What are you doing here, Marsh?" he snapped.

"That's no business of yours."

"I'm paying a fortune for privacy. Your kind isn't wanted here."

"Oh? And what kind is that?"

"A parasite."

"Excuse me? What right have you to speak to an employee of mine like that?" asked Eleanor, looking confused.

He turned his attention to her for a moment, his eyes dilated with anger. "I'd like to know, Ms. Godwin, what the hell you're doing with a journalist on this island? She works for the *Brisbane Morning Globe*. Are you completely mad?"

Sophie angrily interrupted. "Don't speak to Eleanor like that. I'm not here with the paper."

"Rubbish. You wouldn't go on holidays just before the election. But maybe it's for the best. You're a poor excuse for a reporter anyway."

"I made you sit up and listen though, didn't I? And talk about the election. From the look of your dinner companion, it doesn't seem like you're on the campaign trail."

"Why you little…"

"That's enough…both of you." Eleanor's voice rang out with such authority that Fortescue took a step backward. "Please, get in the buggy, Sophie. And you sir, if you don't go away at once, I can assure you I will take this further and that's not an idle threat."

Instinctively, Sophie knew this was not the time to argue. The MP must have realised it too, for with a parting glare, he strode away. Eleanor, without another word, shooed Sophie over with a wave of her fingers and climbed into the driver's seat. The silence was deafening on the way home. She snuck a glance at Eleanor as they turned to climb the hill. The woman seemed as composed as an ice sculpture. By the time they reached the garage, Sophie was so on edge her legs began to twitch—she knew she'd be flat out talking her way out of this one. The best thing to do was to throw herself on her mercy. Grovel, beg, plead.

Inside the hallway of the house, Eleanor's gaze rested on her for the first time since they had left the centre. "You've betrayed my trust, Sophie. Please leave." And with quick strides, she disappeared up the stairs.

Sophie squeezed her eyes shut, trying to absorb what had just happened. She had been dismissed in a blink of an eye, without being able to launch a defence. Her first urge was to run up the stairs, to explain that it hadn't been her idea she come, that she would never write anything derogatory about her. But in her heart of hearts, she knew it was too late. She'd had plenty of opportunities, but had left things drift. And her biggest omission was not to tell Eleanor she loved her. The chance had been there and she'd blown it.

Shattered, she walked to her unit. Where on earth could she go? There was no way she would set herself up for ridicule by asking Lisa or Austen for a bed. She had more pride than that. Then it came to her. There was a place where she could shelter for the night—in the boat shed. Doug had an old stretcher in the back and she knew where he hid the key. It was going to be a battle to drag her belongings there, but at least it was downhill. She'd worry in the morning how she was going to get off the island without a fuss. Deirdre wouldn't be too happy to learn a reporter had managed to get onto the island, definitely nothing she'd want advertised among the guests.

It was well after midnight when her suitcase was finally packed, with the few extra miscellaneous items stuffed into the backpack together with her computer. Automatically, she stripped the bed and tidied the room before she pulled the door closed. As she hurried out of the courtyard, the feeling of loss was so acute, she barely held herself together. She tightened the grip on the handle of her case. There was no time for the luxury of tears, not with streaks of lightning out to sea. Already faint rumbles of thunder could be heard in the distance and the wind was beginning to whistle through the trees.

It was difficult to manoeuvre the wheels of the case down the dark uneven track, but she managed somehow. By the time she reached the beach, she could smell the moisture in the air. No time to try to drag the bag through the sand, she'd have to carry it.

As she struggled along, her heart took a violent leap into her throat when a bolt of lightning hit a tree on the headland. Light rain began to sprinkle. To her immense relief, she reached the shed before it pelted down. After an initial fumble in the dark, she turned the key in the lock and the door opened with a creak.

With a flick of the light switch, the fluorescent bulb lit up the interior. The place was tidy, Doug's tools now packed away in a long grey aluminium toolbox. She walked to the back where the bed was pushed up against the wall, and with a sigh, stretched out on top of the old army blanket. As was her habit, she curled up on her left side to sleep, though she knew it would be useless. Thoughts of Eleanor spun round in her head, together with recriminations and regret. When the tears at last began to fall, it was only then that the full reality hit her. She had lost someone so wonderful that her heart would have a gaping hole forever.

Sophie woke to the sound of the door scraping open. Huddled on the bed, she looked up to see Doug silhouetted in the light.

"Sophie," he said, clearly concerned, "what are you doing here?"

"I…I…" she began, and to her horror, couldn't stop the tears sliding down her face.

He hurried over to sit on the side of the bed. "Hell, girl. What's happened? You look a mess. What's your luggage doing here? Going somewhere?"

With an effort, she sat up and wiped a hand across her face. "Sorry for using your bed but I couldn't think of anywhere else to go." She slid her eyes away as she sucked in a deep breath. *Damn it!* She wished she didn't have to tell him. He was the last person she wanted to disappoint. "You're going to dislike me as much as Eleanor does when I'm finished, so be prepared." She began to tell him her story, only leaving out that Eleanor and she were lovers. When she finished, he studied her for a minute, his eyes narrowed.

"So you're a reporter."

"Yes."

"Do you intend to write about anything that happened on the island?"

She shook her head.

"If I help you, I want your promise on that."

"I swear."

"I'll take you at your word, Sophie, because I respect you. Why Eurydice is so special, is not because it's exclusive or a breath of paradise, it's because people know whatever happens here never leaves the island. It's something everyone understands when he or she comes here. It's what they're paying for. Once that oath is breached, no one will trust us again. People could lose their jobs."

Sophie gulped. Put like that, she felt dirty and small. "Is it possible to get off the island without anyone finding out? I guess the only solution would be to disappear without anybody knowing I worked for a paper. It would be too public to fly out in the helicopter, and I don't want Eleanor blamed for bringing me here, even if she did so unknowingly. We don't have to worry about Graham Fortescue spilling the beans. It wouldn't be in his best interest to make a fuss. He's here with a woman not his wife, so he'd be cutting his own throat."

His quick smile made her feel slightly better. "You're in luck. In an hour, I'm taking the band back to Mackay. The instruments and tech gear are too big for the helicopter, and I have to pick up supplies. I'll put you in the end cabin."

"What if they see me?"

Doug gave a barking laugh. "Slim chance of that. I heard they had a party at Austen's villa last night, so they'll be flaked out. Lie low all the same. I'll make you a cup of tea before we go. The shortbread bickies in the tin will have to do for breakfast."

While he made the tea, Sophie cleaned herself up in the small shower recess.

"Sooo," said Doug as she sipped her tea. "Eleanor chucked you out."

"Yes."

"Pity. You seemed to be getting on just fine."

She paused, catching the gleam in his eye over the rim of the cup. *For Pete's sake, does everyone know how I feel about her?* "She's nice. Who wouldn't like her?"

"Hmmm…I guess you're going to miss her."

"I had a magic time with her, but now it's back to being Sophie Marsh, a nobody." Sophie blinked away the moisture gathering again in her eyes. "You know Doug, life's not fair. I've worked hard to get where I am. I put in more hours than anyone on the paper, but nobody really takes me seriously. My family would prefer I work in the restaurant with my uncle—they think what I do isn't a real job. My bossy aunt, who rules the family, thinks I should have at least two kids by now and another on the way. My boss claims tabloid trash sells better than serious reporting. My best friend thinks clothes make the woman and hates my dress sense. Now I've seriously pissed off a wonderful woman because I was trying to do a job I didn't want in the first place. Hell, I should just shoot myself and put everyone out of their misery."

He stared solemnly at her for a long moment, then rose and placed his hands on her shoulders. She could feel the empathy radiating from him. "Come on. Let's get you onto the boat."

After they climbed aboard, she stood and looked over the island one last time. Then overcome, she bolted down the steps to the cabins below.

CHAPTER TWENTY-EIGHT

Liar! Liar! The words reverberated in Eleanor's head like an old CD stuck in a groove. She tossed in the bed, no nearer to sleep than over an hour ago. How could she have been so stupid? She had been made a fool of, humiliated by a two-bit journalist masquerading as a housekeeper. God, how gullible she had been to be taken in by a lovely body, soft lips, and a pair of dark eyes. Her belly twisted, remembering how those lips had skimmed kisses over her skin, nipping and sucking her tender spots until she screamed out her name. Oh dear lord, what was wrong with her. Even after all Sophie had done, she wanted to feel those lips again, wanted a repeat of the heights they had brought her to.

She fought back tears, trying not to relive the moment she had ordered Sophie out of the house. Her look of surprise and distress shouldn't have upset Eleanor. It vindicated the horror she had felt after that ghastly politician had ripped into her and let her know Sophie's identity. She looked around the room, hating it now. She hated that Sophie's scent lingered in the bed, in the bathroom, on the curtains. It was everywhere. But she hated the bed the most, knowing it was where they had made love, had held each other when the ripples of orgasm faded away leaving profound feelings of love and devotion.

She watched the flashes of lightning through the open door. They were becoming more frequent, the grumbles of thunder louder. The storm would hit soon. She'd better make sure all the windows were shut—with no worry about break-ins, they had become careless about security. After closing the glass door to her balcony, she padded downstairs to check the ground floor.

Once everything was secure, Eleanor strode back to the staircase but then hesitated. Guilt niggled as she looked down the passageway to the back unit. She had been furious when she ordered Sophie out of the house, the sense of betrayal so acute it was as if someone had hacked off one of her limbs. She had given her heart to this woman, only to have it thrown back in her face. All for the sake of a sensational article for some crappy little newspaper. What was it with people that they wanted to read that rubbish anyhow? Why couldn't they mind their own damn business?

As much as she tried to ignore it, a glimmer of reason kept nagging at the back of her mind. If she were honest, she had to take some blame. She had turned a blind eye to what was obvious. It hadn't really gelled that Sophie was a domestic—she was too smart, too well read. Eleanor knew Sophie had been trying to tell her something, but she hadn't wanted to change the status quo, so had cut her off each time. She wished she had listened. If she had been told properly, she wouldn't have reacted so forcefully. The blow would have been cushioned, not such a shock as learning the truth from a rude man in the middle of a parking lot. It had not only been upsetting, but also grossly humiliating.

She took the first step up the staircase and again paused. With the storm brewing, she should check on Sophie. Ignoring her inner voice that said it was simply an excuse to see her, she pushed open the door of the unit. She froze on the threshold, just able to register in the dark that there was no one in the bed.

She fought down panic and snapped on the light. The room was empty, the bed stripped. She flung open the cupboards. The clothes were gone. Eleanor closed her eyes, feeling sick. Sophie had obeyed her to the letter. She had left.

Eleanor ran out back to check the buggy—it was still in the garage. So where would she have gone in the middle of the night? She must have rung either Lisa or Austen to pick her up. But Eleanor hadn't been able to sleep. She would have heard any activity. With a heavy heart, she took a sleeping tablet before she went back up to bed.

The front doorbell roused Eleanor out of a deep sleep. She patted the other side of the bed. It was empty. Groggily, she opened one eye to check the time. Damn, it was half past nine— why hadn't Sophie wakened her. Then she remembered with a groan. No Sophie. With a burst of speed, she threw on a T-shirt and pair of shorts and hurried downstairs. Lisa's cheery face greeted her when she opened the door.

"Lisa, how nice to see you. Come on in."

"Hi, Eleanor. I'm here to pick up Sophie. She wanted to check the pots with me this morning. She was planning to make you a special lobster dinner tonight."

Eleanor's stomach gave a lurch, but she hid her disappointment. Sophie hadn't gone to Lisa's last night. "Umm…I think she went over to Austen's earlier."

"Austen and the band were at the centre packing up their gear and dismantling the sound and light systems. Sophie wasn't with them."

"Oh, then she must have gone for a walk or swim. I took a sleeping tablet and only just woke. What say I give you a ring when she gets home?"

"I'll have a look around the beach. Maybe she's waiting for me there. If she's not, I'll have to go before it gets too late. Can you tell her I called when she turns up?"

"Shall do," said Eleanor weakly.

When the sound of the buggy faded into the distance, she plopped down heavily onto a chair. Where was she? She doubted Sophie would have rung Deirdre or Doug. She had too much pride to air her dirty laundry. So where had she disappeared to? Surely, she hadn't actually walked away with all her luggage in the middle of the night in a thunderstorm. Her fingers trembled as she reached for the phone. It was better to suffer some embarrassment than to sit all day wondering. When the familiar voice came on the end of the line, Eleanor spoke quietly and evenly into the receiver, "Eleanor here, Deirdre. You haven't seen Sophie by any chance?"

"Not this morning. Is she picking something up for you?"

"I slept in and thought she might be there. I expect she'll turn up shortly. Is there a helicopter coming in by any chance today? The studio is sending me something to sign."

"There's one due in at two."

"Fine. I'll come down later on then. Bye for now." Eleanor placed the phone back in its cradle, at a loss how to proceed. Sophie seemed to have disappeared into thin air. If she wasn't on the chopper this afternoon, then the only other way to get out was by sea. And there wasn't a shuttle service to the mainland for guests, so unless she hitched a ride on a boat somehow, she had to go by air. Eleanor's only recourse was to wait until this afternoon.

After wandering lost around the house for an hour, and still tired, she went back upstairs, stretched out fully clothed on top of the bed and dropped off. Hours later, she woke from shivery, disturbing dreams to the whopping sound of whirring blades overhead. After a dash to the loo, she hurried to the buggy.

The helicopter was still sitting on the landing pad when she reached the point. When she saw an elderly couple were the only passengers about to board, disappointment rolled through her. No Sophie.

She felt like screaming out a swearword, but instead smiled sweetly at the pilot who gazed at her enquiringly. "I'm expecting a document, Captain, so I thought I'd pop down myself."

"Sorry, Ms. Godwin. There's nothing for you."

"Oh well," she said overbrightly. "Maybe tomorrow." Fresh out of ideas, despondently she headed home.

By the time evening fell, she was resigned to the fact that Sophie wasn't coming back. Thinking about her only made Eleanor alternately angry and weepy, so she poured herself a glass of red and switched on the TV. The six thirty news had just begun when the doorbell rang. Heart thumping, she ran down the hallway and flung it open. For a moment, Eleanor couldn't comprehend why she was here, but then remembered. *Damn!* She'd invited her to dinner. Self-consciously, she tried to smooth the wrinkles out of her shirt before she stiffened her spine that seemed to want to buckle, and forced a smile. "Austen. Come on in."

Austen's eyes raked over her, top to toe. "What the hell's wrong with you, Ellie?"

Eleanor felt herself deflate. She knew she must look a sight: her eyes felt gritty and puffy, her hair was a mess and her nose runny. It took an effort not to blubber. "I'm a bit sick. I forgot you were coming. Sorry, I haven't prepared anything. I'll get you a drink and rustle something up."

"Where's Sophie?"

"She's…she's not here anymore."

"*What!* How come?"

"I…we…It doesn't matter. She's gone for good."

Austen looked at her with narrowed eyes. "What did you damn-well do to her?"

"Stop playing that blame game," Eleanor snapped, offended. "What makes you think it's my fault? For your information, it turns out she's a reporter. A spy."

"Holy s-h-i-t. I knew there was something suss about her. I've never had a housekeeper that hot."

"For heaven's sake, Austen, must you reduce everything down to sex?"

To her annoyance, Austen chuckled. "And you never noticed?"

"Don't be such a smart aleck. There's beer in the fridge, or a Shiraz is open on the kitchen bench. I think Sophie froze a couple of dinners. I'll microwave something."

"A beer will be good." After twisting the cap off, she tilted her head toward the terrace. "We can eat later. Let's sit outside and you can tell me all about it. You were happy as a pig in mud when you left last night."

Eleanor filled her glass before following her into the open air. Once they were seated, she took a long drink before she set her glass on the silver coaster on the table. "We were ambushed in the parking lot by a dreadful politician. Apparently, Sophie is a political reporter for the *Brisbane Morning Globe* and it seems she wrote a disparaging article about him. Coupled with the fact he hates her, he's here with a woman who's not his wife so you can imagine he wasn't too pleased to see her."

"They had a fight?"

"Very harsh words. He even had the audacity to ask me if I was mad."

Austen gave a whoop. "I wish I'd seen that. Did you peg him back to size?"

Eleanor bared her teeth. "If I have the misfortune to run into him again and he says one more word, he won't know what hit him. I have a few connections who can make his life miserable."

"So what's happening with Sophie?"

"I told her to go."

"Just like that—scram, vamoose, bugger off, you're sacked babe? What did she say?"

Heat flushed across Eleanor's face. She had another drink to delay answering. Austen stared at her for a second. "You did give her a chance to explain, didn't you?"

"Not in so many words. I...ah...felt betrayed, and very angry, so I...um...ordered her out of the house."

"Where did she go?"

"I have no idea."

"You didn't drive her anywhere?"

"No."

"When did she go? Damn Ellie, this is like extracting teeth. Just tell me what happened," said Austen, clearly exasperated.

Eleanor threw her hands up in the air. "Okay I'll tell you. I don't know where she is. She's disappeared. I went down to her room an hour after I said those things and she was gone. With all her luggage. The buggy was in the garage so she must have walked."

"In that thunderstorm?" said Austen incredulously. "Geez, you're one heartless bossy grouch. You'd give the Christmas Grinch a run for his money. You make a big play for her, and in the next breath order her to go without a chance to explain. You have no idea what makes her tick, do you? What did you think was going to happen when you told her to go? Naturally, she wasn't going to hang around. She has more self-worth than that."

Under normal circumstances, Eleanor wouldn't have taken that from Austen. She was hardly one to sermonise on how to treat women. But this time she bit her tongue, knowing there was truth in what she was saying. "Only part of this is my fault. Sophie had every opportunity to tell me who she was. You're forgetting the crux of this unfortunate business. She's a reporter in my house under false pretences, with the express purpose to spy on me for a newspaper article. Whether she would have written a tell-all is immaterial."

"I know. But once you became lovers, it changed everything. It wouldn't have been all roses for her. I can imagine she's been going through hell trying to get up the courage to tell you."

"Yes, I believe she did try, but I didn't really give her an opportunity. What do you think I should do?"

"It's too late, Ellie. My guess is that she'll be long since gone by now."

"How could she get off the island? She wasn't flown out."

"The band went out by boat this morning. I bet she was on it."

Eleanor blinked at her in surprise, letting out a painful breath as she bowed to the inevitable. Sophie was out of her life. "That must be the explanation. She's nowhere on the island."

"This could come back and bite you on the backside," said Austen with a frown. "She knows your secret about Maria."

"She doesn't know who she is exactly."

"She knows you had the affair in Rome. If she's any sort of journalist, it won't take much digging to identify her."

Eleanor stared out over the sea, lost in her memories. "She won't write about it. Sophie won't betray my trust—she's the kindest person I've ever met." She turned to look at Austen with a sad smile. "You know, I don't really care whether she prints it or not. Through my failure to forgive, I've lost the woman I adore and that's infinitely worse. Everything else pales in comparison. I actually don't know what I'm going to do without her."

CHAPTER TWENTY-NINE

"Sophie, why didn't you let me know you were back?" Brie stood at the door with her arms folded, censorious. "Let's have coffee at that new place in the mall and you can tell me all about your assignment. I've been simply livid with jealousy."

"I'm only here to work on the article and then I'm taking a break." Sophie kept her eyes on the computer screen while she continued to pound the keys. "I've got a present for you."

"Something you picked up on the island?" asked Brie. She dropped down into the chair opposite, eagerly.

"Oh, much better than that…you're going to love this one. I'm going to let you publish them in your name, but I'll make it quite clear to Owen I supplied you with them." She turned from the keyboard, opened the folder and spread the pictures onto the desktop.

Sophie was enormously proud of the images of Austen. Photography was one of her keenest hobbies, a pursuit that had come in very handy as a journalist. In fact, she'd considered it as a career at one point. Brie's quick intake of breath confirmed how good they were.

"They're fabulous," Brie said in a hushed voice. "My God, Soph. I've never seen anything like them. How on earth did you persuade her to pose?"

Sophie shrugged. "We became friends."

"You're friends with Austen Farleigh? Really? Wow, go girl! Have you shown Owen yet?"

"Nope. I'm going to finish this article and give him everything. Then I'm going to tell him where he can stick his job."

"What…what did you say?"

"You heard. I've had enough of his crap. I'm off."

"What's gotten in to you?" Her troubled gaze locked on Sophie.

"Nothing. I've just realized I'm wasting my time trying to get ahead here and nobody gives a flying fig about me anyhow."

Brie leaned forward, studying her intently. "What's the matter, kiddo? This isn't like you at all."

Sophie pressed her fingers to her eyes and waited for calm. She'd just blurted that out, but now it made sense. Why was she here anyhow? Her contribution wasn't valued. Being a better writer than her male counterparts meant nothing. They were always given the plum assignments—talk about inequality. "I'm just waking up to a few facts," she snapped.

"Something has obviously upset you. Was working for Eleanor Godwin so dreadful?"

"Eleanor is one of the nicest people I've ever meet. Owen's a proper sleaze for sending me to dig up dirt on her. She deserves privacy." Sophie twisted a pencil in her fingers until it snapped. "If he thinks that's good journalism, he's lost me."

"So what's the article you're writing if it's not about her? Or is it? Owen will hardly print something that's not controversial."

Sophie gave a snort. "It's definitely not about her. I picked up a little tidbit that was right up my alley."

"Are you going to tell me what it's about?"

"Nope. You can read it in the next edition. Now go, I have to finish."

Disapproval mixed with resignation flashed across Brie's face. "Okay. But meet me at the bar at five thirty after work. I won't be resting until you come clean and tell me why you're so cranky." She added with a toss of her head, "Don't be late or I'll hunt you down."

As she waltzed off out the door, Sophie couldn't help smiling. It would be useless not meeting her there. If Brie wanted to know something, she was tenacious. Whether she would tell her anything more, she hadn't decided, but a few drinks with a friend would be welcome. She swayed back in her chair, thinking over the last week and a half.

By the time the boat docked in Mackay, she had felt completely gutted. Not only had she lost the love of her life, she knew it was doubtful she would keep her position on the paper. She booked into a motel, and went online to buy a plane ticket to Brisbane for the following afternoon. The twenty-four-hour stopover allowed her to settle down. She couldn't stop crying.

When she arrived home, she holed up in her flat—Eleanor was due to leave the island in five days and as far as Owen knew, Sophie was still there with her. So she had some time to come up with some miracle, an article that would save her skin. The first thing she did was research Eleanor's films. It wasn't hard to find the one she'd starred in seven years ago in Rome.

After toing and froing from one site to the next, she found some images of the final wrap party, held in the private wing of the Palazzo Doria Pamphilj. And there she was, standing next to Eleanor. Sophie took a hard look at the remarkable resemblance to herself—they could have been sisters. When she clicked on the photo to enlarge it, names appeared beside it. All Sophie could register was the "Princess" before "Maria." It was unbelievable. Eleanor had an affair with a married member of a royal house. What had she been thinking? No wonder it was such a secret.

Sophie slammed the computer lid down. There was no way she would ever print something so damaging. The inflammatory information was dead and buried as far as she was concerned. Not that she was going to write anything anyhow. She'd chop off her right arm before she wrote anything about Eleanor, good or bad.

But what was she going to do about an article? The epiphany came to her while she was watching the nightly news. She could dig something up about that arrogant Fortescue. Though mentioning the island was taboo, she did have some newsworthy information on him. Firstly, he had a mistress or at least a squeeze on the side. Secondly, he was holidaying on a super-expensive resort. Did he pay for everything himself? He wouldn't have been stupid enough, she figured, not to pay his own accommodation, but maybe, just maybe, given his arrogance, he may have charged his travel to his government allowance. If she could get him on those expenses, what a coup that would be. On the public agenda, tax-funded private flights for politicians were a huge no-no. A sackable offence.

It only took a phone call to a friend who had access to the governmental travel claims department and a day later she had the article. Both plane and helicopter fares were paid using his official parliamentary credit card.

Sophie was brought out of her thoughts by the aroma of coffee in the next cubicle. Satisfied her work was done, she punched print, saved it with a click and went to the tearoom. She was going to need some caffeine before she faced Owen. The finished article focused on Fortescue's upcoming re-election, his performance as a minister, and at the very end, she dropped the big bombshell. Instead of campaigning in his city electorate, he was flitting around using taxpayers' money taking scenic helicopter rides in the Whitsundays. No mention was made of Eurydice or his extramarital liaison. The public didn't really care if politicians had mistresses, but they did care if they paid for their elected representatives' recreation. The ride would be enough to sink him.

To her surprise, Owen seemed genuinely pleased to see her when she entered his office. He gestured with a smile to the chair across from him. "Sophie, you're back. I didn't expect you until next week. What have you got for me?"

She threw the photos on the table. "These first of all. I want Brie to have the acknowledgments."

After he stacked them in a pile on the desk, he studied them one by one. The fact he lingered over each shot was a sign he was impressed. "Great work. But why give the accolades to Brie?"

"I have my reasons."

"Now what about Eleanor Godwin. What did you dig up?"

"She's squeaky clean. She was a great employer and there's absolutely nothing remotely controversial in her life."

With an unsmiling stare, he pushed back in his chair. "That's hard to believe. Everyone has secrets. Didn't you write anything about her?"

"No...there are some good people in the world, Owen, believe it or not. It's a pity you never realized that before you wasted my time," she said with a disdainful curl of her lips.

He stiffened, clearly annoyed at her attitude. "What a shame then that there was nothing. It would have been a step up the ladder for you."

"Huh! That'll be the day you'll promote a woman." She tossed the article across the table. "My time wasn't wasted...I earned my money. This is decent reporting, not scandal mongering. It will be my last hurrah."

"What's that supposed to mean?"

"I'm resigning and since I have days-off owing, I'm leaving immediately in lieu of notice."

For once, he looked completely bewildered. "Why? You're one of my best reporters. You can't just walk out."

"Because I'm sick of being treated like a second-class act," said Sophie bitterly. "You never appreciate how many hours I put in, or anyone puts in for that matter. But mostly it's because I want to be a real journalist, not tabloid." She pushed back her chair and leapt to her feet. "Good-bye, Owen." She hurried from the room as she fought to hold back the threatening tears.

After cleaning out her desk quickly, she snuck out of the building without saying good-bye to anyone. Brie was already waiting for her in the cocktail lounge. Sophie would have avoided this tête-à-tête too, but she knew Brie would never let it go.

Brie's gaze rested on her with concern. "What's wrong, Soph? You're starting to worry me. You didn't chuck your job, did you?"

Sophie ordered a double vodka and lime before she sliced her finger across her throat. "You bet I did. I've had Owen up to here."

"He's all right. Just stand-overish sometime. We used to laugh about him. What's got you all worked up?"

Sophie emptied half the glass in one long swallow. "I'm sick and tired of being taken for granted."

"Nobody takes you for granted, kiddo. We all love you."

"Huh! Not from where I'm standing." She gulped down the rest and waved to the bartender.

"Whoa. Steady down. You know you're a three-pot screamer."

"I intend to have a drink tonight. Many in fact." She narrowed her eyes at Brie. "Why do you always boss me around?"

"I do not."

"Of course you do." She took up the new drink and gave a noisy swig. "Everyone does."

Brie gazed at her—a very direct, very unnerving stare. "Come on, out with it. You're really upset about something and I'd like to know what."

"Actually," said Sophie, downing the rest of the drink, "I don't give a stuff about anything or anyone anymore." Suddenly, to her horror, a couple of tears leaked over her lids. She wiped them hastily away with a hand. "I think I better go home to bed. I don't feel very well."

Brie was immediately on her feet and threw an arm around Sophie's waist. "Lean on me. I've only had one drink. I'll drive you home." Her anxiety was palpable as she helped her out the door to the parking lot.

By the time they reached her unit, Sophie was sobbing. With infinite care, Brie helped her change before she tucked her in. "I'll sleep on the sofa tonight. You get to sleep now."

All Sophie could do was grunt before, overcome with exhaustion, she collapsed into a fitful sleep.

As soon as she woke, the memory of her meltdown flooded back. Sophie gripped the pillow tight around her shoulders to control the shudders. What must Brie think? Tentatively, she eased off the bed, hoping her friend had gone home, but no such luck by the noises coming from the kitchen. With a resigned slump, Sophie padded off to the bathroom for a shower, knowing she had some explaining to do. And this time Brie was not going to let her off so easily.

The jets of water went a long way to making her feel human again, although the depression that had settled on her since she left the island still clung like a suffocating cloak. A darkness that left her bereft and wanting. She tried to picture being with Eleanor in her warm bed, secure in her arms, but the more she strove for the images, the more they wavered out of focus like a shimmering mirage. When she emerged from the shower, all she could see was the faded paint on the walls of her bedroom, the threadbare quilt, the shabby carpet. *Ellie would hate it here.*

Sophie hadn't a clue what to do next. She dropped down on the edge of the bed, her hands in her lap, defeated. Nothing could fill the gaping hole in her heart. With an effort, she rose wearily to her feet to dress.

Brie was cooking French toast when she walked through the door. "Hi there," Brie said, warily eyeing Sophie as she took a seat at the kitchen table. "Feeling better?"

"A little."

"Want to tell me what's wrong?"

Sophie shook her head without answering.

Brie dropped down into the chair across from her, folding her hands on the table. Her gaze was sympathetic. "Bottling it up is only going to make matters worse. I'm here if you want to talk it over."

"It's nothing you can help me with."

"Try me."

Sophie wanted to be able to say she didn't have the time to talk, but Brie genuinely looked concerned. And she had stayed the night, so she was owed some kind of explanation. "I met someone on the island but it didn't work out."

"Ah." The word came out like a breath of air as Brie studied her. "So you've finally been bitten by the love bug. Who called it off...you or him?"

"It just didn't work out, and that's all I'm going to say."

"Okay. I won't pry. It's obviously devastated you, but you can't just throw in your job because you're unhappy. You still have to earn a living."

Sophie waved a hand in the air. "Ha! Look at this place, Brie. It's a dump. If I'm ever going to make something of myself, I have to get away from the paper. It's a dead end. Owen's just using me and I deserve better."

"So you're still determined to leave the *Globe*?"

"I am."

"What will you do?"

"For the time being I'll freelance. I've enough political connections to make a living, and later on, I might even try for a position with a TV station or as an overseas correspondent."

Brie reached over and took her hand. "I'm going to miss you. You're my best friend, you know that."

"I'll still be around annoying you for a while yet. We'll be in the same city, just not working in the same building. Now come on and let's eat."

After Brie left half an hour later, Sophie gazed out the window with a trickle of panic. *Quit*—the word reverberated in her brain. She tried to digest exactly what she had done. She had turned her back on a steady position—ripped it out by the roots. For what? To take a ridiculous plunge headlong into the unknown so she could be good enough to redeem herself. To earn the love of someone like Eleanor. She pressed her knuckles to her temples and groaned. Not someone *like* her...she wanted to be worthy of *her*. But it was all too late. She'd ruined her chance, so for the rest of her life she'd have to face the what-ifs.

Just the thought of Eleanor brought back the devastating loneliness. She wanted to cry, to scream, to run. There was only one person she needed to see now, only one person who could soothe the ache.

Her mother.

CHAPTER THIRTY

Sophie loved their sprawling family house, but as she approached the front door, she did so with some trepidation. This was her first visit since Eurydice, and although she sought her mother's comfort, it could end unpleasantly. Today she intended to come out to her.

When Valeria Marsh opened the door, such a surge of love rushed through Sophie that she began to tremble. Could she stand it if her mother was disappointed in her? The welcoming hug Sophie received immediately caused a lump in her throat. "Hi, Mum," she murmured as she sank against the warm bosom.

Her mother stroked her hair, running her fingers lightly through the fine strands. "Sophie dear, why didn't you ring to tell me you were coming?"

Sophie looked up, catching her mother's eye. Even in her early sixties, Valeria, with her warm friendly face, expressive dark eyes, and thick dark hair peppered lightly with silver, was still a beautiful woman. And as was the tradition of her mother before her, she unstintingly showed her affection for her children with kissing and hugging. "I wanted to surprise you," Sophie said. That was true, for she had wanted to see her mother alone. Any forewarning and she would have let the family know Sophie was coming. Someone would have popped over for sure.

"It's a lovely surprise. I see you've cut your hair. It's very chic and suits your face. We've missed you. Come into the kitchen and we can talk over a cuppa."

"Okay." As soon Sophie as settled into a seat, she launched into her prepared speech. "Um…I've something to tell you. A couple of things actually. I…I wanted to have a talk alone without Dad."

"Oh? By the look on your face, the news is important."

Sophie winced, reluctance seeping into her resolve. "It is. I want you to keep an open mind."

"Now that sounds ominous," said Valeria. She looked at her intently. "Are you in some kind of trouble?"

"No…No. I resigned from the *Globe* yesterday."

"You left the paper? I thought you enjoyed your work there."

Sophie watched while her mother poured out two cups of tea. "I did, but I was getting nowhere. I'm going to freelance for a couple of months while I try for a position on a larger publication, or maybe try TV."

"You think you can successfully support yourself with freelancing?"

"I've enough contacts now. At least doing that, I can select my own stories. My last project wasn't true journalism."

"Then go for it. You can always get part-time work at night in your uncle's restaurant until it's paying well," said Valeria with a smile. "I don't know why you wanted me to have an open mind about this. I know you will succeed in whatever you do, Soph. You've always been hard working."

"I'm not worried about money. I was very well paid—what I earned on my assignment was on top of my regular wage." Sophie placed the cup carefully on the saucer, clearing her throat. "It's the next bit that's…um…a bit contentious. I want to tell you something about myself." As her mother waited, Sophie took a deep breath. It was now or never. "You must have been wondering why I've never brought anyone home to meet you."

Valeria blinked, clearly puzzled. "You've had plenty of friends over."

"I…I mean…someone I'm romantically involved with. You know…a boyfriend."

"Are you trying to tell me you've finally met someone? That's wonderful." She narrowed her eyes. "Why aren't I going to like this? Is he married?"

Sophie let out an exasperated puff of air. She was making a hash of it. Better just to blurt it out. "I'm not having an affair with a married man. I'm a lesbian."

Her mother stiffened, her expression stern. Sophie couldn't remember the last time she'd seen such a reaction in her usually unflappable parent. She hung her head, her breathing shallow as she waited for the words to come. She could take anger but not shame. *Please God, don't let her be ashamed of me.*

"Sophie Theresa Marsh. You are twenty-nine years old. Why haven't you told me this before?"

"Because I thought you would be ashamed of me."

Valeria shook her head impatiently. "And why would I be? You are still the daughter I loved, and was proud of, five minutes ago. I'm upset you've kept this secret from me for so many years. I thought you knew you could tell me anything."

Sophie blew out a long breath. "You're okay with this? Really?"

"Well," said Valeria with a wry shrug. "There's nothing I can do about it, is there? And I must admit, I can't say the thought hadn't crossed my mind. You never looked twice at any of your brothers' friends and some were very handsome. I guess I can live with it."

"What about Dad?" said Sophie anxiously.

"I'll have a talk to him, though I suspect he already has an inkling, so don't worry. He was always telling me what a tomboy you were when he took you out fishing. He used to say you were a better second mate than any of your brothers." Valeria twisted the gold ring on her finger with a tight smile. "We both know who's going to be the problem, don't we?"

"Aunt Angie."

"Exactly."

"So how do you think I should break the news?"

"Hmmm. Let's think about it. Maybe you could do it at your thirtieth birthday party. She won't make a scene with all the family present. You could bring a girlfriend. Have you anyone you can ask?"

Immediately the image of Eleanor flooded her mind. With a determined effort she said nonchalantly, "No."

Her mother pounced. "But you like someone, don't you? Hence this out-of-the-closet discussion we're having?"

"I do like someone but...well...I'm not in her league. Anyway, I won't be seeing her again."

"Are you going to tell me who she is? You never did let us know where you've been for the last two months. Now you're back, is it still a secret?"

"It actually is."

"But you met her there?" her mother persisted.

"Yes. Now, no more questions."

"Okay, but you've got me curious. Are you staying tonight?"

"I like to stay until my party if that's all right. I want to take a break away from my flat."

"It will be wonderful to have you home again, dear. Take your bag up to your old room and settle in. When you're ready, come down and I'll fill you in with the family gossip." As Sophie turned to go, Valeria added, "I'll ask Jolene to bring her boss to the party. She's a lesbian."

With a shake of her head, Sophie walked out to the car for her suitcase. Not only had her mother taken her news remarkably well, now she was going to set her up with a date. Unbelievable. She gave a shudder as she visualized her family vetting her prospective lovers. They wouldn't be able to help themselves. Though it would be a step into the unknown for them, they wouldn't take long to formulate a set of guidelines. Eleanor would have been horrified.

* * *

Sophie jogged down to the news agency the following Wednesday morning—today the article was coming out. Next to *The Courier Mail* and *The Australian*, a stack of *Globes* sat neatly on the rack. A picture of Austen took up the entire front page. She picked up one from the top of the pile, feeling a buzz to see her work so gloriously displayed. Paying for the paper, she retired to the bench seat on the footpath. To her relief, her article was on the third page, and to give Owen his due, although it hadn't made the front page headline, he had given it a large spread. An old, unflattering picture of Fortescue was centred above the write-up, one taken at the site of the coal gas controversy. He looked flustered as he argued with a landholder.

She felt a spurt of satisfaction reading the text, aware she had published something that would cause a controversy in Parliament. And it was her exclusive. The Opposition would latch onto this blatant misuse of public funds, especially so close to the election. They would be foolish not to use it to their advantage. Social media would go crazy, and it would likely head up the evening TV news.

She flicked to the middle to admire her photos of Austen displayed in a four-page glossy insert. She really was a fine-looking woman and extremely photogenic. A wave of agony hit as images of Eleanor wavered there too as if they were superimposed on the paper. She snapped the pages shut. Just looking at Austen was enough to trigger thoughts of Eleanor.

Back home, the smell of bacon cooking hit her when she walked down the hallway to the kitchen. Her mother, father, and youngest brother Danny looked at her expectantly when she settled down onto a chair at the table.

"Is it published?" asked her mother.

Sophie pushed over the paper with a smile. "Yep. It's on page three."

It gave her a flush of pleasure to see the admiration in her father's face after he read her exposé. "Good reporting, Soph." She loved when her father was proud of her. Daniel Marsh was a big jolly man, with a wide smile and a twinkle in his eye. When the Italian relations got too much for him, as they often did, he would disappear on his boat, taking one or two of the children for an afternoon of fishing. Sophie missed those carefree days.

"Hey," exclaimed Danny, cocking his head sideways to look at the front page. "Isn't that Austen Farleigh?"

Sophie rolled her eyes. A typical adolescent uni student, more interested in a hot woman than good reporting. "There's a centre insert with a lot more photos." Then not being able to help herself, she added, "I took them."

"Really, sis?" he said, clearly impressed as he ogled the pictures. "There're awesome. How come you got to take these?"

"She's a friend. Now let's get back to my article. Do you think it'll stir things up, Dad?"

"Sure to. The pollies are coming under greater scrutiny these days."

"Austen Farleigh is your *friend*?" interrupted Danny. "Where did you meet her? Shit, she's famous."

"Watch that language," said Valeria sternly, and turned her attention to the photos. "They're excellent. I didn't realize you were such a talented photographer, dear. She's stunning, isn't she? Rather unusual looking though."

Danny gave a snigger. "Mum, she's a lesbo."

Sophie shot him a dark frown. "That hardly defines her. She's an amazing singer, one of the best I've ever heard."

"Of course it has nothing to do with her talent. And I'm not a fool, Danny," Valeria said and turned to eye Sophie thoughtfully. "I presume you met her on your last assignment, because I've never heard you mention her before."

"Yes, I met her when I was away. She's really very nice." Sophie couldn't help smiling. Austen would be appalled to be described as nice.

"So you were taken with her...ah ...personality?"

Sophie felt heat rush to her cheeks as if they'd been suddenly doused with hot water. Damn, this was getting complicated. Now her mother thought her unrequited love was Austen. She'd better nip that one in the bud. "She's fun, but nobody in their right mind would take her seriously, especially anybody with brains."

"Good to hear. She looks rather wild and brazen. Now eat up, Danny. Your ride will be here soon."

After her father and Danny disappeared out the door, Sophie helped tidy the house. When her mother left to visit a friend, she sank on the couch to watch TV. After a flip through the channels, she settled on the *Today Show* to catch up with current events—she'd barely looked at the news for months. There was a lot of congenial banter between the presenters, but not much of interest. She was just about to give it up for a good book, when their next guest was announced. Sophie jerked upright, her heart thumping as the camera panned to Eleanor in a studio chair. She looked poised and elegant as she reclined back waiting for the questions.

"You're here in Australia for the premiere of your new film, Eleanor?" one of the presenters asked.

A smile touched Eleanor's lips, so lightly it was barely there at all. "Yes, it's on Saturday night."

"I'm sure it's going to be a huge success. From all accounts the film is a winner."

Sophie didn't register any more of the conversation as she gazed at Eleanor. On the surface, the lovely cameo face was calm but her fingers moved restlessly on the armrests of her chair. And underneath the perfect makeup, there were stress lines on her skin and puffiness under her eyes. Sophie felt a tremor of concern. Hadn't she been looking after herself properly since she left? Hadn't she kept up her stamina with decent meals? It wouldn't take too much neglect to have a relapse.

Worry raced through her mind until Sophie drew back in alarm. What was she doing? Eleanor wasn't hers to love and cherish anymore. She'd blown it.

She wanted to scream. How long would it be before the dreadful ache vanished? By the way it felt now, it wouldn't be for a long, long time. Surlily, she watched the interview conclude. So much for falling in love. This was the worst agony she'd ever endured.

CHAPTER THIRTY-ONE

In Sydney now, Eleanor watched impatiently as the room service attendant wheeled in her breakfast. Once he'd left, she hurried to pick up her *Morning Globe*, which she had specifically ordered to be delivered every morning with her meal. As yet there had been nothing published about her since she arrived back on Thursday, or in the back copies while she was still on the island after Sophie left. Now three days before her premiere, she wondered if there actually was going to be an article. Sophie surely would have to write something. She was employed to get an exposé and Eleanor imagined if she didn't, she would likely lose her job.

She felt a wave of disquiet. The thought of Sophie not being able to pay her bills was unsettling. Then she told herself to get a grip and face facts. Sophie wasn't hers to look after and love anymore. She had pushed her away.

When she glanced at the headlines, she stared dumbfounded. A picture of Austen in all her glory, took up the entire front page. She was perched on a chair, her guitar resting on her knee as she plucked out a tune. Whoever took this had a natural aptitude for lighting and atmosphere—it was a stunning piece of art. She followed the directions on the top of the page and flipped to the centre to view the rest of the photo shoot. It was an exciting display, not garish and loud, but subtlety captured the essence of the singer in a harmonious and intimate way. Talented, brooding, and dangerous. The photographer obviously knew Austen.

Curiously, she searched for the name of the photographer, finding it at the bottom of the last page: Brie Simmons. Sophie's friend. Eleanor refocused on the shots—this had to be Sophie's work. But when did she take the photos? Then it came, the night she went alone to Austen's for dinner. And that begged the question. What did Sophie give Austen in return for the pictures? Eleanor pushed back the nagging jealousy—it wasn't her business anymore.

Another puzzle presented itself immediately. Why give someone else the credit for such fine work, when she should have taken the accolades herself. Puzzled, Eleanor buttered her toast and settled down to read the rest of the paper. When she came to the picture of the obnoxious politician from Eurydice, she sat up straighter in her chair. Quickly she read the article, which took up most of the page. When she reached the end paragraph where he was accused of paying for his holiday travel out of his parliamentary allowance, she chuckled. He had cooked his own goose.

She read the byline, feeling a flush of pride. There was no doubt Sophie was a first-class reporter and she had worked out a way to fulfil her obligations to the paper without printing a word about Eleanor. She had managed not to mention Eurydice either by giving the rights of her photos to her friend, thus further distancing the publication from the resort. Sophie had been careful to protect Eurydice's reputation as a discreet destination. A wave of loss so acute snapped through Eleanor that she grasped the edge of the table for support. What an imbecile she had been.

But now was not the time to wallow in self-pity—she had to do something constructive to get Sophie back. Taking the phone from her pocket, she dialled the number of her press secretary.

It only took a few seconds for the voice to come on the line. "Anita McMahon."

"It's Eleanor, Nita. I wonder if you'd do me a favour."

"Of course, Ellie. What's up?"

"Would you send an email to Brie Simmons, a reporter with the *Brisbane Morning Globe*, and invite her to the premiere and party afterwards, please? All expenses paid. Drop a line stating I saw her photos of Austen Farleigh in the morning edition and would like her to do a spread of the premiere."

Disbelief resonated in Anita's voice. "You're giving the shoot to an unknown reporter? From Brisbane? We were inundated with requests from bigger publications. And they were willing to pay for the privilege. You knocked them all back."

"I know," said Eleanor soothingly, "but she *is* a talented photographer. The others will no doubt be there snapping away anyway, but I'm going to pose for this woman later in the night. It'll be good publicity."

"Good lord Ellie, what's got into you? I've been trying for years to persuade you to get more exposure. Have you seen the light at long last?"

Eleanor gave a little chuckle. Anita was the exact opposite of Carol. Everything about her smacked casual, from her low flat heels to her loose untidy plait, but she got the job done with a minimum of fuss. "Don't get too excited. I thought I'd be cooperative for once."

"By giving some unknown an exclusive?"

"Did you see the photos of Austen?"

"No."

"Go online and check them out."

"Okay, I will. She better be good."

"She is. Can you set up a room with lighting for some intimate shots?"

"Will do."

Eleanor put down the phone with a satisfied smile. Now all she had to do was work out a way to pump Brie for information about Sophie. She'd have to Google the woman to see what she looked like.

* * *

Eleanor stepped from the limo in front of the Sydney State Theatre. She knew the iconic building well, with its gold and red lavish décor and grand staircases. The early twentieth-century architecture and ornate cultural fabric was like stepping back into history. What better place for a premiere?

With a deep breath, she braced herself for the walk past the gauntlet of press and fans in solid blocks that lined the red carpet. Her dress, of a similar red hue, clung to her slender figure in flowing waves, its strapless bodice covered by the sheerest of short jackets. Sergio Rossi high heels, also red, completed the ensemble. Her hair was loose, left to fall just below her shoulders in a mane of gleaming golden-honeyed curls. She was the epitome of sophistication. This time she rejected a male escort, opting to enter the theatre alone. She was done with all that subterfuge.

No matter how blasé she tried to be about the whole affair, she still had that slightly giddy feeling when she took the red carpet walk. From the catcalls and applause as she progressed to the entrance, she doubted the absence of a man beside her was even noticed. Amidst camera flashes, she took time to sign autographs before she continued to the main foyer. Carol was there to meet her, and stood by her side as Eleanor was greeted by the dignitaries and fellow cast members. Twenty minutes later, they had the nod that the last guest was seated. It was time for the cast to go onstage to introduce the movie.

After the speeches, she was escorted to a seat for start of *On the Edge of Life*. Eleanor had not seen the final print. It was better than she remembered. She squirmed after an hour, not from embarrassment about her performance, but because the seats weren't really made for a tight long dress. After it finished, she waited anxiously for the crowd reaction. When the whole theatre erupted with applause and the audience stood en masse, she breathed a sigh of relief. They had a hit.

An hour and a half later, after doing enough networking to satisfy Anita, they left for the party, which, at her request, was to be a small affair. She was tired of big galas that usually disintegrated into a free booze-up for every hanger-on in the industry. A hive of paparazzi swarmed forward when they emerged from the theatre, nearly jostling them as cameras flashed. Two burly security guards were immediately at their side to force a pathway, and with some dignity intact they managed to slide into the limo.

"Flipping hell," gasped Carol. "I'm glad we've seen the last of those pushy bastards for a while."

Eleanor eyed her in disbelief. "Where's the, *you must be more out there Ellie*, now?"

"Yeah, well. Sometimes it gets a bit too much."

"Like all the time," growled Eleanor. "I'm glad Anita arranged for us to get out of the car in the hotel's underground parking."

"So am I now. Look, we're here already. Be a good star and wave to your fans through the window, just like the Queen."

Eleanor was pleased to see the steel security gate close behind them as they nosed underneath the building. They were ushered out the door to the lift, and with her arm hooked through Carol's, she entered the reception room. Decorated with glitter, it was already full, with waiters moving through the crowd offering refreshments.

"What will you have to drink?"

"One of those glasses of champagne will be fine," replied Eleanor, pointing to a waiter with a tray of drinks. "Let's go outside and you can give me your verdict."

Carol took two glasses and followed her to the balcony. She handed a flute to Eleanor with a wink. "You were marvellous. This is going to net you an Oscar, Ellie."

"You think?"

"You know it, so don't put on that innocent look. From the reaction of the audience, it's going to be a multiaward winner."

Eleanor glanced over the Sydney night skyline. "I hope it will for Nigel's sake. It's a very powerful film. He invested a lot of time and energy into it, besides being the best director I've ever worked with." She turned back to Carol with a sly smile. "You'd have to be happy with your investment."

"Too right. The best thing I ever did was sign you up, my dear. Now we'd better mix to sweet-talk the reviewers. I see that smarmy Walter Drummond from the *Lyric Review* is here. Go make him happy…he's been ogling you since we arrived."

"Ugh! If I must, I must."

"Good girl. See you later."

Drummond watched her approach, arrogantly sure of himself. Eleanor inwardly groaned, but clamped on a smile. If she had to be charming to the know-all, then so be it. They were discussing the movie, or at least he was and she was listening, when she looked over his shoulder and caught a woman studying her. She was attractive, tall, model-thin, and immaculately dressed. Eleanor idly wondered if she was gay—she'd suit Carol to a tee. Then she realised it was Brie Simmons.

She extricated herself tactfully from the conversation as quickly as she could, and walked over to the reporter. "Brie Simmons, I presume. It's lovely to meet you."

Brie inclined her head, though by the way she was rocking back on her heels, she was a little overwhelmed. "Umm, yes, Ms. Godwin. It's so nice to meet you too. I'm a great fan of yours. You were wonderful in the movie."

"Thanks for your support. Now call me Eleanor, please. You did get my message that I would like you to take a few photos of me tonight as well as covering the event? Just something intimate," she gave a little laugh, "but not too revealing. I thought those you took of Austen were superb."

Brie paused, emotions flittering across her face. At one stage, she looked like she was going to confess, but answered, "Thank you very much for giving me this opportunity. Umm…shall we go somewhere now?"

"Come with me. My press agent has lined up a room at the hotel. She's set up some lighting as well. You have your gear?"

"It's behind the bar. I won't be a minute."

As Eleanor watched her weave her way through the crowd, she felt a little sorry for her. She must be worried about the shoot for Sophie's photographs had set the bar very high. Hopefully, if

Anita had supplied them with enough lighting props, the shots wouldn't be too bad.

"Follow me to the lift," she said when Brie appeared with a black camera bag on her shoulder.

On the tenth floor, Eleanor slipped in the card and the door snapped open. It was a sumptuous suite. In the corner of the very spacious lounge, Anita had set up a small photographic studio, with a muted grey backdrop behind a chair, with two lamps either side. A bottle of champagne in an ice bucket and two glasses stood on a side table.

"This is perfect," exclaimed Brie.

"Sit down. We both need to relax before we start. Let's have a drink first." Eleanor popped the cork, catching the first gush of fizz in a flute. She filled it up, passed it to Brie and poured herself one. "I'd like to hear all about your life as a journalist."

"I'm actually the *Globe's* social reporter."

"So you're an old hand at these sorts of things. You like the glitz and the glamour?"

"Oh yes. I adore fashion and the razzle-dazzle that goes with it."

Eleanor studied the reporter. How amazing that she was Sophie's best friend. They couldn't be less alike. "Are you the only one assigned to the social pages?"

"There are two of us. I'm the senior one."

"Personally, I don't like the limelight much."

"Really? But you have such style."

Eleanor gave an elegant roll of her shoulder. "I have to. It goes with the territory. As soon as I'm home out of the public view, I chill out in a tracksuit. I've just been on a long holiday on an island in the Whitsundays, where there was no one to bother me. It was fantastic."

Brie twirled her glass dropping her head. "That sounds perfect."

"It was. I had a very efficient woman looking after me." Eleanor took a sip as she watched Brie closely over the rim. Her eyes were wide with alarm. *Good, she's rattled…time to start digging.* "I read that piece about the politician in your paper. It was a darn good editorial. No wonder it launched an investigation."

Brie nodded dumbly.

"It's all over the news now. Who was the reporter?" asked Eleanor, forcing herself to sound casual.

"Ummm…Sophie Marsh."

"Ah…Sophie. That was the name of my companion on the island. Maybe I should get Ms. Marsh to write up a few words to accompany your photos."

Brie took a swallow of her drink then exclaimed, "No…No."

"You don't think she'd do it?"

"She resigned from the paper after that piece," Brie said, clearly upset.

Eleanor's stomach gave a lurch. Sophie had thrown in her job. After taking a moment to calm, she touched Brie lightly on the arm. "I'm sorry. I didn't realize it was so distressing or I wouldn't have brought it up. You're obviously very fond of her."

"She's my best friend. I don't know what got into her. She had a bit of a meltdown then bang…she was gone."

"Did she say why?"

"Something happened in her last assignment. She never said what though."

"Where was it?"

Brie slid her eyes away from Eleanor's gaze. "Up north. I'm sorry. You don't want to hear all this. I don't actually know why I'm telling you."

"I think you needed to get it off your chest. Sometimes it helps to talk to a stranger. Is your friend coping now?" Eleanor persisted.

"I hope so. She went home to her parents' for a while to sort herself out."

"Then I imagine she's in good hands. The best advice I can offer is to just be there for her."

"We've persuaded her to go out for a drink Friday night. That should cheer her up."

Eleanor put her glass on the tray. "Now, we'd better get on with this photography session or we'll never get back to the party. I'll introduce you to my agent when we get back. She loves fashion too."

For the next half hour while she posed, regret and frustration continued to swirl in Eleanor's thoughts. The news of Sophie had thrown her. One thing was clear. She needed to see her to put things right. And stuff pride. She would get on her hands and knees if it were warranted. Unfortunately, the following Monday to Friday would be taken up with the next movie's obligations—now she was back from holidays her life wasn't her own once more. She'd have to see her sometime next weekend. But there had to be a plan. She'd toyed with the idea of ringing her, but if Sophie refused to see her, she'd be stymied.

It shouldn't take too much to find out her parents' address, but she couldn't just lob up to the front door of her family home and ask for Sophie. If she weren't so well known, it would be fine, but she could imagine the kerfuffle if she just appeared on their doorstep. Completely inappropriate. It was the price of fame.

The best bet would be to find where Brie was taking her on Friday evening. She'd fly up to Brisbane and Blade could organize a get-together with a few of their old friends. Hopefully, it was the bar where the Facebook photo was taken. She'd have to take a punt on it. If it wasn't, it was a night out with friends. But it would mean she'd have to think of an alternative ploy. Brie would think it too odd if she mentioned Sophie again— she'd pushed her a little far as it was.

"That should do it, Eleanor," said Brie. "I've taken more than enough to make it an exciting portfolio. You're extremely photogenic."

"You've finished?" asked Eleanor, slipping back into focus.

"Yes. And thank you very much for this opportunity. It'll be a great boost for the *Globe*. I'll send the pictures over for your approval before we publish them. I did a comprehensive coverage of the red-carpet parade and the ceremony as well."

"I'd appreciate that, Brie. Not that I particularly enjoy seeing my face in print, but my press secretary does and she's the boss."

Brie laughed. "Beauty and clothes sell papers. But throw in sex and you've got a real winner."

"Unfortunately I can't supply you with any tidbits there," Eleanor murmured. "Not yet anyway. Now let's adjourn to the party."

CHAPTER THIRTY-TWO

Now that Sophie's exposé had become a hot topic nationwide, the Marsh household sat glued every night to the evening news. Even her brother, Danny, who had no interest in politics. Fortescue was now under the pump for a "please explain," and it was predicted he'd be forced to resign in a few weeks—they always had to in the end. Having been interviewed on several current affairs shows, Sophie had reached celebrity status with her relations. But now they crowded her too much. Her wish for a quiet time at home was totally thwarted and she was more depressed than ever.

When Brie rang from the airport with the news that Eleanor had given her an exclusive photo shoot of the premiere in Sydney the night before, Sophie felt as if she'd been kicked in the stomach. She held her temper in check as Brie described the night in detail: the stunning clothes, the celebrities, the glitzy after-party, how fabulous Eleanor had been in the film and how gracious she had been to her. After the call finished, Sophie slammed the phone down the table.

"Damn you Ellie. You don't give a stuff about anyone but yourself," she screamed and strode to the computer. It was time, past time, that she left all this rubbish behind her. She opened Google, typed in *great holiday destinations for backpackers* and began to browse. By the time her mother arrived home, she had her top five prospective sites, as well as a casserole in the oven.

Valeria opened the oven door with an appreciative sniff. "That smells delicious. I'm glad to see you're feeling like your old self again, dear."

Sophie grunted but didn't comment.

"What's the matter?"

"Nothing, I'm just …"

Her words were cut off by Danny calling out, "The news is on." With resignation, she followed her mother into the lounge.

Her father gave her a thumbs-up as an embattled Fortescue appeared on the screen, but Sophie sat back subdued. She was beginning to feel sorry for the man. For misusing a few thousand dollars, his career had gone down the toilet. His inefficiency as a minister had nothing to do with his demise.

She was about to get up when Eleanor suddenly flashed on. In a spectacular clinging dress, she was walking up the red carpet in Sydney.

"What a hot babe," snickered Danny and Sophie gritted her teeth.

"Don't be a moron," she snapped. "Eleanor isn't a sex object for a puerile ignoramus who couldn't tell *class* even if he fell over it."

"What bee's up your butt?"

"Grow up."

"Ha! Me grow up. Look at you…loosen up a bit. You're getting to be a boring grouch."

"Quiet," called out her father firmly. "We're here to watch the news."

Sophie sat back brooding through Eleanor's interview. As much as it was too painful to watch, she couldn't turn away. All the feelings of love rushed back explosively. Eleanor was so overwhelmingly alluring…so irresistible. When the weather report came on and her image disappeared, Sophie felt the wrench right to the tip of her toes. She turned to find her mother studying her closely.

With an effort, she leaped to her feet with a cheery, "I'll set the table." Her head downcast, she hurried into the kitchen.

* * *

Friday hadn't come too soon for Sophie. She needed to get out, to get away from the confines of her family. For all their good intentions, they had become suffocating. Not that it was their fault. Sophie had been by herself too long, become too independent to go back to living with her parents for any length of time.

So she had made her decision. Her birthday party was tomorrow night. She had booked a plane to Bangkok next Tuesday to begin her six-week backpacking tour of Southeast Asia. After that, she'd consider the job offers she'd received—the article had opened up a host of opportunities from various publications. She was "hot property" in the journalism world now. But for all that, she was the unhappiest she ever been in her life.

It had taken all week to gather courage to go to the bar tonight, for the time had come to announce her sexuality to her friends. To get into the spirit of things, she decided to wear her old low black leather pants, a deep blue silk shirt and her black leather boots. The pants were a remnant of her first year at university when she passed briefly through an anti-establishment phase. They'd been packed away and forgotten. While she was rummaging through her old cupboard, she was surprised to find her mother hadn't thrown them out.

It took some manoeuvring, but she finally managed to wriggle into them. Ten years on, a few more kilos had settled comfortably on her bottom. She pulled on the shirt, undid the top two buttons and posed in front of the mirror. *Well that looks the part.* After careful attention to her hair, she applied a touch of makeup.

Her mother raised her eyebrows as she emerged from her room when the taxi arrived, but merely murmured, "Have a good time, dear."

As she sped through the streets, Sophie's resolve began to wane. What if the girls were angry—judgmental—dismissive? She had pushed away all doubt by the time the cab pulled up outside the entrance. She couldn't back out—it was now or never.

The room was nearly full and she noted there were quite a few interested looks from both men and women as she slipped through to their usual booth. Her four friends were already seated, quietly chatting.

As she approached, Brie's eyes widened as she raked them over the skintight leather pants. With a bright smile Sophie slid into the seat, though she knew the look on her friend's face. It smacked of disapproval. Brie, despite her professed liberalism, was ultra-conservative.

"Hi everyone," Sophie said. "It's great to see you all again."

Vera leaned over to give her a soft warm kiss on the cheek. "We've missed you, Soph. My word, the break away from the city did you a world of good. You look great, leaner and so tanned."

"I like the pants," chuckled Alice. "Trying to get laid tonight?"

"I thought it was about time I changed my image," replied Sophie, ignoring Brie's frown. "Now I'm going to get a drink. Anyone want one?"

"We've a bottle of champagne in the ice bucket waiting for you," said Janet. "We want to toast your birthday."

Sophie smiled her appreciation as the cork popped. A glass of champers was the ideal fortification for what she was about to reveal. "Just what the doctor ordered," she said, twisting the stem a little nervously.

"Happy birthday," the others said in unison.

After another glass accompanied by lively gossip, Sophie's nerves had settled enough for her revelation. But she needed the right opportunity—she could hardly just blurt it out. Her hands trembled when Janet announced, "You're getting mobs of attention from the guys at the bar tonight, Sophie. With that outfit, you can have your pick."

"I'm not interested."

"Then why did you wear those bloody awful pants," snapped Brie.

"Not to get a man that's for sure."

"And why's that Sophie? Why do you think you're always too good for them?"

Out of the corner of her eye, Sophie could see Vera wave her hand with concern. She ignored her, knowing Vera sensed what she was going to say. "Because men don't do anything for me, Brie. I'm a lesbian."

"Ha!" exclaimed Alice. "I always knew there was something you weren't telling us."

"Good for you, girl," said Janet. "That ex of mine is an arrogant dick. Women will treat you better."

Vera placed a hand on Sophie's and gave it a squeeze. "I've suspected it for a while. Why has it taken so long to tell us? You know it's not going to make any difference to our friendship."

A tear escaped down Sophie's cheek as she gazed with affection, and relief, at Vera. Both Janet and Alice gave her encouraging smiles as well. But so far, Brie hadn't spoken and Sophie couldn't bring herself to look at her. If her best friend deserted her, it would be the final blow in her rock-bottom life.

Then Brie said in a disbelieving voice, "And you think you can get a *woman* tonight wearing those slutty pants. Anyone decent wouldn't be seen dead with you looking like that."

Sophie turned to her and began to giggle. Typical Brie—she didn't care if she was gay, but she did care very much about fashion. "They are ghastly, aren't they? I used to wear them when I was nineteen. They're so tight I can hardly move. I…I kinda wanted to make a statement tonight."

"Honey," drawled Alice. "They make more than a statement, they make a map. Every bump and dip is showing."

"But why *did* you take so long to tell us?" Vera persisted.

"Because it would get back to my family. You know how many rellies I have."

"Are you going to tell them?"

"I told Mum last weekend. She was great about it, but she's not the worry. My aunt is. She's not going to be a happy chappie."

"Tell her to sod off," said Brie. "When are you going to drop her the big L word?"

"There's a family party for my birthday tomorrow night. I'm going to do it then."

"Best of British," said Alice. She held up the empty bottle of champagne. "This is a dead marine. Whose turn to go to the bar?"

"I'll go," said Sophie. "I'll have to stretch my legs. The damn leather is pulling at my groin."

"Here," said Alice, pushing across a fifty-dollar note. "Our shout tonight. It's your big three-O so you're not buying anything."

Sophie picked it up with a smile. "Okay…thanks." With a much lighter step now, she walked down the bar until she found a space. The bartender was busy, which suited her. She was glad of the respite to be by herself for a while. As well, it gave the others a chance to come to terms with her news. Though she knew they'd discuss it as soon as she was out of earshot, she resisted the urge to turn to look. Even though they were so supportive, it would still take time to process it completely. It would be quite interesting to see if they mentioned it or ignored it when she got back. She hoped they wouldn't be like her mother and try to set her up with someone.

She was idly watching the bartender make a complicated cocktail, when someone spoke next to her.

"Hi there. May I buy you a drink?"

She turned to see a spiffy executive-type gazing at her, his interest evident in his eyes. "No thanks, I'm with friends."

"Surely I can tempt you with one." He gave a lopsided grin, no doubt designed to make his clean-lined, almost poetic face irresistible.

She hated to burst his bubble he looked so confident. "Sorry." She turned to the bartender who was waiting impatiently for her order. "A bottle of the Cordon Rouge champagne please."

"Come on," he urged. "Just one."

"I don't want to be rude, but I said no and I meant it."

Then a soft voice spoke close behind her ear. "I think you had better move on. The lady refused your offer."

Sophie froze, the scent of the familiar perfume swirling around her. She felt the soft body press slightly against her back as the would-be charmer, hesitating for only a second, moved off into the crowd. She gripped the side of the bar to keep her back ramrod straight. Was she dreaming? She didn't know, but she didn't want to move to break the spell.

"Hello, Sophie," said Eleanor and fleetingly brushed the back of her neck with her fingertips.

"Ellie," she managed to gasp out. "What are you doing here?"

"I've come to see you."

Sophie swivelled, her heart pounding. Eleanor was dressed in a flowing white dress, her hair elaborately braided on top of her head with strands curling around her ears, and her eyes and nose covered by a glittery black mask. "You're at a masquerade?" she asked incredulously.

A chuckle puffed out of Eleanor. "This was the only way I can go unnoticed." She gestured to a table on the far side of the room. "I'm out with a group of friends from my theatre days. We decided to go in fancy dress so I could have a night out in peace."

"How did you know I'd be here?"

"I cannot tell a lie. I pumped Brie for the information. Would…would you come with me so we can talk in peace?"

"I'm with friends."

"Yes, I understand. We won't be long. I booked a room in the hotel where we can catch up without interruption." Eleanor grasped her hand in a tight grip. "Please, Sophie. Will you?"

Sophie found herself drowning in the warm eyes. They were so mesmerizing she couldn't get her lips to move. Eleanor must have interpreted it as reluctance, because she uttered another, this time more desperate, "Please?"

"Okay," Sophie whispered. "I'll take the bottle of champagne over to the girls and meet you at the lift."

"I'll be waiting."

After Eleanor disappeared to the other side of the room, Sophie picked up the bottle and headed back to the booth.

"Finally," said Alice with a knowing grin, leaving Sophie in no doubt that they had been watching her at the bar. She wriggled her fingers. "Give me your glass."

"If you all don't mind, I'll sit this one out. I have to duck away to see someone. I shouldn't be too long."

"Oh?" said Janet, her eyes glinting. "To see which one? The spunky bloke or the masked babe?"

Sophie rolled her eyes. They hadn't missed a trick. Well, let them guess. "Wouldn't you like to know," she said with a little wave good-bye.

Alice's voice drifted over as she reached the door to the hallway. "I gotta get me a pair of those pants."

CHAPTER THIRTY-THREE

Eleanor waited nervously at the lift. When Sophie appeared beside her, she smiled more with relief than welcome, and hit the button. Once inside, they were both silent as the lift rose to the thirty-fifth floor. Eleanor, reluctant to break the spell, stood against the back wall with her hands clasped together. She had trouble reading Sophie's expression—enigmatic for the usually open woman, more melancholy if anything.

In the room, she switched on the lamp in the sitting area and pulled back the curtains until the lights of the city appeared over the balcony. Then she removed her mask. Sophie watched her without a word, seemingly content for her to be the first to speak. Eleanor began with the question she'd wanted to ask since the conversation with Brie. "How have you been, Sophie? I heard you resigned from the paper."

"As well as can be expected? And you?"

"Not so good."

"Me neither."

Eleanor edged closer and carefully brushed away a stray strand of hair from Sophie's forehead. "I've missed you."

"Have you?"

"Dreadfully."

Sophie studied her closely, her brown eyes even darker in the muted glow of the lamp. "I thought you didn't want to see me again," she said solemnly.

"I was angry. Angry and hurt. I couldn't believe you'd betray my confidence so appallingly."

"I know. I should have told you...no... I never should have taken the assignment in the first place. I didn't really have a choice." She sat down with a thump onto the edge of the bed, her hands roaming restlessly over the quilt. "I'm not here to give you excuses, but I want you to understand what my life was all about. I worked hard to get where I was...very hard. And I couldn't throw it all away by refusing an assignment. I put myself through study by working in the restaurant at night and on the weekends. And on top of that, I wrote voluntary articles for the *Globe* so I'd be considered for a position there after I finished my degree. Sometimes I was so damn tired I'd barely make it to bed. Nobody really seemed to appreciate how tough it was: not my boss or my family. Then you came along, Ellie, and you made me feel as though I mattered."

"You do matter. You're one of the kindest, most loving people I've ever met."

Sophie dropped her eyes. "That sentiment went down the toilet in a hurry, didn't it? I know you thought I was a worthless shit when you found out who I was, but you didn't give me an opportunity to explain. You said you loved me but you didn't give me a chance."

A cold chill swirled down Eleanor's spine as she searched for words that would make everything right, but none came. "I know. I should have swallowed my pride."

"It shouldn't have just been about pride, it was about love too."

"What do you want me to say...that I didn't love you enough?" Eleanor paced around the room. "We both have to share the blame. I know you never said you loved me, but... but I thought you did. You should have told me why you were working for me before I heard it from that ghastly man in a parking lot."

"I know. But I needed to…sorry…I must sound like I'm whining. I'm heaping the culpability onto you, but ultimately I'm the bad guy here. I apologise for turning this into a blame feast. I…I'd like it if we could at least be friends."

"Of course we're friends."

"The ironic thing is," said Sophie with a bitter smile, "in the end I threw in my job. Anyhow, I'm going to put it all behind me. I'm off on Tuesday to backpack through Southeast Asia. When do you start your next film?"

Eleanor walked over to the window and stared out, fighting back the tears. She felt like her heart had been ripped out. Sophie was moving on. "I fly back to Sydney on Monday. We begin walking through the new script next week."

She heard Sophie get up, though didn't turn around. It was too painful.

"I suppose I'd better get back then. The girls will be waiting for me. It's my thirtieth birthday celebration," Sophie said with a distinct quaver in her voice.

Eleanor swung back around with determination. What was she doing letting Sophie walk out of her life? Her dreams couldn't end in a painful "mea culpa" conversation as if they'd never been passionate lovers. "Then I'd like to give you a kiss for your birthday. I have nothing else."

To stall any argument, Eleanor strode forward quickly and grasped Sophie by the shoulders. Ever so slowly, she gently pressed her mouth to her lips. For a brief moment Sophie went rigid in her arms, but then her body became soft and her head fell back. Eleanor gave a low moan, sliding her fingers down Sophie's back to pull her firmer into the embrace. When Sophie opened her mouth to her questing tongue, the sudden burst of her sweet essence flooded every cell of Eleanor's body, and her belly tightened.

When they broke apart, she gasped, "I missed you so much, my love."

"I'm sorry for what I did, Ellie You deserve someone who…"

Eleanor kissed her firmly into silence. This time when she pulled away, she undid the buttons of Sophie's shirt, slid the fabric and bra aside and cupped her breasts. "No more recriminations. I want to make love to you and I hope you want me to. Do you?"

Sophie feathered her lips down Eleanor's neck, then nibbled the tender hollow at the base. "I'm yours, Ellie. I always have been. Please…I need you so bad it's hurting."

Eleanor gave a pleased murmur and took her by the hand to the bed. She slid her hand up a thigh, massaging through the leather. "You may have to help me pull off those pants. Then I won't be stopping until you're screaming out my name."

* * *

Eleanor, still slightly dazed after her intense orgasm, lazily stroked Sophie's abdomen as they spooned together on the sheets. "My sweet, sweet darling, that was wonderful."

Sophie gave a tearful sniff. "I've missed you something fierce, Ellie."

"Me too. I'm only half a person without you." She searched Sophie's face. "I love you."

"I love you too my beautiful Ms. Godwin."

"I know you've made plans, but I'd love you to come with me to Sydney. Would you consider it? I need you with me. You make me complete."

Sophie's hand stilled. "But you're not out. I can't just move in. The tabloids will have a field day."

"I'm ready to make the announcement. Are you?" said Eleanor firmly.

"I told my mother last week and my friends tonight."

Eleanor's heart leapt into her mouth. "And?"

"So far so good. They've all been wonderful. Tomorrow night I'm breaking it to the rest of the family." She shivered. "That's going to be a bit harder."

"Not with me by your side."

"You'd do that for me, Ellie?"

Eleanor propped her body up on an elbow, her gaze level. "Do I have to spell it out again? 'I love you' means being by your side through thick and thin. Anybody messes with you, messes with me. You better remember that."

"I adore it when you act tough. I think Aunt Angie might be about to meet her match."

Smiling, Eleanor glanced over at the clock on the side table then gave a hiss. She scrambled out of bed, snatched up her dress that sat crumpled on the floor. "God…look at the time. The others will be wondering where we are."

"Didn't you tell your crew that you might be a while?"

Eleanor shook her head. "I said I was going up to my room to make a call."

"Help me pull up these rotten pants. I'm never going to do it on my own."

"How did you get into them?" Eleanor asked. Her mouth twitched as she struggled for composure.

"With great difficulty. The last time I wore them I was nineteen. I've put on a few kilos since."

"Ah…I'm glad I met you now, not then. I love your curves."

"Behave and pull," growled Sophie.

* * *

Eleanor grasped Sophie's hand firmly as they made their way back into the cocktail lounge. She could breathe again. Her life was back on an even keel now her mate was by her side. It was, a warm comfortable feeling knowing she wasn't alone anymore. She felt Sophie stumble slightly when her four friends came in to view, but her step firmed as they approached the booth.

"Hi," said Eleanor with a smile. She could see them looking at her curiously, probably wondering what she looked like under the mask.

"This is Ellie, everyone. Ellie this is Brie, Vera, Janet, and Alice."

The women gave welcoming smiles, moving up so she and Sophie could fit in.

"What are you all drinking?" asked Sophie brightly.

"Still on the champers," said Brie. "Stay there and I'll get another bottle and an extra glass."

"What's with the mask?" asked Alice.

Eleanor watched her, interested to see if there were any negative vibes about Sophie being with her. She couldn't feel any. In fact, all the women looked quite comfortable with the situation. But they were clearly protective of Sophie. "We're having a masquerade party. My friends are over the other side of the room."

"So," said Janet. "Are you going to take it off?"

"Janet," admonished Vera. "That's rude."

"Sorry. So what do you do, Ellie?"

"I'm in the entertainment business. What about you ladies?"

"Janet's an orthodontist, Vera's an accountant and Alice is a solicitor. And you know Brie of course," piped up Sophie.

"She knows Brie? She didn't tell us that," said Alice.

"Who do I know?" asked Brie, who appeared with a bottle and an extra flute.

"Sophie's friend," Alice replied.

Eleanor flicked a glance over at Sophie, who looked as if she'd swallowed a lemon. Eleanor patted her thigh reassuringly when Sophie, eyes wide, wrinkled her nose at her. She leaned over and whispered in her ear. "Don't worry. Hold my hand tight…I'm coming out."

"I'm sorry, I can't quite place you. Where did we meet? Your voice does sound familiar," said Brie as she handed her a glass.

Eleanor tipped up the mask with a sly smile. "Now do you remember? Sorry, I'd better put this back on or we'll be swamped by photographers." She pulled it quickly back down.

With a twitchy blink, Brie swallowed noisily. "Eleanor," she gasped.

"Lovely to see you again, Brie. I have to say your photographs were first class. Well done."

Brie preened, clearly flattered. "Thanks. You were a fantastic subject. I just loved your dress. And those shoes were to die for."

"Fuck me," exclaimed Alice. "You went to the bar and picked up *Eleanor Godwin.* Geez!"

"Shush," muttered Sophie. "I didn't pick her up. We met when I was away. We became good...um...friends."

Eleanor brought Sophie's hand to her lips and kissed the palm. "Lovers actually. I've asked Sophie to come to Sydney with me while I work on my next film, so we'll see where it goes. Our romance is a bit new yet, but I think she's wonderful." She looked over at Brie. "Remember what you said about what sells papers. Well, I'm giving you an exclusive interview. I'm coming out of the closet."

"Really," exclaimed Brie. "Me? I get the exclusive?"

Eleanor smiled. "You're Sophie's best friend, so I know you'll give me a very fair go. It'll be a private interview, nothing to do with your paper, so the copyright of the article is solely yours. I'll sign a paper to say as much. Perhaps Alice would agree to be your attorney on this transaction to make sure all legalities are adhered to. Naturally, I'll pay the costs. The women's magazines will give you a great deal of money for it. Globally. I think you'll be able to syndicate."

"So you *are* gay. Merilee Watts is going to be so pissed off," said Alice with a snigger.

"Isn't she just," said Eleanor with an answering chuckle. "That woman needs to be taken down a peg." She stood up, pleased to see Sophie rise unhesitatingly as well. "I have to get back to my party. Would you all like to join us? We're top heavy with men, so I'm sure they'll be delighted if I turn up with four attractive women."

"Just show us the way," said Janet.

Eleanor looped one arm through Sophie's and the other through Brie's. "Come on then. Let's go celebrate with the birthday girl."

CHAPTER THIRTY-FOUR

Sophie wanted to be patient, but patience wasn't her best virtue. Eleanor was due to arrive at seven thirty—still fifteen minutes to go. Even though the party had started at six thirty, they'd planned for Eleanor to make her entrance an hour later. That way, Sophie reasoned, the festivities would be in full swing and guests, with a couple of drinks under their belts, would be less likely to notice when she entered her uncle's restaurant. That was the theory anyhow. They had no other game plan. Nor had Sophie any idea how she was going to do this coming-out-of-the-closet thing. Eleanor assured her they would work out a way, but Sophie wasn't so sure. It was going to take a lot of courage.

Her agitation must have been noticeable, for she looked up to catch her mother's eagle eye. She beckoned Sophie over. "Whatever is the matter with you? You've been glancing over at the door for the last ten minutes instead of attending to your guests. Angie has been trying to gain your attention ever since she sat down and she looks annoyed."

"I've a friend coming and she doesn't know anyone. I'll talk to Aunt later."

"I'm sure your friend doesn't expect to be mollycoddled. She can amuse herself for a while. There's plenty to eat and drink. Is it someone from work?"

"No. Look, I'll see Aunt later, so don't nag. I don't know why everyone is expected to be at her beck and call."

Valeria pursed her lips. "It's your funeral."

"How come you've never stood up to her, Mum?"

"I did once," answered Valeria with grimace. "It didn't end well for me. It's easier not to aggravate her...not poke the tiger."

Sophie glanced across at her aunt. Still an attractive woman in her sixty-eighth year, Angelica Sacchi had a Mediterranean complexion, with liberally silver-streaked hair framing nearly black eyes and a square tight face. Though they looked somewhat alike, she lacked the softness of her sister Valeria. At this moment, she was sitting bolt upright in the chair, frowning at them from across the room. Sophie gave a little wave before she turned back to her mother. "It's about time someone stood up to her."

"I wish. It would have to take a superman."

"Or superwoman," murmured Sophie.

"We can only dream. Now, what do you think of Jolene's boss?"

Sophie chuckled. "Mum, Kathy's more interested in the food. She's a would-be chef, and all she wanted was an introduction to the cook."

"Oh, that's a shame. I had..." A startled expression lit up her face as she peered over Sophie's shoulder. "Santo Cielo! Is that who I think it is?"

The room fell into silence. Sophie turned quickly, knowing who was at the door. When she saw Eleanor, her first feeling was one of relief. She had come. The second was one of wry amusement. So much for slipping in unnoticed—everyone was gaping at her. Eleanor, casually elegant in blue slacks, a turquoise blouse, and dangling retro earrings, stood in the doorway looking a million dollars. She was, in that moment, the embodiment of a fairy-tale princess for Sophie—grace and panache wrapped up in a very attractive package. The best birthday present of all.

Before Sophie could speak, Valeria hurried forward to greet Eleanor. "I'm so sorry. The restaurant is closed for a private function."

Sophie nearly fell over the chair getting to them. "Mum," she hissed. "She's my guest."

"Oh," said Valeria, flustered. "*This* is the woman you've been expecting?"

Eleanor, seemingly not at all embarrassed by the confusion, flashed a charming smile. "I'm sorry I'm late, darling. I was held up." And then to Sophie's astonishment, Eleanor leaned in and kissed her full on the mouth. She let her lips linger far too long for there to be any doubt what it meant. "Happy birthday," she whispered.

Sophie's mouth became dry, her heart raced. *Well, hallelujah! That fixed that! I'm out.*

"Hello. You must be Sophie's mother. She looks so much like you. I'm Eleanor Godwin," Eleanor said, thrusting out her hand.

Valeria clasped it with a bemused look, her colour heightened. "I know perfectly well who you are Ms. Godwin, but I'm at a loss to understand what you are doing here with my daughter."

"Call me Eleanor please, Mrs. Marsh. Sophie and I got to know each other over the last couple of months and we've become close."

"Exactly how close?"

"Very. We've become…ah…fond of each other."

"Oh, Mum," Sophie said in a low voice. "Don't be dense. Eleanor's my girlfriend."

"I saw the kiss Sophie, but I'm still coming to terms with it." She gave a little shake of her head. "I'm sorry, Eleanor, you must think me very rude. Sophie is the one of my children who never ceases to surprise me. Come along and meet the family, all the in-laws and outlaws. I have to congratulate you. This is the first time they've been collectively quiet for years."

Sophie shyly took Eleanor by the hand as Valeria introduced her around. Her father raised his beer in a salute at the back of the room. She grinned and gave him a wink, guessing her mother must have dropped the L clanger before they came.

It didn't take her relations long to monopolize Eleanor, they swarmed around her like bees to a honeypot. Sophie was slowly inched away, and she found herself on the edge of the circle beside Jolene's boss at the punch bowl. She looked at Sophie with a wry grin. "So you two are a couple?"

"We are," said Sophie.

"Good for you. She's a very talented actor and now has your family eating out of her hand. No mean feat," she remarked. "I had no idea she was a lesbian."

"It's not public."

"Then I wish you both the best. It's not going to be this easy, you know. The press will have a field day when they find out."

Sophie looked fondly at Eleanor who was trying to answer a barrage of questions, idly wondering if her relatives would be quite so accepting of their relationship if Eleanor hadn't had such a high profile. "I know. It's something we'll have to face." She looked at her curiously. "You haven't a partner, Kathy?"

"I have. She's over there." Sophie followed her gaze. When it lit on her cousin, she gave an incredulous hiss. "Jolene?"

"Yes. We've been dating for a year." Kathy smiled. "You've paved the way for us to make our announcement."

Sophie broke into a fit of giggles. "My mother was trying to set you up with me. So I guess the family is in for more than one shock." She sobered up when she caught her aunt waving imperiously at her. "I have to go. I can't put Aunt Angie off any longer."

"Best of luck with the old tartar. Jolene's petrified of her."

"So are we all." She searched over the heads of people to catch Eleanor's eye, but to no avail. She'd have to do this alone.

Her aunt pointed to the seat beside her. Those nearby scattered to get out of the line of fire, though Sophie was well aware everyone would eavesdrop on the conversation.

"Sit down," Angie ordered. "Now tell me what you were doing kissing a woman."

Sophie gritted her teeth as she tried to maintain her dignity. "We're together."

"Together? Like a man and woman?"

"I'm a lesbian." Sophie started to perspire. Goose bumps prickled her neck as the image of an ax poised above it hovered in her mind. And by the look on her aunt's face it was about to fall.

"You're carrying on with that…that shameless movie star?"

Sophie bristled, her fear forgotten. "Eleanor's one of the nicest people you'd ever meet. If you want to pick on someone, pick on me, but don't you dare slander her."

"I won't have it, do you hear me. If you don't…"

"Actually, our relationship has nothing to do with you," a soft voice interrupted. "You are neither her mother nor mine."

Sophie nearly cried out with relief as Eleanor pulled up a chair beside her. She put an arm around Sophie's shoulders and drew her close.

Eyes dark and beady like a magpie, Angie stared at them. "You think I'll allow this?"

"Allow what?" said Eleanor. "Equal rights for the gay and lesbian community is no longer a debateable issue for either the church or the state. It's only being kept alive by bigots."

"So, I'm a bigot?" Angie snapped.

"Yes you are. You're obstinately sticking to your outdated opinions and prejudices." Eleanor leaned forward until she was looking her straight in the eye. "This is the twenty-first century, Mrs. Sacchi, so get over it. All you're doing is alienating yourself from your family. For your information, I can't imagine my life in the future without Sophie beside me. There will be trying times ahead of us from the paparazzi and gossip columns, so I would expect Sophie's family to stand firmly behind her."

"It's Ms."

Eleanor frowned. "Pardon?"

"It's Ms. not Mrs."

"Oh, I'm sorry."

"Sophie should have told you," she growled, then drummed a red nail on the armrest of her chair. She looked at Sophie and then back at Eleanor. "I have to say this for you, Ms. Godwin. You have a glib tongue and fire in your belly. It's refreshing to find someone willing to state her case to me. I suppose if I must sanction the relationship, then I must. And I can see you will look after her."

Sophie stared at her in surprise. She had expected more of an argument. For a brief second as she caught her aunt's eye, she was surprised at the odd gleam reflected there. She glanced down at the aging left hand. No ring...she'd never thought much about that. Could she possibly be? She glanced back up, but the shutters had fallen—Angie had moved on. She would never know.

"Now, Sophie, your mother is signalling to be seated for the meal so we'd better move." She looked regally at Eleanor with a half-smile. "You may call me Angie."

"And you may call me Eleanor," she answered with as much aplomb.

Sophie looked at Eleanor, dazzled. The rest of the night passed in a cloud of happiness. Eleanor was everything that she could ever want. Bright, compassionate, loving, and the glow in her eyes reminded her that there was heat inside the elegance.

When she tugged Sophie out into the small courtyard at the end of the night, their mouths met in a long sweet kiss.

"Will you come with me to Sydney? If you were thinking about freelancing with your work, would it matter where you are? There'd be so many more opportunities in Sydney, and eventually perhaps, the States."

"I was actually thinking about moving more into reporting Federal Politics. And as you say, Sydney would be in the hub of things. Easier access to Canberra from there as well."

"Then you'll come?"

"Of course. The family would be scandalized if I left you after you stood up to the ogre."

"Is that the only reason?"

Sophie chuckled. "Now you're fishing for compliments." She rested her head on Eleanor's shoulder, smiling as she felt her lips brush over her hair. "I'm going not because you're gorgeous, sexy, and wonderful, but because I love you."

"Amen to that," whispered Eleanor.

EPILOGUE

Eleanor brushed her fingers down Sophie's arm as their car joined the long queue of limos with darkened windows. "You look beautiful, darling, so don't worry, it'll be a walk in the park."

Sophie wasn't so sure about that—the sea of people on the Hollywood street looked intimidating. When they finally reached the arrival point at the Dolby Theatre, Sophie, wearing a simple black three-quarter length Louis Vuitton dress, alighted first to help Eleanor out of the car for her grand entrance.

One long leg unfurled, and then another onto the fringe of the red carpet. Eleanor rose up like some fairy tale goddess into the blaze of flashing cameras.

"Eleanor! Eleanor! We love you!" the crowd chanted.

When she waved, the crowd roared louder. With hands clasped together, they walked past the myriad of TV crews and banks of photographers, Eleanor smiling to the fans shrieking for her attention. Once through security into the crowded foyer, Sophie had to stop herself gawking at all the famous people. She was barely able to refrain from shouting, "I'm at the Academy Awards!"

The large Oscar statues stood to attention like rows of gladiators as they manoeuvred through to the special areas set aside for photography. Here Eleanor stopped to pose, then turned to allow shots of the back of the dress. Sophie watched her proudly from the sideline—Eleanor looked smoking hot in the lavish floor-length aqua-blue Louis Vuitton evening dress. The photographers must have thought so too, for they spent an inordinate amount of time snapping away. As much as Sophie tried to blend into the background, Eleanor insisted they have a few shots together before they moved into the theatre.

"You look incredible," Sophie whispered, squeezing her arm as they made their way down the aisle. "I'm so proud of you."

"Just so long as you know that you mean more to me than all this, darling," Eleanor murmured back.

Their coming out to the world hadn't been quite the trauma they expected. It amazed Sophie how accepted their relationship had become after its initial sensation. When Brie's article hit the media outlets worldwide, they were engulfed in a storm of tabloid journalism. But months down the track after keeping a very low profile, it was no longer newsworthy enough to haunt their every move. The paparazzi had moved on to more exciting fodder. Now here in Hollywood, no one seemed to be overly interested in Eleanor's sexuality.

As befitted an important nominee, Eleanor was allotted two front row seats. Sophie turned to look behind, hoping to catch a glimpse of Eleanor's parents and Ginny. She gave a chuckle when someone waved from the back stalls—there was no mistaking the pink hair. Next to her, Frances Godwin stood out like a beacon as well, wearing a brightly coloured turban that glittered under the lights. Sophie nudged Eleanor with her elbow. "I can see the old girls at the back."

"God," muttered Eleanor. "Just tell me they're dressed appropriately."

"What do you think? Ginny must have got her hair touched up for the occasion, 'cause it's a vibrant lolly pink now. And your mother…well, she looks like she should be in a kasbah."

"Please don't tell me she's got on that damn gaudy turban she loves so much."

Sophie snickered. "Yep, it's like a beacon."

Eleanor groaned. "I don't know why you think they're so wonderful."

"You do as well, so admit it. What would we do without them? And Ginny actually charmed Aunt Angie, a minor miracle in itself. Who would have thought it could be done?"

Then there was no more time to talk as the Master of Ceremonies began his introduction to the night. When it finally came to the *Best Actress in a Leading Role* nomination, Jennifer Lawrence and Denzel Washington walked on stage to announce the nominees. Sophie wriggled to the edge of her chair when the video clip of Eleanor as an emaciated drug addict flashed onto the screen. She swallowed back the bile that rushed up her oesophagus at the sight. It was harrowing. Even though she'd seen the movie twice, the sight of her love like that was still heartbreaking. A calming hand rubbed her thigh soothingly— Eleanor understood how adversely it affected her.

While they readied themselves for the announcement of the winner, Sophie forced herself not to fidget or cough. She was acutely aware of the roving cameras focused on them and wondered after a sidelong glance at Eleanor, how she could look so composed.

"And the winner is…" announced Jennifer as she slid open the envelope.

Sophie held her breath.

"Eleanor Godwin for her role in *On the Edge of Life*."

The breath sizzled into a long sigh of happiness.

Eleanor swung around to Sophie, giving her a tight hug before she turned to embrace the fellow members of the film. Then she took the famous walk up the steps to the podium to deafening applause, flashing cameras and even a few ear-splitting whistles.

"Thank you," she said with a radiant smile as she accepted the Oscar. "It is indeed an honour to receive this award tonight. It is a tribute to my director, Nigel, who somehow managed to get the best out of me. I couldn't have been blessed with a more helpful crew and fellow actors." She went on to thank pertinent people but Sophie wasn't listening. She was thinking how spectacular she looked, standing there proudly with her trophy.

"And I especially wish to thank with my whole heart, my partner and love of my life, Sophie Marsh. Without her I would be lost."

Sophie's heart swelled with happiness. Hot damn, she loved that woman.

Bella Books, Inc.

Women. Books. Even Better Together.

P.O. Box 10543
Tallahassee, FL 32302

Phone: 800-729-4992
www.bellabooks.com